Anna's Book

by the same author

poetry

Buying a Heart
Poems from Oby
Poems of Love and Death
Penguin Book of Victorian Verse (editor)
Poetry 1900–75 (editor)

fiction

The Born Losers
A Kind of Treason
Cadbury of the Samurai
Cadbury and the Seven Witches

.

non-fiction

Book of Cats (editor, with Martin Booth)

for children

The Rectory Mice

Anna's Book

GEORGE MacBETH

HOLT, RINEHART AND WINSTON
NEW YORK

Copyright © 1983 by George MacBeth
All rights reserved, including the right to reproduce
this book or portions thereof in any form.
First published in the United States in 1984 by Holt,
Rinehart and Winston, 383 Madison Avenue,
New York, New York 10017.

Library of Congress Cataloging in Publication Data
MacBeth, George.
Anna's book.
I. Title.
PR6063.A13A84   1984   823'.914   83-22534
ISBN 0-03-070487-1

First American Edition

Printed in the United States of America
1 3 5 7 9 10 8 6 4 2
ISBN 0-03-070487-1

CONTENTS

1
ANNA
1894–1895

THERE ARE MANY WAYS a love affair can begin. I had a friend who was raped by a sea captain in Malmö, and then married and lived with the man happily ever after. But perhaps that was because he was never there, from one year's end to the next. He was always away ice-breaking, or poaching herrings in the teeth of the Scots fleet that sailed from Thurso.

Anyway, they got on well enough, he with his wee boats and she with her knitting. With most of my friends it was simpler, and more prolonged. Walking out in the poppy fields after evening service in the Lutheran church at the end of the village. Long engagements, and holding hands in cramped parlours. And then a lifetime of hum-drum gossip and steady fertility. The children coming year by year, like the spring daffodils.

It was never that way in my own family. My mother was a frail woman, with what they might now call an inverted womb. I had to be sawn clear, and lifted out by human hands. There was no pushing my skin crumpled to clear the gates of birth. Not for me.

I was born easy, without the usual working through, and I've sometimes thought that stacked up the penalties for all I was going to suffer later. But the penalties for my mother came then and there. She nearly died under the knife, and my father vowed there would never be a second child to put her through the same agony again.

I was the first born, and I was the last. We remained as I first knew us, a small family in a small house, and what-ever love ran down those narrow walls was gathered and given to me.

Klippan was a raw, unformulated village in those days. No more than a thin scatter of wood and brick houses, huddled together as if for comfort in a sharp bend of the river. You had to cross a bridge to enter Klippan, and the water either boiled or froze under the wheels of your carriage, depending on the season.

The sea was only four miles away, the violent, broken sea across which the Norsemen had come and gone in days gone by to Denmark. Nowadays only pleasure steamers and fishing vessels made the voyage, but the great salt mother, as they used to call her, still sent an occasional squadron of gulls reeling and squawking over the ploughland, or the golden barley.

It was agricultural land the village lay in. Undrained, it made excellent pastureland for cows and horses. Drained, it could yield a fertile soil for fields of good corn.

Most of the houses in the village were old, low wooden structures with long verandas and ground parcelled out for goats and chickens. Our own house was the exception.

It stood right at the end of the village, near to the bridge, and it reared up four tottering storeys from piles deep in the clay. What it had once been was part of a mill, but the miller had long since gone bankrupt, and the great over-shot wheel that had turned the stone rings to grind the corn had crumbled and rotted into the stream. There were a few planks and spokes left in our vegetable garden, but that was all.

The main part of the miller's house had been sold to a farrier, and his younger son now ran a thriving iron-mongery business using the vast wooden rooms for storage space. The part we occupied had been a sort of look-out tower at the west end of the property, a bourgeois folly to ape the grander extravagance of our nineteenth-century Swedish nobles.

When my father moved in, the building was in poor condition, with a roof full of holes, and a plot of ground as derelict as a midden. Most of the townspeople used it as a dumping-place for old bottles and rubbish. My father put a stop to that, fierce as an Old Testament prophet with his lifted spade and his angry tongue. In two years, he and his wife and their baby daughter were living in some style and considerable comfort in a six-room mansion with a wash-house and a clean earth-closet and the makings of the best landscaped flower-garden in Klippan.

The house was built round a fine eighteenth-century spiral staircase, with each room coming off on a different level. Through the back door, to the south, you entered a broad, low farmhouse kitchen, with an oak dresser, and an iron range, and cupboards for just about everything you could think of. Our dog, Ranger, a cross between a labrador and retriever, spent most of his days there lounging in front of the stove.

On the next floor, two steps up and around to the north, you climbed through a low lintel down to a small dark room, all decorated in blue, that was normally kept for guests. It had a wooden truckle bed, with fine carved oak posts at the corners.

Above the kitchen, as the spiral climbed, there lay the main living-room, with a gradually improving stock of antique furniture and respectable paintings as my parents inherited and collected what they could.

The fourth room, the one above the guest's bedroom, was our dining-room and parlour, where we ate our meals, and often sat and were read to by my father far into the night. He liked the sound of his voice, and might have been an actor I sometimes thought, despite his rural origins.

The house began to taper after that, squeezing itself thinner into two bedrooms, a splendid double one with a view across the bridge and the fields, where my mother and father slept, and would sometimes sit and talk when they wanted to be alone; and, right at the top, a baroque, wood-raftered pinnacle, my own wee sanctum, a little room with a brass bed and gauze curtains, flowered wallpaper, and my own stock of precious ornaments and toys and games and books.

I could see a long way from my little room, albeit only to the north, across the dulled slate-red tile roofs of the village, and into acres of green and gold, dotted with feeding beasts, the farming hinterland of Klippan.

And beyond that, the mountains, and the road to Norway, and then the sea again, and the bitter grace of the

Arctic ice at Spitzbergen. But I never thought of that, when I was sixteen.

My father was a typical man of his time, in more ways than one. He'd met my mother first at Sunday school, and she'd been his childhood sweetheart. There was never any question that when they were old enough their parents would agree to a marriage. For the second son and the third daughter of two modestly successful local farmers the match was a suitable one.

So the bells rang in the wooden tower of the church on a fine May morning in 1877, and the young couple plighted their troth, and made their vows before God, in the same plain pews as their grandparents had done. My father worked on his uncle's land, and my mother helped milk the cows and make the cheeses.

But then, one day in the winter of 1881, my father was chopping wood for the stove, and caught his two end fingers in the blade of the axe, and they had to be amputated. The nerves were permanently damaged, and his hand was never the same again. It broke his heart, but it meant he could no more do the regular work on the farm.

Various people spoke to each other, and eventually something was found for him to do. The postal service had been expanding rapidly in the 1870s, and our local postmaster in Klippan was growing old, and needed an assistant. My father got the job, on the understanding that when the older man retired, in only a few years' time, he would have to undertake the full responsibility on his own.

By 1885, when I was seven, my father had become the local postmaster, and so he remained until I left Klippan in 1901. He was never, I think, entirely reconciled to the work. He was an outdoor man, never happier than when pruning rose bushes or digging flower beds. He had the blood of centuries of farmers in his veins.

But he made the best of his new post. It grew more and more important as time went on, and my father enjoyed the position of authority it gave him in our little community. He had letters and parcels to manage and sort through and see safely delivered, and by the mid-1890s there was the expansion of the new postal telegraph. Sending cables became quite a craze.

12

For every occasion from the death of an uncle to the birth of a daughter, the wires hummed with condolence or congratulation. My own birth, on the 25th July, 1878, was celebrated in hushed voices, and with heartfelt prayers for my mother's recovery.

I grew up realizing as the years went by that I'd been a burden to my mother before I was born, and I think I always felt some kind of guilt towards her because of this. I know that my father deeply resented the necessity of forgoing the son and heir he'd always wanted, the strong unmutilated boy who could walk back into the fields, and regain the claim on the land those broken fingers of his had lost.

Of course, I was shown love, and the kind of love an only child inevitably enjoys. What money there was to spare could be spent on new clothes, or books or dolls, and even an occasional holiday in Gothenburg or into the mountains. I had a room of my own, and plenty of attention to my physical health and my moral well-being.

But there was a strictness, almost a vindictive strictness it seems to me now, in the way my mother would insist on my helping her out with even the least onerous of domestic chores, emphasizing her own frailty against my burgeoning adolescent strength. I was made to make beds and to cook meals, to clean floors and to do washing. It was good for me, I suppose, and it saved money on having a maid living in. But I hated the drudgery, even though I did perform my tasks with an outward appearance of good grace.

My father was a distant figure compared with my mother, a stern, uniformed presence in the post office, with terrific moustaches, and a large gold signet ring on his hairy knuckle. At home, he seemed more approachable, but only in the way one might approach a lion that had temporarily escaped from its cage.

I was frightened of my father. Frightened of his great bulk, and the evident physical strength he could demonstrate whenever he swung me off my feet into the air. I hated to feel I was losing my safe grip on the ground, and I used, even as a tiny child, to kick and scream when I felt the earth sinking away.

My father would laugh, amused and scornful of my fear. A man child would scarcely have been so timid. Even in my teens he would still, in his cheerful moods, hoist me out of a chair as I sat sewing, and hold my squirming waist at arm's length, watching my boots lunging for something to catch on.

Put me down, father, I would scream, pretending to giggle, and loathing every minute of it.

Nowadays, to judge from that book by Sigmund Freud they're all talking about in Glasgow, you'd have to say there was something sexual about it, I'm told. My poor frustrated father working out his desires on his teasing young daughter.

But it wasn't that. I wasn't trying to tease when I kicked my legs for a grip. I desperately wanted to be back on the ground. And my father wasn't frustrated. He knew well enough how to get what he needed from my mother without having to put her in the family way. Sweden was an enlightened country, even in those days.

It was bitterness that made him lift me up in the air. He had to take it out of me for not being a boy. His affectionate gentleness was a kind of contemptuous dismissal.

There were other ways it came about as well. He would sit me down beside him after dinner in the drawing-room, and try to excite my interest in agriculture, the complex process of weaning spring lambs, or the various points in favour of feeding cattle on sainfoin or lucerne.

I knew about farming life as other country girls do, in a natural, unaffected way, and I'd learn a lot from wandering through the fields and talking to the reapers in August, and the men sowing barley in March. It was all haphazard knowledge, though, not book-learning.

You have to read, Anna, my father would say, turning the pages of the heavy, maroon-leather-spined encyclopedias in his huge hands. You have to know the names.

But the books were always too heavy for me to lift, and my boredom at their insensitive cataloguing of what ought to be magical and instinctive, as it seemed to my adolescent mind, made the pages flutter closed as I let the great tomes fall from my fingers onto the floor.

14

Be careful, Anna, my mother would say, carping always at what seemed to her to be carelessness. Your father had to pay for those books, you know.

I could understand my father's dream of the land, his ingrained sadness at having had to put it behind him. But I knew it was never the place for me, or not, at any rate, as the placid wife of some sombre local yeoman.

To do him credit, however, my father was no narrow concentrator on farming matters. His intellectual interests were wide for a local postmaster, and he bought and read periodicals and books on a large range of subjects. He was an avid follower of the news, too, and the *Aftonbladet* would always lie beside his plate at breakfast-time. It was one of my many jobs to make sure of that.

One morning a few days after my sixteenth birthday, in late July 1894, I was drawing on my boots to go out for a walk when my father looked up from the inside pages of the paper. He looked at me with a slight smile over the tops of his oval gold spectacles.

This might be your salvation, Anna, he said, and then he read aloud, spacing the words with a solemn slowness. 'Young man of good family, and excellent education, seeks position as tutor for the months of August and September. Living in preferred.'

My school holidays had begun some eight days earlier, and there had already been talk between my mother and father about whether I might profit from some extra tuition before the following term. The thought of acquiring a captive audience, albeit only of one, was a further inducement to my father in deciding to look about for some suitable person to enlarge my education.

I'll write and ask to see his references, my father concluded. He certainly sounds exactly what we require.

So that was that. In due course, a letter was dispatched to the newspaper, and another returned fat with eulogies. Mr Nils Strindberg (a very respectable name, as my father judged it) was a graduate of the University of Stockholm. He was exceptionally qualified in natural sciences. His hobby was photography. He was twenty-two years old.

Very good, my father said, as he thumbed through the documents. I admire an interest in these new studies. I shall suggest that Mr Strindberg presents himself for an interview. He can take the train down from Stockholm to Malmö. I shall buy him lunch there at the railway station and explore his mind.

So my father was driven in to Malmö, and met the prospective tutor, and spent an hour discussing with him the effects of rainfall on root-crops, and was very favourably impressed. There was no question of either my mother or myself, or indeed the tutor himself, needing to meet and discuss arrangements.

My father returned on the evening of August 6th, stepping down from his cousin's two-in-hand with an armful of magazines on fertilizers, and the deal completed.

Strindberg will arrive on Thursday, he pronounced, and went straight up to bed.

I suppose all adolescent girls keep a diary. Mine was thronged with vague, dreamy sketches, and pressed flowers. They still seem to retain some odour and feel of those lost summers of the 1890s when I turn over the lavender pages and finger the crumbled petals.

The words are less evocative. The ways of describing things are derived from the books I was reading, the primness and detachment of the officially recognized Jane Austen, and the highly coloured romanticism of the wildly improper and definitely not recognized Ouida. I used to acquire a second-hand copy of one of those wicked English romances at school, swapping a treasured pair of gloves for it, or even, perhaps, a locket with a photograph of Jenny Lind. She was still our great hero in Klippan, in the 90s.

Whatever happened to me came out sounding either too decent or too lurid. I have to raid my memory to give weight and order to those far-off days. The bare entries, respectable or hectic as they are, no more than hint at the real turmoil and wonder of my life. That needs the skill of hindsight.

It helps, though, to read what I wrote at the time. I have the pages for that first, remote meeting with my dear Nils open here as I sit by the window. The gentle Victorian covers, with their gilding and their blue marker ribbon —

they look very incongruous against the hard, Aztec lines of this modern wireless set.

I wonder, though. Such a piece of up-to-date equipment, with all its fragile grey valves and its power, seems much more the natural accompaniment for Nils than an old-fashioned, floppy-backed and very imprecise girl's day-book. Those valves, too. With their screw bases, when you open the back of the set, and their filaments, like lightbulbs. They're the same shape as balloons. Little, hard, eternal memorial balloons, locked in stiff plywood coffins to keep the voyage of Andrée and Strindberg alive.

Nils would have liked the idea.

Be exact, he used to say, when I showed him one of my drawings. Look down and see the internal nature of what you're drawing. Compare one thing with another until you understand. It's a matter of thinking. That's what Leonardo did. Think, and then draw.

Then he put down the book, and held his hand to one side, in that very actorish, dismissive gesture he used to have, as if he was brushing crumbs from a table.

It might be loosestrife, he said. But you say it's rosebay willowherb. It might be any fairly tall weed with reddish petals. Whatever you do, be accurate. It's the same when you write as when you draw. Think first, and get it right.

Well, I've thought about that first meeting with Nils, and this is how it seems. It must have been about half past three, and I was in the garden, sketching. It was a hot, oppressive day, and I was wearing a straw bonnet, tied under the chin, to protect me from the sun. The garden was looking fresh and bright, as it always did in August. It seemed to get its second wind then, largely because my father took infinite pains to plant all his flowers with an eye to when each would open and be at its best.

I was in a corner I liked as well as any, under the shadow of a blossoming ceanothus, with a torrent of little dark-blue coconut cakes mounting on their stems behind my head towards the cloudless sky. My pencil and sketching-pad lay beside me on the rustic bench.

I'd heard the carriage come over the bridge, though I couldn't see it from where I was sitting, so it was no surprise when I heard the sound of voices, the light, slightly whining tones of my mother, and the deeper, more vibrant interventions of another voice.

I smoothed my dress down, and lifted my pad. I was trying to draw the view across the stream, purling by a few feet away, and presenting a flickering squadron of blue dragonflies as a foreground to the more distant prospect of grazing Holsteins.

Here she is, my mother was suddenly saying, at my elbow, and then, Anna, this is Mr Strindberg. He's just arrived.

That kind of irrelevance was typical of my mother's conversation. It was as if she needed to justify any given statement with some backing information to support and condone it. But I wasn't bothered by my mother's foibles that day. My eyes were all for the new tutor.

I was confronted, I realized, by a very dapper, slightly plump young man, wearing a dove-grey three-piece suit, unobtrusive in its elegance, and a pair of cotton spats a little less unobtrusive in theirs. The plain, bone-tipped cane the young man was carrying added a final note of a slightly swashbuckling flamboyance to his dress. At any rate, it seemed so to me. But I was a country girl, as I say, unused to seeing fashionable young men from Stockholm. It may be that this particular example of the genre was no more extravagant in his appearance than most.

I'm very pleased to make your acquaintance, Miss Charlier, the young man said, with a steady smile, bowing gently over his cane.

I was very taken by this. I wasn't used to such graceful ways. I blushed a little, I remember, and shuffled my papers on the pad.

Anna, my mother said, smoothly seating herself on the bench, and motioning to me to rise. I know that Mr Strindberg would like some tea. I know he would.

This repetition was designed to forestall the implicit demur in the new tutor's gesture, as he moved a gloved hand from his cane. My mother was very keen on her tea. She wasn't going to postpone this essential afternoon ritual on the grounds that my education needed to be commenced at once.

18

I'll get some tea, mother, I said, laying my sketch-pad aside.

How very kind, Anna, my mother said, sighing a little to indicate that her own tiredness inevitably prevented any assistance being given in the provision of this tea. Then, rapidly adding some tone of gracious condescension to this preliminary move, she patted the seat beside her. Please, make yourself at home, Mr Strindberg, she continued. I'll explain what Anna knows, and needs to know, while she makes the tea.

The new tutor smiled at me as I rose to go.

Thank you very much, Anna, he said, seating himself and laying his gloves and cane on the ground.

I liked this attentiveness, but I was just old and shrewd enough to see that the young man was trying almost too hard. I was amused by this, I discovered, and went in to make the tea with an opening impression mingling a feeling of being flattered with a feeling of being watched and teased.

I made the tea, and took out a tray with our best silver service, and a plate of fruit cake I'd baked myself. Under the generalship of my mother, this tray was found a place on the grass, while I was dispatched again to the house to look out a small table and a basket chair. Throughout these arrangements, and comings and goings, my mother maintained a flow of what she evidently took to be appropriate tea-time gossip, and the new tutor maintained an expression of what he, I thought, evidently took to be appropriate attentive concern. This mood was broken only when he would leap to his feet and offer a comparatively useless helping hand in the establishment of the bamboo table or the spreading of the tea-cloth.

At last, all was ready. The tea was poured, the cake eaten (largely by my mother, who pronounced it too nutty) and the conversation maintained at the same slightly unreal tea-time level. An hour went by thus, pleasantly if boringly enough. Then, rising to her feet with another of her prepared sighs, my mother announced her departure.

I always need to rest for an hour or so before dinner, she explained, drawing the skin down from her forehead, as if

19

indicating an appalling headache. Anna will augment what information I have already given you, Mr Strindberg.

After my mother had gone, the sun seemed to burn hotter for a moment. The birds were singing, I noticed, and there was the occasional hushing of a breeze.

I was sitting with my back to the stream, in the basket chair, and Nils was facing me on the bench. He bent down and lifted my sketch-pad, where it lay on the ground. He turned the sheets, idly.

You know, he said. There's an English painter called Marcus Stone. He's always painting couples in Regency clothes in beautiful garden settings. Very like this, he added, with one of those actorish waves of his hand. The girl is usually on a rustic bench. The man is standing adoringly by. Sometimes you have a basket of fruit, or the remains of a meal, like this. The titles are always very simple, and rather touching. The most famous is called 'In Love'.

The new tutor looked up from my sketch-book, and smiled at me. I realized for the first time that he had a very marked pair of lines round his mouth which gave him an air of smiling when he wasn't. His features were smooth, unformed, with a kind of girlish softness about them. I later realized that it was often, as now, the contrast between what he said and how he looked that gave his personality much of its charm and distinctiveness.

For the moment it was all I could do to hide my confusion. I wasn't used to young men talking so abstractly about matters of the heart. I sat very still, staring down at my hands clasped in my lap.

'In Love', the young man repeated. Then he laughed. Everyone in Europe imitates him, he said, scornfully. His paintings are rubbish. Don't you think that's marvellous? Isn't it marvellous?

I didn't think it was marvellous at all. I thought it was confusing, almost frightening. I looked up at the new tutor, and I think he saw that he'd had the effect he wanted to have. He laid aside my sketch-pad, making no comment, or no further comment than the one he'd already implicitly made.

20

You work very hard, he said, lifting his glove and cane, and rising. Your mother is very fond of you, you know. She wants me to turn you into a young lady. But I think you're probably enough of a young lady already. So I'm not going to do what she wants.

She won't like that, I said, suddenly fearful that I'd said or done something to cause this young man to decide, after all, not to accept his engagement as tutor in our house.

No, he said, striding to and fro on the grass, and poking at specks of mud with his cane. I'm going to turn you into a young gentleman. Exactly like myself. What else can one do? A tutor is like a machine for copying things. He copies what he knows from others, from books and from people. And then he makes copies. Copies of what he knows. Copies of himself. And that's exactly what you shall be. It's the best I can do.

Then he went into the house, and I didn't see him again until dinner-time, when he ate and praised my fish-pie, and discussed some new developments in wireless telegraphy with my father, and promised to get some French silk sent to my mother by his aunt. He was the perfect guest, the perfect companion, and I found him mysterious, remote, and, albeit fascinatingly so, a little pretentious. I decided, as best I could, to be on my guard.

The following morning I had my first tutorial. The breakfast-things had been cleared, and we were sitting opposite each other at the dining-table. In front of Nils was the copy of *Aftonbladet* my father had left behind when he went to work. It was folded down at one of the centre pages.

Read this, my tutor said, leaning over and pointing with his finger to a news item he had ringed in red.

'BALLOON ASCENT,' the item said. 'Yesterday the well-known aeronaut, Mr S.A. Andrée, made his seventh ascent in the dirigible balloon supplied to him by the Lars Hierta Foundation. The ascent was completely successful, and Mr Andrée is planning a further one later this year.' The item was headed, Gothenburg, and the paper was dated August 5th, 1894.

You know nothing about balloons, Nils interrupted,

seizing the paper from my hand, except as brightly coloured toys to be tied and burst at children's parties.

I was nettled by the reference. I considered myself a long way from the sort of party where balloons would be in evidence.

Make notes, Nils continued, leaning back and closing his eyes. And then he proceeded, slowly, as if dictating. In view of his seven balloon ascents, we may prima facie consider Salomon August Andrée as the type of the modern hero, the Nietzschean superman. I'll explain Nietzschean. Nietzsche is the greatest living philosopher. The superman is the man who transcends the ordinary. Who — metaphorically — rises above the everyday world in the balloon of his genius.

I had not taken in all of this but I'd taken in enough, and become irritated and thus bold enough, to make some objection.

What about the superwoman? I asked. Does she rise above the everyday world in the balloon of her genius, too?

It would be most improper, he said, for a lady to go up in a balloon. Woman is like a tortoise, she is helpless when laid on her back. That's what Nietzsche said. But then, he added, pursing his lips, Aeschylus, the greatest of all Greek tragedians, was killed by a tortoise dropped on his head by a passing eagle. And it must surely have been the shell that crushed his skull, the tortoise upside down. So perhaps Nietzsche was wrong. Or rather — surprisingly for him — he didn't go far enough. Woman is not so much helpless, as evil, when laid on her back. What do you think, Anna? Are you evil when laid on your back?

This kind of obliquely sexual badinage was to be a common feature of Nils's educational technique, I soon learned. It was a kind of can-opener, a means of disrupting one's normal expectations. Later, I thought it might have been flirtatious, too, but it never struck me as so at the time. It was all done so coolly, with such panache and aplomb.

I don't know, I said to the present sally. I have bad dreams when I sleep on my back.

The weather-clock on top of the small-boy in the corner

22

was chiming nine, and I watched the little Swiss man in his knickerbockers and Alpine hat roll out on his board and then retire through the closing door of his chalet.

Dreams, Nils was saying. Do you ever dream in colour? Have you dreamt the same thing twice? Dreams are our sins, Anna. Tell me one of your sins.

I remembered the nights I'd wakened in the small hours, watching the shadows of the trees moving on the wall in the moonlight, sweating with a nameless fear, sweating with another even more nameless feeling I now call bare need, and some may call perverse desire. But I wasn't going to tell my new tutor about that.

I once dreamt I was dancing, I said, choosing an innocuous dream, and no one was paying any attention. It was in a big room, full of mirrors, and my hair was all undone. It had to be, for the dance. And all the people were talking and laughing on little gold chairs all round the room. And the more I danced, the more they ignored me. I took my shoes off then, and danced in bare feet, and then all the mirrors broke, and I cut myself on the glass. And I still danced, and they still ignored me.

That's beautiful, said Nils, matter-of-factly. But it's vague. Far too vague. I want you to draw me a picture of it, and only put in what's clear.

I thought for a moment.

It's not the sort of thing you can draw, I said, after a time. I mean, not clearly.

You can draw anything clearly, said Nils. What isn't clear, doesn't exist.

This was his creed, I see now. It came out in a hundred ways. He would question anything and everything, always anxious to bring the matter down to a series of hard facts, almost mathematical formulae. It was an obsession with him, almost something mystical.

He had none of the German vagueness that used to be so common at that time in Sweden. The cloudy majesty of Wagner, and the convoluted horror of Grimm's fairy tales, these were not for Nils Strindberg.

Think of that black balloon up there, he said, against the clear blue sky. Draw that for me. Be clear, Anna. Be clear.

But I wasn't clear. I was a muddy brook, teeming with

23

elvers and newts, and with subtle unknown crawling tiny creatures there at the bottom of me. Things too evasive and darkly fearsome to come up and simplify themselves to the daytime shapes of compass and ruler. Nils never realized that. Or rather, he realized it, but he thought it might change. All he had to do was fish, and dam, and drain. The waters would come clear, and be the better for it.

They never did. They never have. That raving madman there on the wireless, the one they say's become Chancellor of Germany, with his blood and toil, he knows more about the human soul than ever my poor Nils did. My poor Nils. I loved him, though. Even then, I think, in our dim dining-room, pacing to and fro in his spats and his grey suit. Even before the feeling surfaced into the will to change what he was. To become his own tutor, as he'd been mine. Or tried to be.

It passed quietly, that long August, and we each came to respect each other's qualities. I learned about photography, and Nobel, and Nordenskjöld, and his trip round the edge of Russia in the *Vega*. I learned about Leonardo and Lewis Carroll. I learned about Uncle Johan, the eccentric relation of Nils's who wrote plays and was said to hate women. And I learned about Andrée.

One of Nils's most impressive characteristics, I soon discovered, was to absorb and retain an immense amount of factual information in his head, and then produce it, like a silk scarf out of a sleeve, when one least expected it.

This often gave him the air of seeming to know everything about everything, and he clearly enjoyed, and cultivated, this air. One of his tricks was to bring the conversation round, by some casual remark, towards whatever subject he had it in mind to enlarge on, and then launch forth into his discourse as if the topic had come up by accident.

It was thus, about half way through his time as my tutor, that he returned to the theme of Andrée and his balloon journeys.

It was the only really wet day we had, I remember, one of those freak summer storms of rain that often come in late afternoon in Scania.

24

Normally our hours in the schoolroom, as the dining-room had become for the month of August, would be nine to twelve and the afternoons were usually left free for more casual talk in the garden, or while out walking. But on this day, for some reason anticipating the bad weather, we'd stayed at home, indoors.

I was leaning with my chin in my hands, gazing out through the long, horizontal, Gothic-leaded window across our strip of front garden and wishing the sky would clear. But the rain swept in sudden gusts, and I watched the passers-by with their umbrellas up, and their faces turned down into their coat collars to keep dry.

Nils was standing by the tall cylinder of the corner stove, fingering a piece of material, in fact a fragment of a Japanese kimono, that my mother was working on to incorporate in a patchwork dress.

Silk, he said, suddenly. The most wonderful stuff in the world. Woven by worms, worn by queens. You can dye it any colour. Water runs off it. They use it to make wedding-dresses, umbrellas, even balloons.

I was already making notes with my little silver pencil in my copy-book. Nils had made it abundantly clear that he expected his least utterance to be carefully written down and pondered.

Andrée again? I queried.

I'd grown very forward and quick in the last two weeks and I knew that Nils appreciated my power to connect things up. He laid down the piece of material now, and put the tips of his fingers together, touching the underside of his chin and lips before speaking. It was another mannerism very frequent with him.

Seven journeys, he said, frowning. One. On the 15th of July 1893 he takes off from the barrack-yard of the Royal Svea Engineers, in Stockholm. At 3.34 a.m. During this first ascent, which lasts more than two and a half hours, he is carried forty-two kilometres, and attains a height of 4,500 metres.

Nils paused.

He rose in the darkness, I said slowly. Landed shortly after dawn. Was higher than most of the mountains in Sweden. Travelled faster than I could run.

25

Three facts of interest are recorded, said Nils, ignoring this cleverness. One. At his highest point, he distinctly heard dogs barking. Two. During the descent, he discovered that, when the gas was allowed to escape in part from the balloon, the lower part of the envelope was forced in by the pressure of the air, so that, in some degree, it acted as a parachute. Three. He noted that, so far as scientific observations were concerned, the ideal crew would have been three: one to observe, one to record, and one to manage the balloon.

I went over to the window, and watered the pot plants along the ledge. They seemed to yearn towards the streaks of drops on the further side of the glass, very near, and yet very far. I stroked the slim copper spout of the watering-can.

You'd like to fly in a balloon, I said. Which would you be? Observer? Or recorder?

Nils was lolling back on the wooden settle along the wall. He smiled.

You're right, he said. I couldn't manage the balloon myself. I'm not the type. I leave that to the Andrées of this world. I'd be the recorder.

I came and sat down again at the table. My hair was done in long plaits that day, and I twisted one in my hands.

What makes you so fascinated with Mr Andrée? I asked.

Nils twirled an imaginary moustache.

He is a very, very good-looking man, he said. He would make an excellent husband, and a splendid father of your children.

Seriously, I said. I want to know.

Seriously, said Nils, with an openness that was very typical of him, I wrote away to the paper for further details of his flights the very day I saw the report. They put me in touch with the Swedish Anthropological and Geographical Society, and this very morning I received through the post an abstract of an article from their journal, setting out the details of Andrée's voyages in his own words. That's why he's in my mind.

He's your superman, I said.

Nils shrugged his shoulders.

Just one of them, he said, off-handedly. Just one of them. But I'll tell you this, he added, leaning forward on his hands. There are three things about him I like. One, he's a patriot. He wants to do something for Sweden. So do I. Two, he's a scientist. He wants to discover more about the structure of the universe. So do I. Three, he's an adventurer.

Nils paused.

What he's doing with this balloon, he said slowly, could provide the means for a completely new kind of exploration. Penetrating to the very depths of the African jungles. Crossing the frozen ice to the North Pole.

I had a sudden vision of a great ruined church. I was in the nave, shivering in the wind, surrounded by broken graves, white tombstones. I raised my eyes. At the north side, there was a tall stained glass window, constructed out of blocks of multicoloured ice. I felt myself swinging through a hundred and eighty degrees, like a bell on a rope. I was upside down, close to the window, staring at a drop of rain, seeming to float, suspended in the deepest blue. Three tiny figures, men or flies, were waving to me from the drop's tip.

I don't like balloons, I said.

Somewhere no one has ever been before, said Nils, not seeming to hear. That's where Andrée wants to go. I admire him for that. Even if I could never follow him.

I shook my head. I wasn't entirely convinced by these explanations. There seemed to be something else, a missing link. But I couldn't think of the right question to ask, and I knew that Nils wanted to go on. I let my vision slide.

Tell me about the second balloon journey, I said.

Seven hours, said Nils, more casually now, and a hundred kilometres. It took twelve hours to fill the balloon with gas. The balloon spun round and round in air currents, especially when it was rising rapidly.

I closed my eyes.

I'd get very dizzy, I said. I'd be sick.

I know, said Nils, nodding. I'm very worried about that. You'd have to practise. Vomiting, I mean. It's a matter of holding your stomach back, and leaning well forward, so as not to spoil your clothes.

27

With an unfolding movement, he was on his feet, bending over the table at me, and retching loudly in an awful parody of a man being violently sick. It was typical of his boisterous, deliberately shocking humour.

Mr Strindberg, I said, matter-of-factly. I shan't be in the balloon. I'm not a man.

Not quite, said Nils, wagging his finger, and resuming his seat on the settle. But very nearly. You're getting more and more like I am every day. Ninth carbon already. Still very muzzy at the edges, but a perfectly legible copy. I am earning my money, Miss Charlier. I do assure you I am earning my money. You are almost the young gentleman I said I would make you.

I wasn't, of course. But I allowed Nils his delusion. It was all part of the mutually teasing stimulus that the process of learning with him had become. He was a good teacher, and he knew how to make an adolescent girl work hard, and feel wanted, and pay attention.

Let's go for a walk, I said. The rain's stopping.

But Nils was having none of that.

The third voyage, he said, lowering his voice to a sepulchral whisper, was the most exciting. It was also the most dangerous. The balloon was carried right out to sea, towards the Finnish archipelago. You see, the direction of the wind had changed.

Nils puffed up his cheeks, and expelled his breath in a low wind-whistling noise, then turned his head and repeated the noise in another direction.

Imagine Andrée, he said, in mock horror. His vessel is proceeding at a great speed into the middle of nowhere. All round him is open sea, above him nothing but air. What does he do?

Throw out ballast, I suggested, stroking my cheek with the hair at the end of my braid.

Nils shook his hands in the air, as if frantic.

But this will drag him down to the sea, he said. The cold, weltering sea. The icy grave of so many mariners before his time. No, said Nils. He waits until he sees a ship. He decides to seek its aid. He uses his drag-line to reduce his speed. It slows his progress. But it isn't enough. He attaches two empty ballast-sacks to his landing-line — that's another rope he has — and these drag some more. It's enough. He hovers near to the ship. He hopes that they'll catch a rope and haul him down. But it's going to be tricky, very tricky. He notices that the captain wants to lie athwart the balloon's course, and he realizes that this may result in the rigging getting damaged, or even the funnel. He daren't take the risk. So he tries to increase his speed and get away. He tries to raise the landing-line. But he can't. It's too heavy. He has to cut it free. His speed increases. He heads for Finland at thirty kilometres an hour.

This narrative, delivered now with staccato speed, had drawn Nils into a real feeling of involvement. His manner had changed. It was no longer a macabre tale to amuse a teenage girl he was telling, it was the bare facts of a grim journey he had lived through himself step by step.

I felt his intensity, gripped by his passion.

Go on, I said, my chin cupped on my hands as I listened.

He passes more vessels, Nils continued, his eyes focused on the window, but not seeing the skies clearing. He notices that the balloon dips and swoops like a kite, as the gas diminishes, and the wind moves it forward now. Darkness has fallen, and he has no idea of the time.

Nils shook his head, as if surfacing from a dive. He grinned at me.

But he knew what time it was when he landed, he said. You see, the landing took place with such force that his watch stopped. In the morning he realized that this had happened at 7.18 p.m., and that he was on a small island.

From which he was later rescued, I said, after living for many months with a beautiful native girl who washed his socks and made him tea.

My socks don't need washing, said Nils, but I'll have some tea.

Later as we sat drinking from flowered English china, and nibbling biscuits, he told me about the other four voyages.

The importance of the third voyage, he said, as he tapped his biscuit on his saucer, was this. It had demonstrated for the first time how guide-ropes could be used to control the progress of a balloon more precisely than ballast.

Like braking a cart down a hill, I suggested, and then lifting the brake on the level ground. That's easy, I scoffed.

No, said Nils, bridling. It wasn't so easy. Carts run on roads, and brakes are short. It took imagination to think of ropes, and using them over water. Anyway, he added, dipping his biscuit in his tea to annoy me, knowing that I thought this was vulgar, it hadn't been done before.

The sun was shining again now, sending a shaft of light in through the small panes onto the open door of the stove, through which it made the rim of the kettle glitter on its hob.

That voyage was made in October last year, said Nils. On the 26th of February this year, Andrée took off from Gothenburg on his fourth voyage. This time he succeeded in filling his balloon in only two and three-quarter hours.

It's very bracing at Gothenburg, I said. No wonder that he was so quick. He'd have frozen stiff out there in the cold for his usual half a day.

Facetiousness, said Nils, will get you nowhere. Oddly enough, this fourth voyage did indeed have a comic ending. The balloon landed in a tree, south of Jönköping, and Andrée climbed out and went to a nearby farm building for assistance. But the woman and boy there had locked themselves in. They thought he was an evil spirit.

I smiled, amused by the story.

Of course, Nils added flippantly, he might have been after the woman's virtue. Or the boy's. Do you think he was after the boy's virtue, Anna?

I shook my head, and blushed at that, still able to be outraged a little at my tutor's impropriety.

More tea, said Nils, and waited while I poured.

The fifth ascent, he said, was on the 7th of April. On this occasion Andrée attained his greatest height. Some 4,500 metres. From 4,000 metres he experienced a slight headache, and the beating of his pulse produced a faint singing noise on the left side of his skull.

I've heard my uncle say you get the same kind of thing when you climb mountains, I said. The higher you go, the worse it is.

A matter of the supply of oxygen to the blood, I suspect, said Nils. If you went high enough, your brain would burst, and you'd die in agony. Just imagine going up and up, with all your ballast gone, and not being able to stop.

I played with my beads, the long string of black glass ones my father had given me for my birthday. They were cut in facets, little crystal balls on a thread.

Mr Strindberg, I said. I sometimes think there's something very morbid about you.

But there wasn't. I was the morbid one, even then, fascinated by the lethal image of the three men in an upward spiral, twisting like a paper taper in the draft of a flue, from the fires of purgatory to the terrible darkness of eternal heaven.

No, said Nils, it isn't the danger that appeals to me. With proper precautions, voyaging in a balloon should be no more dangerous than a ride in a pony-trap.

I know a boy who fell from a pony-trap and broke his neck, I said. He was only eight.

The dog had come in, and was flapping his tail to and fro against Nils's legs.

He wants a walk, I said. Let's take him down to the stream.

Nils groaned, and put his head in his hands.

The sixth ascent, he said, rising to his feet, and fondling Ranger's neck, will have, I see, to be swift. Fortunately, it was. It took place on the 14th of July, only a few days before my advertisement for work as a tutor appeared in the *Aftonbladet* and brought we two soulmates together. There are only two things to say about it.

I was drawing my gloves on, and furling my parasol.

One, said Nils, holding the door open for me, and watching Ranger bound out, was the use of a sail, to direct the balloon with. In some trials, the deviation was more than 30° from the main course.

I had unlatched the wicket now, and we were stepping through into the street. The sun was bright and warm in a sharp, clear sky, and the gaily painted wooden buildings were shining like dolls' houses in the light. Our dog was leaping ahead, eager and joyful.

31

Just like a sailing-boat, I said. With the guide-rope employed as a kind of rudder, I suppose.

Nils raised his hat to a passing neighbour.

The girl is a wonder, he said, addressing an imaginary friend in the hedgerow. She is really a wonder. Eleven marks out of fourteen. Three off for insolence.

We turned left and then right again, and strolled down towards the river. Everything was fresh and rinsed-looking after the rain. Small beads glistened on the privet flowers and the lilac leaves.

One last thing, said Nils. He threw down balloon-cards, to be filled in and returned by the finders, as a means of plotting the course of the balloon.

Let's look for some, I suggested. After all, they might have been blown a long way off course by the wind.

Remembering the buoys, it seems a prophetic remark now, but it didn't then, in the warm August sun, in Klippan.

They were weighted, silly, said Nils. How else could they stay where they fell?

We were walking now along the river-bank, and the dog was nosing ahead, snuffling into every nook and cranny of the water-side. I put my parasol up, and walked a little apart from Nils, twirling the stem in my hands. I thought the parasol made me seem a very mature and sophisticated lady, but I suspect in retrospect that my management of it was a trifle childish.

Nils walked right over by the water, staring at his boots, kicking at things, whistling, or throwing sticks for the dog. He'd become much more casual and countrified in his manner over the past few weeks.

I heard from my Uncle Johan today, he said, apropos of nothing. He's thinking of moving to Paris.

Nils's Uncle Johan, the writer, was one of the recurring themes of our more casual conversations. I had been instantly taken by the story of his long and embittered romance with Siri von Essen, and now by his exile in Germany in a stone cottage on a great Moravian estate with his new bride, Frida Uhl. It seemed the very stuff of an English novel to my hectic young imagination and I was always asking Nils to tell me more.

32

How is the baby? I asked.

Uncle Johan and his wife had recently become the parents of a noisy and troublesome child, and the domestic idyll was about to break up into a familiar pattern of hatred and withdrawal.

He can't bear it, said Nils, cheerfully. The old boy wants to have it baptized a Catholic, but Uncle Johan says that he won't be hurried. And Frida. Frida apparently still says that he smells of sulphur.

But he won't give up his chemical experiments, I put in, intelligently.

I knew that this had been a severe bone of contention between these warring dogs, Uncle Johan and his German wife.

We Strindbergs do as we choose, said Nils. Like Lucifer, the Prince of Darkness, we always carry a smell of sulphur about with us. It's our natural element.

I wonder, though. With Nils it was the natural chemicals, the traces of hypo or glycerine on his fingers, from working with film plates or dyes, that gave him his characteristic odour and tone. There was none of the metaphorical sulphur, the stink of fire and brimstone, that hung round his mysterious and fury-driven Uncle Johan. That was my own province, then and now. The cloudy depths. The muggy waters of the nether lake. The crude airs of the place my tutor never touched.

The seventh ascent, I said, as we turned at last to walk home. That was the very day you came.

Nils raised his eyes to the sky, and carolled a tune.

That magic day, he said. That very magic day.

Then his mood changed. He tucked his arm through mine, arranging the parasol behind our shoulders.

Miss Charlier, he said. I believe that one day my uncle, Johan August Strindberg, will be known as the greatest writer of his day. His plays will be performed all over the world.

At the time, this struck me as family pride, but in retrospect it stands out as a sober enough prediction.

The funny thing, said Nils, appearing to speak confidentially into my ear, is that Uncle Johan wants to be remembered as a botanist. A botanist! He wants to be able to show that plants can think and feel in the same way as people can.

We were back now beside our own garden wall. Nils leant over, and plucked a budding rose. He handed it to me, with a slight bow.

Do you think this rose can think and feel, Anna? he asked. I mean, like a woman can. Like you, perhaps.

I kept the rose in a little three-cornered glass jar in my room, and it bloomed and died, shedding its dark red petals over the white wood of my window ledge; and later, when Nils had left us, in early September, waving to me from the swaying seat of the two-in-hand as the horse clattered away across the bridge, I folded the remains of that wilted blossom into my diary, and pressed it down, and with it stamped the memory and the image of Nils Strindberg, the summer tutor, hard and for ever into my heart.

Yes, I was already in love. It may have been the moment when he took my arm, or when he plucked the flower. I don't really know. But the irreversible movement had begun.

It wasn't, of course, the first time, and I was just old enough, and sensible enough, to realize that it might be no more than a passing infatuation. I was a shrewd, practical girl, and I'd had a depressing obsession with the son of a local farmer, who'd given me no cause to suspect my feelings were reciprocated, or even noticed, and had in due course become engaged to a dumpy hoyden from Malmö, and gone to work in a cement factory, to earn sufficient money to win her hand.

I'd been hurt by that, and I didn't want to be hurt again. There were boys at school I flirted with, and older men I'd had a crush on. But that was to be expected, I knew, at my age. What I didn't want again, or not so soon, was the great love of my life, the unrequited passion that would ravish me through and through and last for ever.

Somehow I knew that it had to be unrequited. Such love, in the kind of books I read, nearly always was. The man was either unworthy, a villain and a rogue, or inaccessible, because married or pledged to someone else. It was these barriers that gave the passion its intensity.

34

Having lived through such an isolated, and rather abstract, affair, and one still fully documented in my diary for the mature eyes of sixteen to recall and learn from, I had no desire or readiness to repeat the experience.

Of course, Nils was neither unworthy, nor inaccessible. Not in principle. But in practice, in my heart of hearts, I knew that the chance of him ever responding to my private little passion was pretty remote.

Needless to say, any response would have had to be romantic, ideal. I had no notion of the bodily satisfactions to be got out of being in love. My father, though a deeply religious man, was in no way a prudish one, but he would have drawn the line, like most of his contemporaries, at allowing a girl in her early teens any acquaintance with the seamy facts of life.

I grew up ignorant of these, like the rest of my generation. What little I picked up was frightening, and improperly understood.

There had been a disturbing incident one day on my uncle's farm, when I was no more than twelve. I'd been taken into a disused barn, by a boy of fourteen or so, who'd already shown a perverse enjoyment in tickling under my arms when I wasn't looking, and once, when I lay in the sun beside a stream reading, teasing my bare feet with a feather.

The implications of this meant nothing to me, nor perhaps even to him. But what he did in the barn was less ambiguous, though equally puzzling. We were standing in a lane of sunlight by the door, while he was sucking a straw in his thick lips.

You know what a French letter is? he asked suddenly.

Of course I do, I said, skipping. It's a letter, written in French.

The boy sniggered.

No, it's not, he said. It's a scum-bag.

I had no idea what this meant.

Oh, I said. Of course, I knew that, too.

The boy looked at me slyly.

Have you seen one? he asked, slipping his hand in his pocket.

I had a sense, I think, of something momentous about to

happen, and I know my heart was beating faster. I stopped skipping, and stared at the boy.

Show me, I said, softly.

I remember now the sense of anti-climax I had when he pulled what seemed like a flattened, uncoloured balloon out of his pocket, and then slid his first finger inside it. The skin glistened over his flesh.

It's just like a balloon, I said, uncertainly.

The boy nodded.

Well, he said, waggling his finger, my uncle says you can go right up in one of these, and it's perfectly safe, whatever happens. Right up. Those were his very words.

I watched him lifting his finger into the air, inside the skin. Then, suddenly he brought the finger down and made a series of quick jabbing movements with it, into my ribs.

Stop it, I said, stop it at once.

He did stop, awkward, and grinning. He unrolled the skin from his finger, not sure, I think, exactly what to do next.

I watched him put the lips of the thing to his mouth, and pretend to blow. It swelled a bit, and his cheeks grew red and tense as he puffed.

It's a pretty poor balloon, I said. It won't blow up.

O, but it's not for blowing up, the boy said, with a twisted grin again. It's for going up in. Going right up. That's what my uncle said.

I ran away then, confused, and irritated. I knew that something dirty was involved, as it often seemed to be when a boy, particularly an older one, communicated some unclear piece of information. And that was enough.

I imagined the damp, collapsed little balloon, soaring into a clear sky, with two tiny figures peering out from a basket underneath it, expressions of pure, unclouded joy on their faces.

Right up. And, perfectly safe. I had no idea what that meant. I went away from the barn, though, and back into the stink of the farm-yard, with a lasting sense of disturbance about balloons. They seemed to me far from safe, from then on. They seemed to me threatening, and dirty.

There had been nothing dirty, even remotely so, about

my relationship with Nils. His flirtatiousness, and his outrageous remarks, were all very carefully balanced on the right side of decency.

Our conversations throughout the four weeks of his stay in the house had been frivolous and teasing, close and lively, intimate and unbridled. There had been nothing about them to suggest a restraint, or to create a sense of repulsion. But, on the other hand, there had been nothing to suggest any real depth of feeling either.

I wanted to feel that Nils found me beautiful, and attractive. That he thought me witty, and sophisticated. That he saw me as, one day, the object of his attentions. But I couldn't.

Sometimes, after he'd gone, when I was alone at night in my tiny bed, reading by candlelight, I'd finger the ruins of my rose, and wonder if, after all, that had been a sign of some deeper interest, even some unconscious commitment to my well-being and my future happiness.

But I knew I was playing. My love was real, but its object was remote, and made no response. I was doomed, once again, to that awful adolescent hell of a total passion, a form of love consuming its own bearer, and bringing no solace or recompense.

That winter the snow fell early, in late November, and I dragged my way to school each day in my fur boots and my red cape, knowing that months must go by before there was any chance of hearing from Nils again.

He did write once, a jaunty, flippant letter I kept pressed in my diary like a sacred relic. It was full of information, empty of feeling, as I might have expected.

It's still here. The pages have yellowed, and the green ink he used has gone dry, and dulled. But the words retain their spirit.

My dear Miss Charlier, he begins. My life is a desert without you. Do you miss me? You will not, I know, be at all interested in a boring account of my life, which is largely cast in the mould of Lewis Carroll's *Hiawatha's Photography*, a parody of a parody. I shall tell you instead about Uncle Johan. He is living in Paris now, in the Quartier Latin, where he has a little room in a small hotel. Across the road there is a home for the deaf and dumb, and he watches the mute children communicating by sign language in their garden. Silent as flowers, he says. I gather that he has made a crucible of his grate, and attempts to manufacture gold by the use of mercury, as a consequence of which his hands are blackened and charred. He has proved to his own satisfaction that sulphur contains carbon and he is concerned to establish that hydrogen and oxygen are also present. His wife − the redoubtable Frida − has come and gone. As with Siri von Essen before, he becomes insanely jealous. She interferes with his work. She spies on him. What a man he is! Too mad to live, too much of a genius to die. He is the very type of the superman. I admire him next to Nietzsche and Andrée. You are to read all his plays, and to burn this letter. After all, it may turn into gold. By the way, my regards to your mother and father. Tell them that I may be coming to Malmö in spring, for a conference on the use of aerial photography in map-making. Your satanic friend, Nils Strindberg.

Perhaps there really was a conference on map-making. Perhaps Nils made it up. At any rate, he never came.

The winter passed, as others had done, with only the books in their leather strap under my arm to provide some distraction, only the finches coming to the bird-house in our frozen garden to supply some outlet for my affections.

Day after day I went out in the morning to place bread for them on the porch of their little villa, breaking the stalactites off with my fingers, and sometimes bringing a knife from the kitchen to scrape the wood free of encrusted ice.

On Saturdays and Sundays I would watch them circling and fluttering, plunging and jabbing voraciously at the dry bits. I was envious. They had more to satisfy their hunger than I had, I thought.

On weekdays, I got home in the afternoon after dark, and there was only the feel of the cold hollow under my hands to remind me of where the birds had been. I would go indoors, and make tea, and wait for my father to come in, smelling of horses, and eager for the comfort of his old slippers on the floor beside the stove.

Our nights were often spent in the dining-room. You

came into it down a pair of steps off that high spiral stair, opening the two halves of the door, like the gate of a stable. In one corner was the high, squared white mass of the stove, usually with the front open, and a kettle simmering on the hob. With the curtains drawn against the night, and the grandfather clock ticking against the wall, it made a cheerful refuge from the Scandinavian winter. But it didn't much help to take my mind off Nils.

There was no wireless or gramophone in those days, and my father regarded cards as the picture-book of the devil. But my mother, when she felt well enough, would sometimes play the piano, for which she had a surprisingly sweet touch. And there were always books.

Books, and of course the newspapers, and my father's weekly gardening magazine. I was turning over the pages of this one night, and learning about the excavation of ponds for planting lilies, when I heard my father cough, and lay his pipe aside.

I knew the signs. He had found something in the *Aftonbladet* that he wanted to read aloud. I remember noticing the date of the gardening magazine – February 16th, it was the issue out that day – as I dutifully looked up, and prepared to hear what he had to say.

My mother was sewing, with her feet up on a stool, and a hooded oil-lamp burning brightly at her shoulder. It cast a lemon glow on her lined face and the black sheen of her high-collared dress. She, too, paused in her work to listen.

It happened two or three times, perhaps, each evening, but this was the one time that winter that my father wanted to read out something about balloons.

There's a man here who's been lecturing about trying to fly to the North Pole, he said, crackling the paper in his hands. Listen to this. 'Is it not then more probable', he quoted, 'that we shall succeed in sailing to the Pole with a good balloon than that we shall be able to reach it with sledges as our means of transport or with vessels which are carried like erratic blocks, frozen fast to wandering masses of ice?'

My father looked up, over the tops of his half-spectacles.

That's Nansen, of course, he's referring to, he said.

The papers had been full, a month or two back, of the

Norwegian Fridtjof Nansen and his bold plan, then in progress, to drift right across the polar sea in his ship the *Fram*. We'd had earlier readings from the *Aftonbladet* to keep us in touch.

'Yes,' my father continued, still quoting, 'I am certain that it will be justly acknowledged that we have far greater prospects of being able to penetrate into polar tracts by means of a balloon than in any other way.'

Is the man who wants to use the balloon called Andrée? I asked.

It was a shot in the dark, really, but it served my purpose. If I was right, my father would be impressed by my knowledge. And the source of that knowledge would bring Nils's name into the conversation. I could speak it freely aloud. I could hear him talked about. Such crumbs are often the feasts of love.

How did you guess? my father asked, laying the paper aside.

That nice tutor I had last summer, I said, greatly daring. Mr Strindberg. He told me all about Andrée, and his voyages in balloons.

The name was out. It hovered with all the brilliance of a kingfisher in that winter room, ready to plunge and spear the beating fish of my thoughts. But that other name, its own dark shadow, was the first to strike.

Indeed, my father said. So tell your mother and me about Mr Andrée and his voyages in balloons.

I told what I knew, word perfect almost, as I was by now in all of Nils's lessons. The clock ticked, and the stove hissed, and my mother and father were soon as well briefed as I was in the flights of the *Svea*.

Most impressive, my father said, as I finished my account. As always, Mr Strindberg emerges as a most instructive tutor. I admire what he has done for you, Anna. Don't you agree, my dear?

Naturally, said my mother, a little resentfully.

She never liked to be made to agree in praising somebody, although, if that were possible, she'd been even more of a supporter of Nils than my father had. It was not, alas, a support that helped me. They saw Nils, I knew, as the grown son they both wished they could have had, not the potential bridegroom of their still pimply daughter, their wayward child.

Mr Strindberg would like to become a balloonist, I said. We discussed the idea together.

A noble ambition, my father suggested, and then, picking up the paper again, he continued to read aloud. 'It cannot be denied but that, by means of a single balloon journey, we shall be able to gain a greater knowledge of the geography of the Arctic regions than can be obtained in centuries by any other way. And who, I ask, are better qualified to make such an attempt than we Swedes? As a highly civilized nation, characterized for ages by the most dauntless courage, dwelling in the neighbourhood of the polar regions, familiar with its climactic peculiarities, and by nature itself trained to endure them, we can hardly altogether help feeling that we have a certain obligation in this matter.'

My father lifted his pipe, tapped out some dead ash, and then puffed in silence for a moment.

I agree with every word of that, he said, and then, completely incongruously as it seemed to me: We can still beat the Norwegians at their own game.

So with that remark, the balloons, and Andrée, and what Nils had had to say about them, were dropped like a handful of stones into the bottom of the cold winter's night, and there they remained, untouched and undiscussed, until the snow had melted, and the daffodils come and gone in spring.

It was on a mild afternoon in May that my father reverted to the subject of Andrée's plan to make a voyage to the North Pole by balloon. I was helping him in the vegetable garden, weeding the onions and dressing them down with soot.

That fellow Andrée has got his money, I see, I heard my father say.

I straightened up, feeling my back stiff, and blinking a little in the glare. My father was leaning on his rake, a hard bony figure, with his jacket off, and his shirt-sleeves rolled up. He always looked healthy and at ease out of doors. I had some of my best conversations with him then.

So the balloon journey will take place, I said.

41

Nobel has given him over £1,000, my father said, rubbing dirt from his nail. The rest of the money will follow. It's only a question of time.

My father was obviously predisposed to talk. He would often make a break for conversation in the midst of a long spell of gardening, and then attack the job in hand — mowing or hoeing, planting or trenching — with renewed vigour.

Your grandfather once worked for Nobel, he said. It was during the recession in the 70s. He took a job in the dynamite factory at Vinterviken. From what he used to say, Alfred Nobel was the most remarkable man he ever met.

Making money out of killing people, I said scornfully. That's not very clever. It's been done throughout history, since ploughshares were first beaten into swords.

My father laughed. He squinted his eyes up at the sky.

Looks like rain, he said. Then: No, there's more to it than that. Nobel made work for a lot of people who would otherwise have starved. And he looked after them, too. He pays well. He has medical care for his workers.

He can well afford to, I said. He's a gangster.

This was a common enough view among young people at the time. I was saying nothing very original.

He's been very generous, my father said. And he's an honest, plain-spoken man. Your grandfather tells a story of one time when they asked the old man for a photograph, to put in an anniversary publication for the factory. His reply was: as soon as my assistants, every single workman, have been asked to send their portraits, then I will send a reproduction of my pig's bristle bachelor snout to the collection, not before.

He's better looking than that, I objected. At any rate, if we're to judge by Emil Osterman's portrait of him in his laboratory.

Never mind, my father said, starting to rake over the soil again. He's a hero to me, is Alfred Nobel. A man with a real creative brain, who made money, and helped other people. He can write, too. You should read his book *On Modern Blasting Agents*, Anna. I'll get it for you.

I brushed some soot off my apron, and lifted my palm in the air. A drop of rain fell on it.

You'll soon see, my father said. The King will give Andrée some money now, and Baron Dickson, too, I'll warrant. Where Nobel leads, the rest will come.

Another drop of rain fell, then another. Soon it was falling steadily, and we went indoors to wait for it to stop. It didn't stop, not soon, any more than the steady flow of money coming for Andrée's polar flight. In due course, as my father had predicted, King Oscar offered a sum of £1,680, and a few days later Baron Oscar Dickson gave an equal amount. By the 4th of June, the sum necessary for the expedition was fully covered.

So the polar flight was going to take place. Perhaps, after all, it was not entirely out of place that dynamite should have been the force to set all in motion. The destructive powers cling together.

2
STRINDBERG
1897

IT WAS AMAZING when we were off. All those weeks, years, of waiting, and then to be finally in the air! I could hardly believe it when I looked over the instrument-ring and saw the faces down below growing smaller, and then when I looked up and out and saw the rocks and the snow on the cliff side, and there to the north the ships in the bay, and the height of Amsterdam Island.

You stood in the car with Andrée, Anna, I know. But you never felt what it was like when the basket left the ground. It's an eerie feeling, like being whirled off your feet in a fast waltz at a ball. You lose all sense of balance, you have to go with the flow.

There were four of us, really, I knew that when the roof of the balloon-house drifted away below. Andrée and Fraenkel and I and the *Eagle*. Andrée announced the name through a megaphone when we all stood in the car. There was cheering. I expect you've read the reports in all the papers.

Lachambre used to say that you steered a balloon like a man weighing gold dust in a scale. Open the valve a fraction and you rise, from the loss of gas. Tip out an ounce of ballast and you fall, from the loss of weight. It's a kind of exact measuring.

I used to think this, too, in Paris. But at Spitzbergen, it was different. The balloon was more like a wild thing than a tame one. You shuck the reins, and a horse moves the way you want. You can make it teeter on a penny, in the ring. But fire a rifle, or start a forest fire, and it runs and jumps to its own will. You can't stop it.

The balloon was the same. Anna, I have to tell you how it was. You'll know the way it seemed, the first part, anyway, to those watching. I don't doubt that the newspapers will have carried many paragraphs of eye-witness accounts. Most of them contradictory, and none of them knowing how it felt, really felt, in the air.

I'm writing this now, much later, in a place I shall tell you about, in time. I'm well fed, and in good spirits, and we're all alive, and safe. I'll give you the details in their proper order.

I want to start with the morning of July 11th, exactly as it was. It seems a long time ago now. It takes an effort to think back and remember. But I have to try. So. Have you got your pen and paper ready, Miss Charlier? Here we go.

It was only three o'clock in the morning when the bay was ruffled by the first cat's paws from the south-south-west. The wind grew stronger, and seemed steady. Andrée rose early and went on shore from the *Virgo* to examine the balloon. The rest of us followed, and had a conference in the balloon-house.

Two sealers had put into Virgo Harbour to weather the anticipated storm. The wind was expected to last, which was good. But it was likely to be very squally, which might be dangerous. Nevertheless, all of us wanted to go, and the decision was soon made.

So when Andrée went through the formality of asking each of us in turn what we wanted to do, we all said, go. Even Swedenborg, who was going to stay, said go.

He and I were lucky enough to be able to eat a last breakfast together. We'd gone back on board the *Virgo* to compare chronometers, and they persuaded us to stay for bacon and eggs, and a bottle of champagne. Fraenkel and Andrée had to make do with beer and sandwiches in the car of the balloon.

I took a lot of photographs of the preparations. A number of small balloons were sent up, the little ones you like of that goldbeater's silk, and they all seemed to confirm the strength and direction of the wind. The gas-tightness was checked, and seemed fine. You know, we developed a new test near to the end. We'd lay a strip of linen soaked in acetate of lead over each seam. If it grew black, we knew that there was a leak. It worked well.

Finally, we attached the car, and all three of us took our places. The wind felt very strong, even inside the balloon-house, and there was quite a banging and shuttling noise. Everyone cheered the announcement of the balloon's name, as I say, then the moment had come.

Cut away everywhere, said Andrée.

Three cutlasses slashed through ropes attached to the carrying-ring, and we started to rise. Three men, and thirty carrier pigeons. It made me remember for a second our last night together in the loft of Pike's House. Well, well. Perhaps it will help me to watch my consumption of alcohol on the expedition!

I shall have more to say about the pigeons, but that, too, in its place. I scribbled a note to you very early on, over the bay, and meant to let it drop when we were over the far point of Amsterdam Island. But I forgot. I let it fall instead in a little cylinder over Vogelsang Island. I wonder if it's been found, and if you have it now, with my love, my undying love, in the shorthand that only you can read? I hope so. The rest of what you get will surely come, if at all, by pigeon post.

Now, Anna, I have to tell you about the first setback. It happened very quickly, and quite by surprise. The papers will have said, no doubt, that the balloon was seen to dip, and some may go so far as to say that we sank half under water, like a drowning elk. We nearly did.

It wasn't a dip, though, in the air. It was a sickening sudden drop. One moment we were gently rising, carried along by the wind across the bay. Fraenkel was attending to the sail. Andrée was making a meteorological observation. I was checking the ballast-sacks.

The next moment, without warning, we were plunging like a toboggan down a slide. Straight for the sea. I may have called out. I don't know. I felt my stomach gripped from above and wrenched violently out. Then I was thrown against the rail, hanging on for dear life, and I could see the water rushing up from below.

We did stop without going under. But only just. I don't know how. Fraenkel, perhaps, doing something with the

49

sail. And then we were back on an even keel, and then rising slowly again, and over Amsterdam Island.

It took us a moment to realize what had happened. It was Andrée who voiced the news. His face was ashen, and not just from sickness.

The guide-ropes have unscrewed, he said. The balloon's flying free.

I looked over the rail. We were higher now, and the first section of the guide-ropes all dangled loose well above the water. There was nothing left to drag on the surface, and enable us to direct our course. We were no longer in a dirigible balloon.

Fraenkel laughed.

We're in the hands of the gods, he said bitterly.

I put my head on the cold brass.

We can't go back, I said.

There was a silence. Only the sound of a soft hissing from the large valve. Then Andrée, in his quiet methodical way, summed up what must have happened.

We should never have used ropes with a screwing-mechanism, he said. They must have got twisted when we laid them out on the beach. When the car rose, they untwisted, and the thread on the upper section was too slight to hold them on.

So we're done for, Fraenkel said. We have to drift where we can.

He didn't sound very worried, I must say. Fingering that imaginary beard in the way he does.

Andrée was looking over the side at the ballast-ropes. Then he looked up at the sky, and over at Amsterdam Island.

No, he said. We have one more chance. We can try splicing together the ballast-ropes and the guide-ropes. That way, we can make a smaller number of greater length. We may still be able to make the balloon guidable.

So we set to work. It took us three hours to do the best job we could, and it never helped much. But it took the curse off our sense of failure, and by half past four, when we'd finished, and cast the makeshift guide-rope over the side, our confidence was back to a high ebb.

50

Let's have a drink, said Andrée, and we split a bottle of beer amongst us.

We were over the first of the pack-ice then, and I took a range of photographs. There was no sign of the *Express*, which we ought to have sighted on its way to the Seven Islands with provisions for our emergency base. But we didn't worry. Swedenborg was to follow with the *Virgo*, and he would check.

After the beer, Andrée threw the bottle overboard, and the balloon rose ten metres. We were drifting at about two hundred metres then, and he and I went up together into the carrying-ring to follow the needs of nature.

Andrée was very direct, opening his buttons and standing close to the hole. He seemed to have no difficulty. I saw a steady stream come gushing out and spray away into the wind.

Look out, Fraenkel, Andrée called. You'll get a shower-bath.

Fraenkel had stayed down below in the car. I heard his guttural laugh.

All right, he called. I'll watch out.

Andrée turned in, shaking drops away. Then he buttoned up, and bent at the knees and up again to make himself comfortable. Exactly like an old and rather disgusting member in a Stockholm club.

I did the same myself, but I'm afraid with much less elegance.

Ballast, you see, is the crucial thing in a balloon. Lachambre was right. It responds, like a horse to the prick of a goad. You spit in the wind, and it falls a little. You need to lose some height, and that day you don't empty your bowels.

To maintain height, we threw out sand, all that first day. We let fly four carrier pigeons and, light as they are, it made some difference. And finally, with much reluctance, we let loose two of our buoys.

By the evening there was some mist about, but away to the east the sea was still free of ice. At just after seven o'clock Andrée decided to go down and take some rest. He'd been up all night for several days, and he needed to conserve his strength.

51

Call me at two o'clock, he said, and then climbed down through the trap-door to lie on the sleeping-bag at the bottom of the car. There was just room to stretch out there, and I expect he slept well enough.

We sat on baskets, after Andrée had gone, just the two of us. The sun burned down, and it was bright and warm. Fraenkel put on a pair of dark glasses, and we sat as comfortably as a couple of resting skiers at an Alpine resort.

It was one of the quietest moments of the balloon journey. Our height was about six hundred metres, and everything was still and calm, except for the occasional creaking of the wicker in the car, and the steady escape of gas from the low valve.

I wish I could smoke a pipe, Fraenkel said.

Try this instead, I said, and passed him my snuff-box. It's better for your lungs.

Fraenkel took some, laid it in the crook of his finger, just as if we were back at home in a drawing-room, and inhaled.

Not bad, he said, brushing grains from his lapels. But smoking concentrates the mind. I miss the stimulus of tobacco.

It would be stimulating, I suggested, if the hydrogen gas caught fire, and the balloon went up in a puff of smoke.

Fraenkel stretched his long legs out, and his boot caught me on the shin. When you stand upright at the rail, it's fine. There's ample room. But you tire, Anna. And when you sit, as we were doing, it's easy for legs to get entangled. I didn't like the constant irritation of being bumped. This time was just the beginning.

Sorry, said Fraenkel.

He got up, opened the trap-door, and peered down into the base of the car. Then he closed the trap-door, and sat down again.

He's fast asleep, he said, quietly. His legs are drawn up like a child's.

I was suddenly aware how loud our voices were sounding in the clear air.

Perhaps we ought to talk in whispers, I said. He's very tired. We don't want to wake him.

I don't think we will, said Fraenkel. He's a weary chicken.

But he spoke in a whisper, and that was how we continued to speak. We were more at ease together, it seemed, and there was a companionable silence for a while.

What do you think? said Fraenkel, at last. You know him better than I do. Will he get us through?

I thought for a time before I spoke. He'll get us through, I said. And then: If anyone can.

Fraenkel put his hands behind his head, and leaned back on the rail. He looked very relaxed in the sun.

Well, he said, I don't much mind. It's the journey that matters. And how we behave to each other under pressure.

But the destination matters, too, I said. Surely. You want to get to the Pole.

Fraenkel smiled, inscrutable behind his glasses.

I want to, he said. But will I?

That night, about ten o'clock, it began to get colder in the balloon. The sun was losing heat, and we were coming down about two hundred metres in height for every fall of half a degree in temperature.

We were just above the cloud cover when Fraenkel suggested that we throw out the first buoy. Andrée had left a message with me before he went to lie down, but I'd held it back. It had seemed wiser to conserve ballast then, and retain the power to control our height.

Now we were falling every minute.

Be quick, said Fraenkel.

I took Andrée's message out, read it through, and added a brief note of my own. Then together we lifted the little rope beehive and tipped it overboard.

After the buoy had gone, we gained height, and the balloon was soon back at about six hundred metres, and we had sunshine and stillness once more.

But not for long. The cooling of the sun kept reducing our height, and we had to throw out more ballast, rungs of rope, and then kilos of sand.

53

It was after midnight when the crucial change came. We entered a large cloud, and the balloon dropped slowly through mist until the guide-rope we'd fashioned in the afternoon began to trail on the ice. We reached equilibrium at about a hundred metres.

I looked overboard. We were over blocks of pack-ice, no more than floes, really, clustering together and separated by wide leads. The guide-rope made a rough, hawking noise as it dragged over the ice, and then a cool, lapping one as it furrowed water. We were near enough to hear quite clearly. I had a sense that I might have reached down and, yes, cuffed the ear of some larger blocks.

But the height remained at a hundred metres. We tried to navigate, using the sail, but there was little wind. The sun was invisible, and the balloon had begun to collect moisture from the mist.

This was the beginning, Anna, of the first major change in the tenor of the voyage. So far we'd managed to keep a good height, rising whenever we fell by losing ballast. Now we could no longer do that.

For the remainder of the time in the air – and, yes, I must tell you plainly, it *is* now over – we could only stay aloft at all by discarding baggage, and there was no longer any hope of gaining real height. We began to skip at low level over the pack-ice, like a sparrow hawk in a hedge.

This meant that we were no longer high and warm, suspended in calm air, and with a good view of the polar sun. We were jerked through a soggy low-lying mist, and everything began to get soaked and wet.

The word voyage took on a real meaning. Before we'd been flying high, creatures of air and wind. Now we were birds of the sea surface, hooking the solid waves, and frozen by a kind of Arctic spray. We were subject to the pitch and roll of the ground currents, and to sudden whirls and dips which would alter our course without warning.

I felt like the captain of a leaking trawler in a bad storm. Fortunately, it took time for this new mode of progress to reach its worst. To begin with, there was the struggle to gain what height we could, and to attempt such navigation as might maintain some kind of course to the north.

54

We were busy, suddenly, after hours of peace and calm. Once a black bird, a strange alien creature, circled the car at some distance. We had our double-barrelled shot-gun hung on the rail, and I wondered about a shot.

It looks like a raven, I said.

Maybe, said Fraenkel. But remember the albatross.

It's too small for an albatross, I said. And I don't think that they're ever black. Unless this particular one is in mourning.

But I left the shot-gun where it was, and the bird flew away, and disappeared in the mist.

By then the balloon had sunk very low. The moisture was gathering on the net and the car, on everything. Its weight was bringing us down.

We threw out another buoy, with another simple, banal message. But we were still losing height. Fraenkel began to unbuckle his trousers, then he pulled them down to his knees, and eased the long underpants to his thighs.

I'll do what I can, he said, with a grin.

Then he climbed up onto the instrument-rail, took a grip on the car-ropes, and leaned back over the two belts of webbing put there. I watched him lying back like a small boy in a swing.

One metre and sixty centimetres, I said, hauling in the lead-line. Have we a laxative on board?

At exactly two o'clock in the morning, as promised, we woke Andrée from his sleep. He climbed up through the trap-door into the car, driving his knuckles into his eyes.

The balloon was still. For half an hour there had been no wind, and we'd hung about eighty metres above the ice. There was a chill in the air, a thick mist, and the steady sound of dripping.

It's wet, said Andrée, putting his finger in the air. I feel soaked already, as if I'd come up in a Turkish bath.

But without the heat, suggested Fraenkel.

Andrée was gripping the rail, looking down.

I'm thirsty, he said. Let's have a drink.

It's very curious, Anna, this balloonist's thirst we all get. There we were, surrounded by water, in a dank, soaking wicker basket, under a great globe of dripping moisture, like a sort of overhead whale, and all we wanted was something to drink. You'd think we'd have needed a dry biscuit, or a slice of toast. But we weren't hungry.

Fraenkel opened a bottle of beer, and passed it to Andrée. He drank from the neck and passed it back. We all stood, leaning on the rail in the mist, speaking in a muffled silence.

You'd better both get some sleep, said Andrée, after we'd given him a brief account of the last few hours. I'll take the next watch alone.

I wanted to stay with him, and share a few hours on the roof, but he wouldn't hear of it.

You're both tired, he said. You need sleep. I'll need your young arms later. I'll play some patience if I get bored.

I didn't feel tired, but I knew the reaction would come soon, when I got down into the bottom of the car, and stretched out. I followed Fraenkel through the trap-door, and we made ourselves as comfortable as we could.

Andrée had closed the trap-door almost before I'd ducked my head, and Fraenkel put covers over the two small windows. It was almost completely dark. I leaned back against the side of the car, and closed my eyes.

Goodnight, Fraenkel, I said, in a whisper.

I didn't expect him to answer, and he didn't. He lay well away from me, flat on his belly, his face with its dark frown towards the wall. He looked even more powerful asleep than awake. And he seemed to sleep like a stone, or a tree. In a kind of absoluteness of repose.

It's become more normal now. I'm used to it. But that was the first night I'd ever slept in the same room as a man. That close. That much alone. It felt very strange.

I lay for a long time that night, Anna, our first night in the air, thinking about the expedition, and where we were: thinking about you and I, and where we would one day be. I heard the wicker creak, and I breathed in the dank, moisture-filled air, and I thought of Sir John Franklin, out there with the *Erebus* and the *Terror* in 1847, trying to find the North-West Passage.

He must have had the same soaking voyage, before the winter froze him up, beyond Hudson's Bay. Franklin, Fraenkel. I felt the two names merge and blur in my mind, as I eased away towards sleep. I was there with Franklin and his English crew, drifting through the heavy mist and the silent fog, not knowing where I was going, or where I would finally reach. I was here with Fraenkel and Andrée, alone in our drifting, soggy balloon, whirling at rest in some weird air current south of the Pole.

Franklin, Fraenkel. Which of the two would survive? I rolled over, and took a corner of Fraenkel's blanket, and heard him grunt with discomfort or protest, and then I was a little warmer, and then I was asleep.

It was just after seven o'clock when we woke. I checked the time by my chronometer, and stretched my stiff limbs on the sleeping-bag. Then I reached over and shook Fraenkel by the shoulder. He was a heavy sleeper, and he turned and grunted before opening his eyes.

Morning, I said, smiling.

Breakfast, he replied, flaring his nostrils.

Then we climbed up through the trap-door, and stood once again on the roof of the car. Andrée was seated on a basket, shuffling a pack of cards. He put them in his pocket, and nodded.

We're stationary, he said, answering the question that was in both our minds. The balloon has scarcely moved all night. I estimate that our height is about thirty metres. In the hours while you two gentlemen have been sleeping, we may have sailed about one nautical mile.

In what direction? I asked, hoping.

Andrée looked at me.

Dead west, I'm afraid, he said.

So it dawned on me, there in the chill, dripping day, that the voyage towards the Pole might already be over. We were drifting now with the wind, such as it was. But not any more in the direction we wanted to go. It was hard news to wake to.

Let's have breakfast, Fraenkel repeated, and he began to busy himself with the water and coffee for the Goransson apparatus.

It works perfectly, Anna. You remember all our doubts? They were quite unfounded. Whenever we wanted to cook — I mean heat up soup, or make coffee, in effect ¬ it served our purpose admirably.

57

Fraenkel tended to do the cooking, although in theory we had a rota, and I must say he has quite a culinary touch. It's odd to see such a big man working with a woman's tools, but he does it really well.

That morning I shivered in the mist, watching him lower the apparatus down the rope, and then pull the little lever to light the flame. It was about eight metres down, to clear the lower valves. We waited, not talking much, until the coffee had boiled, and then Fraenkel hauled up the apparatus, tasted the brew, and pronounced it drinkable. Then he blew down the rubber tube to extinguish the flame, and served the coffee round in our tin cups.

I found some cheese and sardine sandwiches, and they were soon shared into equal portions. We sat on the baskets, and occasionally a watery beam of sunlight broke through the pervading cloud as we ate and drank. There wasn't a great deal to do for a moment, and we took our time.

The guide-ropes are the trouble, Andrée said, after a while. The attachments, I mean. We ought to have put them to one side, not under the sail. Whenever the ropes drag, the balloon turns, and the sail won't work.

Fraenkel was sipping coffee.

Be thankful for one thing, he said.

What's that? asked Andrée.

But for the ropes unscrewing, said Fraenkel slowly, the balloon would have been drawn down into the water as we left Danes Island. It's a mercy we lost them. Otherwise, you'd both have been drowned.

What about you? I asked.

I'm a better swimmer, he said.

We all laughed.

You know, said Andrée, thinking. You may be right about the ropes. I wonder.

Then he took out a piece of paper and began to make calculations. I lost interest. I got up and went over to look down at the pack-ice. I could see it vaguely through the rifts in the mist, one solid jagged sheet of yellowy white. Fraenkel was leaning back with his eyes closed, occasionally sipping at his coffee.

A lot of time passed. There was little we could do for the

58

moment to guide our destiny. We had to wait for the wind. It was boring, Anna, in a way the balloon journey was never again to be boring.

Hours went by, and little happened. We spoke little. Fraenkel took our bearings with the theodolite. Andrée was reading, and sometimes pausing to draw or calculate. I spent much of my time just watching the ice, Anna, and thinking.

Once, late in the morning, I saw a patch of blood on a small ice floe. It was almost circular, and by far the most vivid colour we'd seen, except for the sun's occasional orange, since we left Virgo Harbour. I pointed the patch out to Fraenkel and Andrée.

There was a great battle there, said Fraenkel, reaching for the binoculars. Then, laying the glasses aside, he added, I think it must have been two polar bears, fighting over a seal kill.

I watched the dull red in silence. There seemed to be no signs of bone or flesh. Only the stain of red remained to commemorate whatever had died there. It was a melancholy sight.

Supposing Nansen had been surprised by bears, I said. They'd have eaten every scrap. Only the bloodstains would be left on the snow.

Andrée put his hand on my shoulder.

Nansen's alive, he said kindly. And so are we, Strindberg.

Fraenkel had turned away, and was sitting again on a basket with his back to the rail.

We have plenty of ammunition, he said. Any blood left on the snow by us will be bears' blood. Not our own.

So the red patch receded, into the drifting mist, and the subject was left alone. That was the only thing of significance until the middle of that afternoon, when the car hit the ice. Twice.

I was jolted by the shock. I'd been half dozing on the basket, and I came awake, stiff and cold, with a jerk. I looked at my chronometer.

Three o'clock.

That was the end of the easy time, Anna. We began to throw out sand to gain height. It came out of the bags this

59

time, and for some reason that none of us quite understood, it hung in the damp air, clammy and able to float better, it seemed, than the balloon.

It began to drift back, and stuck to our lips, our eyes, everywhere. We spat it out, irritated. It clung to the insides of our shirts and stockings. For the first time, I started to feel dirty. I longed for a bath, even a bowl of water to rinse my face in.

It's like the plagues of Egypt, Andrée said, as he heaved another bag over. First of all, the plague of moisture, cold and dripping water everywhere. Then the plague of sand, gritty and drying and sticky like marmalade. What next, I wonder?

The locusts, I suggested.

At last the sand did drift away. But it wasn't the locusts that came next. It was the bumps. Each time the car hit the ice, it seemed to bounce, and then rise a little, as if it were a hare jumping across a field, or a stone skimmed across a pond.

It began to feel wet again. The car, the net and the balloon were loaded with moisture, like a sponge that hasn't been squeezed out. We were still travelling west, but slowly, and very low.

Whatever we threw out, the balloon continued to hang low, and bump the ice. At last, Andrée climbed up into the carrying-ring, and came down cradling the polar buoy in his arms. He held it close against his chest, as if it was a precious toy, like a kind of doll, or a fur dog.

It isn't necessary, said Fraenkel.

We still have sand, I said.

There were tears in Andrée's eyes. He blinked.

Yes, he said. But sand can be shed in amounts that vary. We need to hold what sand we have to the last.

He put the buoy down at his feet. It bulked very large on the roof of the car. With its wire net around the cork, it was like some gigantic pine cone. As if the forests of Valhalla had shed one final seed.

Gentlemen, said Andrée, quietly. We can no longer hope to reach the Pole. But we may still travel further north than anyone has done before. That chance will be increased if we lose this buoy.

60

The weather may change, I said. With some sun to dry up the water, and a good wind, we might still be over the Pole tomorrow.

We're drifting west, said Andrée, wiping his brow. Not north.

Besides, said Fraenkel. The important thing is to plant the Swedish flag. The news will get back, in time. Either from our own mouths, or out of our dead bodies. We don't need the buoy.

So we heaved it overboard, and it spun round and was lost to sight in the mist and snow. The others turned away, but I watched it whirling in the air, and then bouncing on the ice, for as long as I could. It was like a wooden teardrop. A kind of unfelt grief for what we had lost.

Shortly afterwards, the balloon came to a standstill. One of the ballast-ropes had got caught in a block of pack-ice. Each of us struggled to tug it free, but without success. The balloon swung slowly round, as if at a mooring-mast.

We should have kept the buoy, I said. It did no good to throw it out.

Andrée put his hand up on one of the ropes by which the car was suspended. He ran his fingers down, and water spurted between his joints. Moisture was everywhere.

We could get free, he said, slowly. If we lost another hundred kilos of ballast, the force of the wind would loosen the rope.

We could slice the rope through, said Fraenkel.

That was when I knew he was really tired. So was I. So was Andrée. It wasn't the loss of sleep. It was simply the strain of a completely changeable and unusual environment. Our nerves had no protection against this.

No, I said, making a big effort. First the polar buoy, then the rope. It's too much. Supposing that this was a voyage at sea. We'd simply lie at anchor until the wind rose. When it filled the sails, we'd be back on course.

We were shouting at each other now, standing up with our hands in the rigging. Our faces were streaked with dirt and sweat. There seemed to be a lot of noise in the balloon. The wicker creaked, the wind soughed in the sail, the ropes were rustling and scrawling on the ice.

You're right, said Fraenkel. But we're not at sea, Strindberg. We're in the air. That makes a difference. If the wind comes, we can't work the sails. We've tried and failed.

The wind's from the east, said Andrée. If we break loose, we should reach Greenland by morning.

Greenland, I said bitterly. Greenland.

None of us had signed on for a flight to the west. The last Viking had died in Greenland centuries ago, starved for grain. His body, from the skeleton, was only four feet six inches tall. He'd shrunk to a dwarf. In a barrel beside him, that had once held corn, there were the bones of hundreds of mice. The last mice in Greenland. I had bad associations with Greenland.

Never, I said, clenching my teeth. You go there by steamer, not by balloon.

Andrée smiled. He hadn't shaved, and his bristles were a hard, iron grey.

We'll lie at anchor, he said. I was only seeing what you would say.

That night, Fraenkel and I slept again in the car, and Andrée kept watch. I sat against the wall, with a bottle of mineral water open to quench my thirst.

He won't rest, I said. And he won't take any risks. What kind of man is he?

Fraenkel was trying to shake some sand out of his boot.

You're tired, he said. We're both tired.

I drank some mineral water.

There's time to wait, said Fraenkel. When Charles XII was in Turkey, he learned that. Andrée knows it, too. He has energy in reserve.

But throwing out the polar buoy, I said. Why do that?

Fraenkel had turned over onto his stomach. He lay prone as if waiting for someone to come and massage his back.

Strindberg, he said. You'd better get a grip on yourself. Get some sleep. It's been a hard day.

I drank more mineral water, and said nothing.

Buoys are a luxury, said Fraenkel. We don't need buoys.

Then the trap-door opened, and Andrée's head appeared in the gap, a fierce mask, like the gargoyle in a church roof.

Stop talking, he said sharply. That's an order. You're there to sleep.

It was the first time he'd shown signs of losing his temper, or exercised his authority as our captain. So I lay down obediently, and turned over on my side, and went to sleep. And all that night the balloon lay stationary a few metres above the ice, and Andrée sat on his basket above our heads, like God Almighty in the clouds, the origin and guidance of our world.

The thirteenth is always an unlucky day, Anna. I rose too early, and left Fraenkel snoring until four hours later. I spent the time taking our bearings with Gleerup's azimuth compass, and examining the ice.

We remained stationary in latitude 82°2 north and 15°5 east of the Greenwich meridian. Andrée told me how the wind had blown during the night.

It wasn't strong enough to free us, he said. But it was blowing from the north.

I laid the compass aside.

So if we'd broken loose, I said, we'd have landed back in Spitzbergen, where we started.

Andrée rubbed the grey stubble under his chin. He pursed his lips.

Yes and no, he said. The wind might have veered.

It seemed an ironic thought. Here we were, tied in place for want of a strong enough breeze, and knowing that if we did get one, we might well be further back, and worse off, than we were now.

What are we doing, Andrée? I asked.

It was a rhetorical question, I suppose, but he had his answer ready.

We're trying to beat Nansen, he said. It's only four degrees.

We never did beat Nansen, Anna, and I think I knew even then that we wouldn't. Whatever powers ruled, the fretful winds had decided that our presumptuous balloon was to be toyed with, and teased a little, and then taught a bitter lesson.

I left Andrée and went up into the carrying-ring. It was quieter there, and curiously cut off. I had a great need to be alone for a while, and think. So I made myself comfortable amongst the baskets and bales of stores, and I took out a book, and tried to read.

Fraenkel rose at 10.30, and I flicked a ball of hoar-frost at him through a trap in the floor. He looked up, and shook his fist. He and Andrée settled on the baskets, and I closed the trap again to be more alone.

Time passed, and I must have dozed, or been daydreaming. I was jerked suddenly awake by a series of violent bumps. I was cushioned from the shock by the surrounding baggage, and I didn't realize at first what had happened.

Then I opened the trap and peered down. Andrée and Fraenkel were lolling back in the car-ropes, grasped in each other's arms, like two men wrestling for life. There was something almost funny about it, exaggerated in its posture.

Then the car bumped again, and I was almost thrown down through the trap. I lurched back against a pile of boxes, my head singing. I felt a sudden sense of freedom, and I knew the balloon must be rising.

I shook my head, and clambered down onto the roof of the car. Andrée and Fraenkel had unclinched themselves, and Fraenkel was busying himself with the sail.

We were nearly thrown overboard, he said. You were lucky, Strindberg. You had some protection in the carrying-ring.

I checked our height. It was fifty metres now, and the balloon was drifting east at about three metres per second. The ballast-ropes were just long enough to drag on the ice. They made a reassuring rustling sound.

Andrée rubbed his hands, grinning.

This is better, he said. This is how it ought to be.

Except that we're drifting east, I said. Not north.

I was feeling rather groggy from the shock of the bumps. The visibility was terrible, it was dank and chill, and I could see no reason for good spirits.

Let's have lunch, said Fraenkel.

I'm not hungry, I said, but I helped him get the cooking apparatus out, and prepare the soup. Somehow the work helped my queasiness, and I had quite an appetite, after

64

all, when we sat down to eat.

It was an excellent, three-course meal. First of all a hot bowl of steaming hotch-potch soup, nutritious and appetizing. Then, another drop of the apparatus, another kindling of the flame, and, lo and behold, our main course, three chateaubriand steaks, done to a turn. For dessert, there was a third drop, a boiling of hot chocolate, two mugsful apiece. And finally, to fill up the last crannies of hunger, we had biscuits with raspberry syrup.

I think I'll take a short rest, said Andrée, after this meal. But, first of all, the pigeon post.

He took a stub of pencil, and wrote our brief dispatches, which we placed in their cylinders, and attached to the legs of four of our remaining pigeons. They were loath to fly, and spent half an hour circling the balloon, and settling on the guide-rope, before finally taking off, in what seemed a southerly direction.

Let's hope they arrive, said Andrée, and then he went to lie down.

After that, the mist grew thicker, as if it had only been waiting until Andrée disappeared, and the showers of light drizzle became more and more frequent. The temperature was below zero, and the balloon began to lose height. The drops of rain froze into ice when they met the car, or the net, or the calotte.

Let's throw out the reserve medicine chest, I suggested.

Fraenkel was doubtful.

Medicine, he said, superstitiously. It seems wrong.

We won't need it, I said. One's enough.

So we heaved over the box of bandages, and ointments, and jars of aspirin, and hypodermic syringes, and morphine. It seemed a waste, and a kind of nose-thumbing to the gods, too. I could understand how Fraenkel felt, of course. But we had to be rational. We had ample for any expected needs in our main box.

It's always the problem. What to throw away. It's like having a storeroom, or a filing-cabinet, that's grown too small for your needs. You know how hard it is to choose what has to go, Anna. Your grandmother's photographs, or your own school reports. Each have their claim.

I do believe that on some occasions Andrée would

65

have tossed Fraenkel or me overboard rather than lose any of his precious sand. The measurable, so various sand. The grains of the jeweller's scale. The balloonist's life blood. It was like a loss of will to lose sand.

Nevertheless, with Andrée asleep, we did lose more sand and the balloon kept afloat. Half an hour before he woke, and rejoined us, we even drifted a point or two towards the north.

It was about then that one of the pigeons returned. I saw it first as a small dot on the horizon, and, when it flew closer, I thought at first that it might be an ivory gull. But at last the shape, and the sit of the flight, was beyond dispute.

The bird circled the balloon a few times, and then settled on the guide-rope, a metre or two below the car.

It's hungry, Fraenkel said, leaning over.

But he couldn't reach. The bird was frightened as well as hungry.

It's going to die, I said. There's nothing that we can do.

Fraenkel reached right out, hanging head down, with his leg looped in the ropes. But the bird stepped away down the line. It sat there for a while with its head under its wing. Then it seemed to nod and sway, and then fall off.

Its wings didn't open. It fell like a stone into the snow, and disappeared.

Fraenkel hauled himself back into the car, and dusted frost off his clothes.

Requiescat in pace, he said softly, and he crossed himself.

We both stood staring down into the snow for a long time. But the pigeon didn't rise.

Andrée reappeared on deck just before six o'clock, and shortly afterwards I took a turn below on my own. I lay down on the sleeping-bag, and drew the blanket over me, and closed my eyes.

But it was a short sleep, and a rudely broken one. I came to with violent nausea. The car was bouncing, it seemed, on the ice. I tried to lie still and count. Every fifty metres or so, like a buck leaping, it seemed to come down, and slap its bottom hard on the ground. Each time I felt all the breath knocked out of my body, and a great wave of sickness lift and then fall in a soggy torrent over my brain.

Tired as I was, I realized that I had to get up and climb onto the roof of the car. Down there, I was getting the worst of the bumps, and they obviously weren't going to stop.

I got to my feet, in a red mist, and climbed through the trap-door. Andrée and Fraenkel were hanging onto the car-ropes. The car bumped once again, as I stood aloft, and I was thrown hard against the side. I felt Andrée reach out to steady me with his arm.

But it made no difference. I wasn't afraid of being thrown overboard. I was too far gone for that. I leaned over the instrument-rail, vomiting.

The car bumped once again, and I was shaken by another fit of sickness. I clung on, icy cold and shivering. My heart was pounding, and my legs were weak at the knees. I half collapsed on the floor.

You'd better go up in the carrying-ring again, said Fraenkel. It's calmer there.

I felt his hands under my armpits, and I staggered to my feet. With Andrée's shoulders under my legs, I managed to reach through the trap-door and haul myself aloft. I felt Fraenkel's hand on my thigh, shoving me in, as I rolled over and lay gasping for breath between the baskets and boxes of stores.

He was right. It was calmer there, and I lay still, trying to recover my strength. The car was still bumping, and the intervals were more frequent. Fortunately, I didn't feel the force of them with anything like the same intensity in the carrying-ring. I closed my eyes and tried to rest.

Once Fraenkel climbed up beside me, and hauled out several crates of food. They'd decided to jettison even these, to keep afloat.

Fraenkel saw my eyes watching him.

Food, he said. Yes. It's come to that, old chap.

It seemed even worse than medicine for a moment. I had a vision of us starving on the ice for want of bread or meat. I closed my eyes again. I was in no state to protest. And, anyway, of course, they'd made the right decision. We had plenty of spare food, so far as we could tell. The expedition had been given crates and crates of free biscuits and tins by firms wanting to advertise their wares, and much of this was bound to be surplus.

But it still felt very bad. I heard the thumping as the boxes of cake and molasses, tinned chicken and Bovril, tea and fruit juice, went rocketing over the side and down for ever into the snow, food for polar bears, and Arctic birds, when the cardboard rotted, and the tin, maybe, rusted and could be pierced by beak or claw.

Finally, hours or days later, I was too weak and delirious to know, they threw out more of the precious sand, and I knew that Andrée was ready to give in. I felt the hatch thrown open, and managed to look down at their two heads, lank and grizzled, staring up, yellow-eyed, at me through the gap.

They looked bad, I could see. Almost as bad as I felt in my sickness. There wasn't much fight left in any of us for more hours in this pitching, hop-scotch-playing balloon. We needed a rest, and a break for thought.

Listen, Andrée said. We have plenty of gas. But the winds are all from the north. If we stay in the air, we shall almost certainly be carried to Russia, dead or alive. What do you say?

I summoned up all my strength. I reared myself on my arm, but I felt my fingers trembling.

I need rest, I said. I'll be fine if we land. Or if this bumping stops. But the nausea is beyond control.

Andrée stared at me. Then he nodded.

Yes, he said. I see.

Then he turned to Fraenkel.

What do you say? he repeated.

I heard Fraenkel's voice as if from a very long way away. It seemed to be distorted, and made thin and weird, like the voice of a ghost, by some freak of the balloon's construction.

I say land, he said. If we drift further, we go too far away from the coast. Either the islands or the mainland of Siberia. Those are our only chance of getting home alive.

He paused. It didn't sound like the old Fraenkel, this kind of survivor's caution. And then he added,

We can try again next year.

68

So that was his myth now, the chance of a new expedition in 1898, I thought, as I lay groaning in my sickness. Fraenkel no longer wanted to die famous in the snow. He wanted to be one of the first men to reach the Pole.

All right, said Andrée. We'll land.

He said this as if the decision had not been his, but ours, as if he was rehearsing a future when he could say to the reporters that he'd wanted to go on, but had been overruled by his more cautious colleagues. I saw the politician in him, even as the last wave of nausea hit me, and I lay back while Andrée opened the valves.

The gas hissed, and Fraenkel controlled the speed of fall with the last of the sand. There was a very slight thump, quite unlike the others, and then the car was still. The balloon journey was over.

3
ANNA
1895–1896

EVERY LOVE AFFAIR, I suppose, prospers by setbacks, and mine was no exception. The year wore on through the blossoms of June, and the languors of July, and once again, as before, the question of a summer tutor was discussed.

Of course, I'd known for months that my father and mother would be well disposed to the idea of Nils reassuming the post. I'd used whatever opportunities came up to keep his name in mind, and my father had once, indeed, specifically mentioned his hope that Nils might be persuaded to repeat his visit.

So when my father's letter of invitation went off in late July, I began to anticipate and prepare.

Of course, I was only seventeen. A romantic age. I had no way to deal with the prospect of an emotional encounter from my own experience. Or rather, I had no internal resources to protect me against the forces of illusion.

Ours was a religious town. The Lutheran Church was well filled each Sunday morning, and the bell rarely called for a wedding or a funeral without ensuring that the ceremony was duly supported by the local community.

At school, the girls of my age grew up in the fear of God, and the dream of salvation. Life on the farms gave them some information about the hard realities of love and marriage, and there were few who hadn't seen a boar coupling, or a goat castrated.

But these physical necessities were held in separate compartments of the mind from the airy truths of religion,

73

and the romantic hopes of passion. As in other countries, a gaudy Sunday literature of moral comment, and fervid relationship, had grown up to mask, and transcend, the brutal coarsenesses of everyday life.

So I read and re-read all the trashier romantic and religious novels I could beg or borrow, and my mind filled with the easy and blurring language of the day. I lived in a world of trysts and recognitions, of impossible liaisons and surprising encounters, of true love and thwarted passion, of stalwart, handsome men and ruby-lipped, entirely devoted women.

I would translate the situations, even the names of the characters, until they fitted more closely my own mood. All that mattered was the tone of yearning, the sense of a world drawn in colours of rose and powder-blue.

It was exactly the world of Marcus Stone I had slumped back into, the trashy inaccurate world Nils so much despised. I would take a passage from a novel, say George Macdonald's *Home Again*, to name one of my favourites, and the touching encounter between the recuperating poet and his childhood sweetheart would soon become part of my own, and of Nils's, existence.

I would read the words aloud, whispering to my rag-doll, as I lay in the window-seat overlooking the herb-garden, squeezing the red covers of the little volume as if it were the strong hand I so much wanted to touch.

'It was a sweet day in the first of the spring. Walter lay with his head towards the window, and the sun was shining into the room, with the tearful radiance of sorrows outlived and winter gone, when Molly entered. She was at once whelmed in the sunlight, so that she could see nothing, while Walter could almost have counted her eye-lashes.

'Stand there, Molly, he cried. One moment. I want to look at you!

'It is not fair! returned Molly. The sun is in my eyes. I am as blind as a bat.

'I won't ask you, if you mind, Molly! returned Walter.

'In these days he had grown very gentle. He seemed to dread the least appearance of exaction.

'I will stand where you like, and as long as you like,

Walter! Have you not consented to live a little longer with us! O, Walter, you don't know what it was like when the doctor looked grave!'

O Walter, O Molly! It makes me blush with shame as I read this passage I copied out into my diary. I was totally the prisoner of my infatuation. The very unreality of the comparison seemed to release the power of the emotions. It was the triggering power of the words I needed, not the facts, or the moral, of the narrative.

Sometimes I would imagine Nils arriving in the same mood as last year, and instantly surprised, even amazed, by the change in my looks, I would picture him coming through the orchard and finding me reading beside the soft fruit bushes, a volume of Hall Caine in my gloved hands.

He would start, look confused for a moment, and I would know. He would be at a loss for words, unlike himself in his confusion; and then he would gather confidence, and reveal his new sense of closeness to this older, more mature and beautiful Anna.

There would be more jokes, yes. More playful sessions in the dining-room. The old Nils would be slow to die. But a new Nils would rise in time from his ashes. A Nils less frivolous. A Nils more involved. A Nils on the edge, perhaps, of being in love.

The magic words would sometimes draw me to a kind of trembling as I worked with hoe or riddle in the garden, as I scrubbed floors, or forced recalcitrant clothes through the mangle. They would make my heart beat faster, and the blood rush to my cheeks, exactly as they did in *Home Again* or *The Lady From Flanders*.

But I knew, really, that all this was fantasy, mere empty speculation. What would happen when Nils came would happen in its own way, and no doubt quite unpredictably. I could only wait, and be ready.

As it turned out, there was nothing to wait for. At least not initially. One day in early August I was washing up the breakfast dishes in the big zinc bowl beside the kitchen window.

It was hot already, although it was only ten o'clock, and there were flies buzzing and smacking the wooden walls as I tipped a fresh pan of hot water from the tank into the bowl. We had no running water in the house, and the barrel in the corner had to be filled each morning from the pump in the yard. Hot water for washing had to be drawn from the tank by the stove and, alas, this meant that we had to swelter in a boiling kitchen throughout the hot weather. There was no other way we could get hot water except by boiling it.

I was wearing a light summer dress, with the sleeves rolled up, and my face was flushed with exertion and warmth. I liked washing up, because it was one job that always showed some positive results − a pile of dirty dishes when you began, and a rack of clean ones whenever you'd finished. But it was hard and sweaty work.

My father came downstairs with his jacket over his arm, and his peaked cap already on. He was holding an envelope and a letter in his hand.

We shall have to look elsewhere for your tutor this year, Anna, he said. Mr Strindberg has written to say that he goes up to Norrland on Saturday to do geodetic work for the summer.

My father was glancing through what appeared to be a letter of some considerable length.

Very sorry not to be able to come, he murmured. Says how much he regrets any inconvenience. Sends his regards to mother and to yourself.

My father made a tut-tutting noise with his lips.

A great pity, he said, in evident annoyance. Your mother will be most upset. Most upset, I know.

Outside the window, I began to focus again on the crab-apple tree, on the tubs of aubretia on the terrace. It was odd. They were still there. The mist had cleared, and the world was still the same. The thunderbolt had struck, and yet the garden had not, after all, been burned to a sudden cinder.

Only the organs, every one of them in my body, had been seared to a solid conglomerate mass. Only the flesh and bones of Anna Charlier had been charred and blackened. The rest of the world's material was all the fresh colours it had been before.

76

Not coming, I whispered, feeling the water gripping my wrists like two manacles of fire. You mean, he's not coming at all.

No, said my father briskly. Not at all, I'm afraid. I should certainly have been prepared to take him on for a shorter period, but he makes it quite clear that his whole summer is already committed.

My father turned his eyes back to the letter.

One piece of good news, he said casually. Apparently there's to be an exhibition of photographs at the Industrial Palace in Stockholm and Strindberg has had a number of his own efforts accepted for display. He sounds very pleased. It's evidently quite an honour.

My father held the letter out at arm's length, and read aloud.

I should be overjoyed, he says, if you and Mrs Charlier and Anna were able to come down to Stockholm as my guests for the Private View. That's what he says.

My father half closed his eyes, and looked at me sideways with a slight smile. He must have seen the comet leap in my face, and soar through the darkness.

Well, now, he said softly. You're seventeen, my little Anna. Time that you saw the capital city, I'd say.

You mean we can go? I asked, incredulously.

I'll book us three tickets on the train, my father said. We'll have a couple of nights in a good hotel, and you can see the Royal Palace and some of the museums. The Private View of Mr Strindberg's photographs can form the culmination of our trip.

Then he did what he so often did, reached out and clasped me round the waist as if I was still a child, and once again I was swinging, off the ground, high up and then down, a parachute of a girl, afraid with her usual terror, delighted with a new excitement.

O, Daddy, I said, uneasy and yet happy. What a wonderful trip we shall have!

That night, in the quiet and privacy of my bedroom, I lit a candle, and took out the faded red volume of *Home Again*, and rubbed the incised bough of gold oak-leaves with my finger. It was like the first step of a ritual.

I made myself comfortable on my wooden bed, propping

the pillow under my back, and then I did what I now found best of all. I opened the book at random, and began to read. As always, my mind skated away and around the words, fitting my own situation to the dreamy world of Walter and Molly.

'From Comberidge a dogcart had been sent to meet him at the railway. He drove up the avenue as the sun was setting behind the house, and its long, low, terraced front received him into a cold shadow. The servant who opened the door said her ladyship was on the lawn; and following him across the hall, Walter came out into the glory of a red sunset. Like a lovely carpet, or rather, like a green, silent river, the lawn appeared to flow from the house as from its fountain, issuing by the open doors and windows, and descending like a gentle rapid, to lose itself far away among trees and shrubs. Over it were scattered groups and couples and individuals, looking like the creatures of a half angelic paradise. A little way off, under the boughs of a huge beech tree, sat Molly, reading, with a pencil in her hand as if she made notes. As he stepped from the house, she looked up and saw him. She laid her book on the grass, rose, and came towards him. He went to meet her, but the light of the low sun was directly in his eyes, and he could not see her shadowed face. But her voice of welcome came athwart the luminous darkness, and their hands found each other. He thought hers trembled, but it was his own . . .'

I laid the book aside, and looked up at my coloured photogravure of Bronzino's 'Annunciation'. The Angel Gabriel was separated from the Virgin Mary by a low brick wall, and the white dove lanced across it like a streak of cream. O Nils, I murmured, and was soon asleep.

I remember the first time I saw Edinburgh. I'd landed at the port of Leith and taken a diligence up to the Waverley Railway Station. I walked half way down Princes Street with my two bursting suitcases, just staring at everything – the Scott Monument, the Castle, the Gardens. They were like buildings from a fairy story.

I had to sit down and rest for a while in the Gardens, breathless with admiration, as many another young girl had been before me, for sure. I didn't properly recover, I remember, until I'd had a cup of hot Scottish tea at Jenner's, and a potato scone.

Stockholm was just the same. Even more so, I suppose, at the impressionable age of seventeen. It was a long journey in those days from Malmö, sixteen hours by the night train, and more by day.

My father had booked us three berths in a sleeping-car — the first time I'd travelled in anything so extraordinary, all brass and porcelain, and starched sheets and little folding tables — and we arrived at Stockholm about nine in the morning.

I didn't sleep a wink, of course. I lay awake in my upper bunk, with my eyes fixed on the ceiling, and my body tuned to the rhythms of the wheels. In the darkness I pictured Nils there in the bunk below me, awake as I was, and separated only by the blissful reticence of love.

I had still no idea of the physical satisfactions of passion. Those dirty games the girls at school had shown me were no more part of the world of love I lived in than the wooden walls of this moving train. They were gross adjuncts, base meals for the body. Love lived somewhere else.

I felt the stiffness of the hard bed under me, and dreamed. Nils, Nils, Nils, the train wheels seemed to say. Nils, Nils, Nils. I felt the name beat up and into my head. It took me over, it lulled me, and then, yes, for a time, I know, I fell fast asleep and woke only to the sense of stillness, the train halted and the busy, jostling morning sounds of a great station.

We ate new rolls and drank coffee on the platform. My mother found the butter rancid, and complained, and sent it back. My father watched the throng of passengers, lighting his pipe and relaxing. I was all trembling alertness, eager to see Nils, by some magic accident, in every face that passed.

The Hotel Rydberg, where we were to stay, was only five minutes walk away, but my father — in a mood of expansive luxury that lasted throughout the holiday — insisted on taking a carriage. So we arrived in style, the wheels rattling to a stop in a small cobbled courtyard, and the horses reining in with a fine fluster and whinnying.

The hotel overlooked a busy quay, and our room was on the first floor, a large sunny space, with a curious high bay window in an alcove, and shutters carved with hearts to show the daylight through in the mornings.

I had a little bed beside this alcove, and my mother and father were in a bold half-tester against the wall. There were flowered curtains, and some clean, well made old furniture. I loved the room. It had an indefinable salty, maritime air about it, and there was a feeling of suspended voyages in the hotel, of ships about to put out, or soon to put in.

Stockholm is very much a city of the sea. It was so then, forty years ago in the 90s, and I don't imagine that much has changed. There were always captains in the streets, with peaked caps and gold braid on their sleeves; always views down thin alleys or across open prospects to water; always vessels at anchor or in full sail, or steaming between pine-clad islands towards the sea.

For a girl in her teens, romantic at heart, and in love as I was, it offered the perfect background for every kind of dream and speculation. I would sit in some small café, over a tall glass of lemonade or soda water, making notes for my diary, or drawing baskets of fish or coiled ropes. Whatever I touched or thought about assumed some role in the adventure of my heart's desire. The fish were symbols of Christian marriage, the ropes were to rescue princesses from ivory towers.

I would walk by the quays, lifting my skirts to avoid the swill of guts or rotten vegetables in the markets, twirling my parasol, of which I was inordinately proud, and assuming the air, though I doubt scarcely the style, of a fine lady of town out shopping or on the way to meet a friend.

Usually, of course, one or both of my parents would be with me, or close behind, and I expect that to most eyes I presented the spectacle of a gawky teenage girl in plaits, all angles and jerky ways, learning as best she could to adapt her growing body to the mode of a woman of the world. There were many such girls in Stockholm at this holiday season, and I can hardly have stood out much above the crowd.

80

My mother with her plain country face and her sensible clothes had an energy of lassitude, if such a thing be possible, that gave her rather idle progress a certain drawing power, and there were always strangers to lift her bags, and open doors, and in general pave the way for whatever intention she had in mind. She could manipulate the world to do what she wanted with the minimum of wheedling.

So whether accompanied by my father, or alone with me, she was adept in arriving at the front of waiting lines, and in being served before other people in restaurants, and in obtaining exceptional service for her money. I despised this proficiency in her, and, of course, profited by it.

My father was happiest when we could avoid the expensive shops in Norrmalm, and spend an afternoon in one or other of the museums, where, with guide-book in hand, he could lecture at his will on the merits of Donatello, or some early type of steam threshing-machine.

The time went by very quickly. Six days passed in educational conversation, in healthy walking, and, on my part as I say, in glorious dreaming. Well nourished in mind and body — the smörgaasbord in our hotel was excellent — at last we reached the day our whole holiday had hinged on, the occasion of the Private View for the Amateur Photographic Exhibition.

The Private View was a notable Stockholm occasion; less perhaps for the established society of the day than for the younger, more brilliant set, the artists and writers, who were setting the tone for the new century. The Industrial Palace itself, a stale antique now, I suppose, had all the smartness then of novelty. It had been erected the previous year, to the designs of a young architect from Austria, who'd worked with Otto Wagner, and it bore the marks of that sinewy elegance already becoming known as *Jugendstil*, or *art nouveau*.

There were thick, elephantine columns, covered in a wealth of plant and flower forms, and a roof bulging and tormented into the curves of an opulent Aladdin's cave. In this emphatic venue, the guests moved in their long coats and their bright dresses, pausing with programmes and glasses to inspect the series of black-framed photographs hung along the walls.

The whole affair was done with a lot of style, and there was even a traditional flunkey in a green jacket who took our names and announced our arrival in a sonorous bawl.

Mr and Mrs Victor Charlier, and their daughter, Anna.

I felt the eyes of the whole room swim towards me. I was wearing a brand-new dress, in fine cream satin, with tiny pearl buttons all the way down, and a necklace of old amber beads my mother had kindly, and rather surprisingly, agreed to lend me. I felt very elegant, and extremely conspicuous.

My mother in her dark-blue bombazine, and my father in his frilled shirt and his tail-coat, seemed no more than a foil to my brilliance. My eyes ran to and fro in the room, searching for Nils, sure that he would suffer an astounding − and exhilarating − shock when he saw how much I'd changed.

But of course I hadn't, and he didn't. He did emerge from the crowd, hearing our names, and hurry across the room, all politeness, and bobbing good will. But his first approaches were to my parents.

How very kind of you both to come! he insisted, holding my mother's gloved hand in his own, and smiling in pride at my father. What a real honour this is.

It was the old Nils, the first Nils I'd known, a little precious, a little excessive in his compliments, a little nervous evidently on this important occasion in his life. But it was a new Nils, too, in a tiny physical way that surprised me.

You've grown a moustache, I said.

Even as I spoke, his original, softer face seemed to break out under the bristling hair, making the twisted points of the new moustache twirl up and underline his smile. I felt my heart leap, and then melt, and drip away to my feet, as he turned and looked me in the eye.

Observation, Anna, he said smartly. That's what counts. I grew it last winter, in Lapland. To keep me warm in the cold.

Nothing had changed. In that quick, light speech he had re-established our old jaunty relationship as if no time had elapsed since we met. It was wonderful. I felt close, and at ease with him again.

Show me your pictures, I said boldly, sliding my arm through his. I want to know all about them.

Anna, my mother said, most shocked by this forwardness.

But I knew my Nils. He saw me still as a child. I had to accept and live with that. Any love he was going to feel for this little country mouse must burgeon and flower later. But affection, yes. That was still there. And genuine liking for my willingness to be as outrageous as he wanted to be himself.

I must shelve my passion, and be the flirtatious child I had been before. In that role, I had a chance to be shown attention, and even flirted with. In any other role, I was going to be overlooked, and soon forgotten.

My lady, said Nils, in mock deference, and then, casting his eyes up to an imaginary heaven for the benefit of my parents, he allowed himself to be dragged away through the press of scented necks and perspiring arms, the flutter of idle talk, the restless movements of fan and programme.

Iceberg One, he said suddenly, pulling to a halt. Notice the tonal values of the dark blacks in the foreground shadow.

I leant forward, oblivious of the thrusting shoulders, the heavy odour of musk and ambergris. It was a small photograph, dwarfed by those on either side. The white curve of the berg reared like a Roman nose from a dead black sea. It seemed to shimmer; to beckon and to threaten.

On either side, the complex spring landscapes with their pre-Raphaelite detail of trellis and roses looked suddenly meretricious, and out of date. It was this stark white berg that seemed the wave of the future, the beak of the twentieth century.

It's wonderful, I said.

Nils looked at me sharply. For a moment, he seemed at a loss for words. He could see I was really moved. After all, he must have been thinking, she isn't too young to see what it means. But then his irrepressible jauntiness took over.

No, my dear Anna, he said, steering me on through the crowd. Not wonderful. Just new. NEW. Taking a photograph is like performing a scientific experiment. It requires patience, luck, and an aim. It must work, or fail, either showing something that has never been seen before, or simply repeating an earlier image.

Nils paused.

Like most of these, he said scornfully, waving his hand in that strange dismissive gesture he had, as if slicing off the heads of stalks of corn.

I have seven photographs here, he continued, seizing a glass of champagne from a passing tray, and pressing it into my hand. The one you've just seen is the best, the most clear. The rest are approximations. Look. Over there.

He pointed through a gap in the crowd, to where a stout, florid-looking young man was bowing along a line of photographs with a red rosette above them.

Homage to Nordenskjöld, said Nils. My other six. They've won first prize. That's why they're hung together with that rather silly red rosette. And it's also why my boring sculptor brother is here to give them his blessing. Tore, he said loudly, as we came up behind the young man. I want you to meet my former student, Miss Anna Charlier.

I took against him, even then. He was a solemn, over-heated young idiot in those days, with an awkward attempt at sideburns, and a supercilious grin.

Why, charmed, I'm sure, he said, lifting my hand and brushing his lips along the skin.

He did this glancing at Nils, as though to prove he was humouring a child. I didn't like the feel of his lips, though, and he let his tongue slide in the niche of my fingers, a brief, lecherous touch of a kind I'd never known before, and felt very disgusted by, from him.

Amazing work, he said to Nils. You deserve your prize. Those masts.

He gestured, without words, at a picture of a tall sailing-ship, seeming to be embedded in ice.

Quite amazing, he ended.

Well, said Nils, amused clearly, but also, I thought, a little flattered. And what do you think of my seventh picture? Iceberg One. Over there.

Tore took Nils by the shoulder, and shook his head as he squeezed. Then he plucked a handkerchief from his pocket, and blew his nose.

Too bare, my boy, he said. Very much too bare. Take my word.

He was digging the dirty handkerchief back into his trouser pocket, and eyeing my dress in a way I didn't at the time quite understand but now realize meant studying the shape of my breasts. I only knew I was faintly discomfited, and unhappy with his stare.

Stick to ships, Nils, he said. You have a talent for those. Come round and see me one day at the studio. Bring your young friend.

Then, leering at me, and finally, yes, I'm sure, winking, he pushed away in the crowd, waving his programme to make air in front of his face. He looked hot and loathsome, I thought, a toad on legs.

Tore, said Nils confidentially, is by way of becoming a sculptor. But not, I fear, in the wake of the French Rodin. More in the style of that crawling insipid English Alfred Gilbert.

I knew neither of these names, but I was gratified to hear Tore Strindberg's work so obviously denigrated. I looked quickly along the group of prize-winning photographs. They were good, I felt, even very good: romantic evocations of the great voyage to find the North-East Passage which had taken Baron Nordensjköld from Spitzbergen to Yokohama in his ship, the *Vega*. He was still the greatest polar explorer of our time, so Nils had told me. It didn't surprise me to find his achievement so boldly celebrated here.

Well, said Nils.

It was a question. I felt, suddenly, an important question. Once again, I was being tested as an adult.

They're good, I faltered. Very good.

I sipped my champagne. I'd never drunk any before, and the heady beverage was going to my brain. I felt sure of my judgment, free of restraints. But not so good as Iceberg One, I said.

Nils took my cheeks in his two hands and kissed me swiftly and drily on the forehead.

85

Hail, Anna, critic extraordinary, he said solemnly. You're absolutely right. These are tricks, he said, waving his hand at the prize-winning row. The ice is good, the shadows are fine. But the ship was collaged in. Superimposed, he added, seeing I didn't understand. I photographed the ice in Lapland last winter, the ship here in Stockholm. I developed the prints one on top of the other.

That's very clever, I said. I couldn't have told.

Nils touched my cheek, serious in the milling crowd.

Yes, you could, he said. Intuitively, you saw. You knew it was a fake. A clever fake, but a fake.

I saw my father approaching across the room. There was something I desperately wanted to know.

Does it matter? I asked. Why does it matter?

A photograph is a record of first-hand experience, said Nils slowly. Not a dream, but an actuality. At this very moment Nansen and his crew are trying to drift across the Arctic in the *Fram*.

Nils tapped the frame of one of his photographs with his finger.

These photographs are theirs, he said quietly. Someone in that ship is the man to make them real. To turn my dream into a real experience.

Anna, my father said, arriving a little breathless. I think we must go. I hope she hasn't been monopolizing you, Mr Strindberg. You know, I think, that we're returning to Klippan tomorrow, but I should be honoured if you could spare the time to eat lunch with us at our hotel before we go. My wife would be quite delighted.

I waited with caught breath. Say yes, my heart said. Say yes, O please, say yes.

It will be a pleasure, said Nils, bowing, and that was that. The alcohol took over, and I remember very little of our getting coats, bidding farewell, finding a carriage, or returning to the Hotel Rydberg, where I pleaded a headache and went straight to bed.

The lunch took place, of course, out on the terrace in the sun, with Nils in a lovely red alpaca jacket, very much the town dandy, and my mother dominating the conversation with questions about the social life of the summer. I sat in silence, rubbing crumbs into the table, or toying with my salad. It was only in the hall, after my mother had said her farewells, and my father had gone to find a book on irrigation techniques in Holland he wanted to lend Nils, that I was able to have a word on my own with my former tutor.

You're very quiet, my beauty, said Nils, lightly, as he flicked at the tiles with his cane. Are you sorry to be going home?

I'm sorry not to have had your help as my tutor this summer, I said, very quietly.

I'd rehearsed the speech, and it had sounded quite respectable, and proper, in the privacy of my room. But downstairs here amidst the potted palms, with their faint hothouse atmosphere of Ibsenic adultery, it seemed forward.

Yes, Nils said, it's a pity. And then, idly flicking at the leaves of an aspidistra: You remember our conversation about Andrée, and his balloon voyages?

Yes, I said.

Shall I tell you a secret?

Yes.

You're the first to know, said Nils, taking a deep breath. I applied to be one of his two companions on his flight to the North Pole.

A bell-boy went past with a telegram.

I heard this morning, said Nils. I've been accepted.

I took to looking at myself, with critical eyes, that winter, in the little swing walnut mirror that stood on my chest of drawers. It showed a lean-faced girl, with high bones in her cheeks, and skin stretched white and clean from tall forehead to chin.

I would turn my head, and watch the profile of my face, making the straight long nose move towards and away from me, like the prow of a ship, slicing air like brine. Then I would let my eyes drop over the brink of that nose, flicker along those cheek-bones, and then glide into the rich depths of my hair, coal-black, lustrous, and, when I let it down, before blowing my candle out and going to bed, long enough to fold under my slim buttocks.

I knew, I think, I was good-looking, but not how far I

was attractive. Other girls had long hair, and thin faces, and one or two had even a lovely sweep to their necks, with their hair up, and jewels in their ears, that I knew I lacked.

So what was I like, in a man's eyes? I faced myself in that little walnut looking-glass, and I saw the answer. I let my eyes droop to the sensual, ruby curve of my lips, and then rise and focus, fascinated, on their own blue, bottomless depths. Yes, I could eat men up, with those. Yes, I could drown men's hearts for ever, in these.

One night, when my mother and father were out at a church meeting, and I was supposed to be fast asleep in bed, recovering from a cold, I crept downstairs, greatly daring, in nothing but my shift and slippers, and stood, examining my full length, in the long cheval-glass that fronted the door of my mother's wardrobe. I stood back on the carpet, kicking off my slippers, and rising on tiptoe.

Lifting my thin arms above my head, I made a quick turn, like a ballet dancer, on my toes, nearly falling into the double bed as I lost my balance. I got my breath, feeling my heart beating nineteen to the dozen, and then I stood up again, and put my hands on my hips.

I lifted one arm, and looked up and under it to the pit. There was hair there, in a thick, wiry forest. How would that appear to a man? It seemed to me repellent and coarse, but something told me that a man might not find it so.

I put down my arm and, on impulse, shucked up my shift to my waist, shutting my eyes tight as I pulled the whole thing over my head, and let it fall to the floor. It was cold in the empty bedroom, and I shivered, feeling goose-pimples coming all over my back and belly.

I kept my eyes shut for as long as I could, then opened them, and stared. I was very shocked by what I saw. I was in the habit of taking a bath by candlelight in my room two or three times a week, but I used to sit half-clothed in the zinc tub, first doing the top half, and then the bottom, and I'd never paused before to examine myself like this while I washed. It wouldn't have been decent.

It seemed grossly indecent to me now, and I found myself blushing, right down from the cheeks to the navel, and on beyond. I put one hand over the bush in my groin, another over my two young breasts. I looked very much, I suppose, like the famous Greek statue of Venus disturbed at her bath.

But it wasn't a Greek physique I had. I saw that now. I was thinner, by far, than the classical ladies I'd seen pictures of in art magazines at school. Thinner and also, in a curious way, more improper. I had pink little teats projecting from my fat breasts, and this terrible uncombed, uncut growth in between my legs. It had never felt so rough or so prominent before, when I sat in my bath water with my eyes on 'The Annunciation'.

Now it looked huge. Grotesque and yet in some way alluring. I realized, without wanting to, that a man would be drawn by the sight of this, as I saw it now. He would want to reach out, and, yes, perhaps, fondle and caress that special place. I did that, too, myself, I knew, but I never spoke or thought of that. It was washing, after all, a kind of washing, anyway, and I had to be clean.

So why did I want to do it now, here in my mother's bedroom, bare-naked from crown to toe, with my two nipples stiff as buttons, and my legs pressing wetly together when I slipped my hand into position, and closed my eyes again?

Afterwards, drawing the slip on again, and realizing what I'd done, I knew that it wasn't only ugly girls who wanted themselves, and practised the places to touch. It was girls like I was, too. Girls who knew, as I now knew, that they could have all the men they wanted. Their bodies were theirs to use, their secret places were theirs to make their fortunes with.

That night, I wrote my letter to Nils. It had long since occurred to me that I might do this, and I'd made many abortive attempts, all burned, and forgotten. But now I knew the tone I had to adopt. It had to be something connected with what had happened in front of the mirror, in my mother's bedroom, but it had to be vague, too, in some way suggestive, and yet reticent, on that subject.

So I took my pen, and my school atlas for a support, and I wrote the following letter.

Dear Sir, it began. You must get many letters from

adolescent girls, I know, and you must forgive me for adding another to your growing pile. I have no excuse, of course, for approaching you out of the blue, as it were, like this, but you will perhaps understand my reasons when I tell you of the fearsome dream that ruined my slumbers only this last night. O, sir, will you listen to a young girl, distraught as you must judge her to be? I know from the vivid work you have displayed at the Industrial Palace what a bold enquirer you are into the hysterical undertones of our Scandinavian unease. Your 'Homage to the *Vega*', with its desperate bark so cruelly implanted in the over-riding ice of an unfeeling world, is a work evidently, from all its careful malformations, its blending of elements from many a source, wrenched, I would say, from the depths of your own hectic misery and pain.

Dear Sir, I know how you feel. I, too, have been that frail ship, have lain, unable to move or feel the breath of clean wind in my sails, in that dry ice. I have been the beleaguered *Vega* of your so rightly acclaimed master-piece, and not, alas, only in my dreams. It is, however, on the subject of those, and in particular of the one I touch on, still lurid and dreadsome in my mind as I write, that I wish to address you now. Let me be brief. I was lying in the depths of an enormous white sofa, an enveloping and in some way sinister vehicle of repose, less the repository of sweet dreams and restorative ease than the turbulent vessel of a distracting range of sensations. I lay on my back, aware of nothing through the sense of sight or smell or hearing. Bodiless, as it were, apart from my mouth. With this one sense I was active to the full, chewing, with a slow, meditative intensive enjoyment, some form of white caramel, a kind of mint confection, that filled my throat with a light, pure effervescence of flavour.

Thus, as I chewed, stripped of all sensation, except the rounded, fluffy feel of the sofa under my back, and the clear taste of the caramel in my mouth, a curious inver-sion, a sort of disorientation of the sensory balance, a kind of Menier's disease of the palate, gradually — I say gradually, but it may have been almost in that famous instant while the milk runs out of the milk bottle — trans-ferred the taste to the feel, the feel to the taste, so that, willy nilly, and before I knew this, I was lying, yes lying, *inside* the mint caramel. Being eaten by what I was eating. Being felt by what I was feeling.

Dear Mr Strindberg, you of all men, with your grasp of your own disordered imagination that your photographs so remarkably evidence, you, I feel sure, will be able to read this tormenting image for me, to unpack its full range of associations, and to relieve me of the obscurely worrying sense of uncleanliness and misuse it has left me with. I feel dirty, I scarcely know why, after this clean dream.

I was pleased with this letter. It cost me a lot of effort. I knew that it would offer Nils the kind of extravagant fancifulness he so much enjoyed. At the same time, it poked fun at his photographs, and might be expected to elicit a sharp response on that subject. It also, of course, and most of all, provided a symbolic vehicle for the expression of my recent experience.

It was also, in a curious way, quite true. I had indeed had an odd dream of the sort I described, though not the night before I wrote. It had come to me in the Hotel Rydberg the morning after Nils's exhibition.

I can guess now at the passion and sensuality such a dream will always mask, more easily than I could then, in my eighteenth year in Klippan, with no more knowledge of psychology than its derivation, as a word, from the Greek root for a soul.

Nils's reply was quick to come, in a plain cream envelope, inscribed with those flowing rather messy capitals he affected as a young man. Our shorthand, with its bold, spiky diagonals came later.

Dear Madam, the letter began.

Your letter has wrung my heart. I do, as you hint, receive my fair quota of over-coloured, romantic effusions from the young. Yours combines the mood of the hothouse with the tone of the French novel. I recommend more than a glance at the verses of M. Rimbaud, and some study of his doctrine of the *dérèglement de tous les sens*. As for my photographs, you are well aware, you ungrateful young hussy, that I set no store by the *Vega* trash. That solitary study of the iceberg, that's the one that matters.

By the way, I am well, you will be glad to hear. Unlike

you, I have not been dreaming. I have been reading, most interestingly a paper by Ernst Ek, on the way to manufacture hydrogen gas for filling balloons in the Arctic. For him, the applications are military – an invasion of Russia by hot air, no less. For Andrée and me there are likely to be polar implications.

The gas is obtained by the action of sulphuric acid on iron shavings. You pour it on, it hisses off. It needs diluting with sea-water, and then you wash, purify, and dry it. Its quality is the best imaginable. The tests that have been made, to the total of more than one hundred, show not the slightest trace of free acid, nor of hydrogen sulphide in the gas. It means that we could make the gas we need for the balloon in Spitzbergen, and save the labour and the wastage of carting it all up there in steel cylinders. Three cheers for Ernst Ek! Your eye-averting interpreter, Nils Strindberg.

So the correspondence had begun, a weird lickerish one on my part, and a joky, down to earth one on Nils Strindberg's. I was poorly satisfied by the jaunty tone of what he wrote, but it was better than nothing, and it helped to give more body to the rosy-coloured images I allowed to drift across my starry eyes as I squatted in the bath-tub.

Enough of that. I learned about balloons, and ballooning, too, and of the gradual development in Nils's own experience of them. After Christmas, as the first step in his education for the polar trip, he was sent, at Andrée's expense – lucky fellow as I considered, with my dreams of perfumes and furbelows – to make a number of trial balloon ascents with M. Lachambre in Paris. News of ballast and of dizziness at great heights, and of crashes into the high branches of trees, began to arrive, mingled with further comic-opera responses to my own famished advances.

And later, a provisional schedule for the balloon journey began to emerge. After Nils had completed his training, which, in my over-stoked imagination would inevitably be enlivened by the caresses of French prostitutes, he would set sail with Andrée and the third aviator, Nils Eckholm, for a remote island in Spitzbergen, where a balloon-house would be built, and a hydrogen gas apparatus installed. The balloon, which would travel with the aviators from Norway, would be filled in the balloon-house and the flight attempted, weather permitting, in July or August, 1896.

In effect this would exactly cover the period of my eighteenth birthday. I didn't like the dating. It meant that Nils wouldn't be there to see me come of age. I should step from my chrysalis, a full-grown butterfly, and he wouldn't be present to know.

This put me off balloons, and everything to do with them, more than ever. I was already very suspicious of the expedition, even before I went up to Stockholm again, to hear Nils lecture, on April 24th.

It had been, by then, a long-planned trip. My father was by now a keen student of Andrée's plans, and he followed the newspaper reports of what was intended as closely as the information in Nils's letters. He was proud, he said, to be an acquaintance and, indeed, an employer, of one of the three heroes who were to carry the banner of Sweden to the North Pole.

Mr Strindberg has proved a friend indeed, he would say, rubbing his hands in delight, each time he read Nils's name in the *Aftonbladet*.

This not unexpected interest − after all, much of Sweden was by now fascinated with the idea of flying to the Pole by balloon − was both boring and helpful. Boring because it just was. And helpful, because it forwarded my aim of seeing Nils again.

I am to return to Stockholm, he said, in one of his letters, on April 12th. I shall, by then, have made seven ascents. You will be delighted to know that The Swedish Anthropological and Geographical Society − yes, none other − has invited me to follow in the master's footsteps (he meant Andrée's, of course) and lecture to its members on the construction and equipment of the polar balloon. This is a great honour, needless to say, and I am paralysed with nervousness. I can hardly face the thought of the occasion without the moral and, I hope, physical support of − and I now through you, dear Anna, address your mother and father as well as yourself − my dear friends from Klippan. Will you take pity on a poor man in his hour of need, and say you will come and be in my audience? I await your reply with eager, nay desperate, hope.

Needless to say, my father was deeply flattered by this invitation. My mother, though equally so, was smitten by a spring flu much nearer the date, and thus, to her great chagrin, her place in the dual representation that my father thought appropriate, had to be taken by me. Had it not been so, I think I would either have had to pawn my necklaces, few as they were, to find my own fare, or drowned myself in the stream, rather than stay at home.

So once again, places were booked in the sleeping-car, and this time my father and I, like a vigorous older lover and his young mistress, as I feel sure many a stranger seeing us together thought, set off with our bags and our umbrellas, for it was a wet spring, towards Stockholm.

Many a lascivious or speculative eye was cast on the slender young beauty in her high boots, and her long fur-edged coat, as she swept off the train with her handsome moustachioed father, clattered through old Stockholm in her carriage, and stepped proudly into the portico of the Hotel Rydberg, where the porters hardly, I think, recognized the quiet little mouse they'd known the year before.

I had come of age. If not in years, then certainly in body; I was a woman ready for whatever the world had to offer. Nils would know it. He was bound to. And there would be changes. A new relationship would sprout, and the world would never be the same again.

And so, indeed, it proved.

I won't say very much about the lecture. My father and I arrived by hansom, over-dressed, on a night of fizzling rain. All I remember of the building is a vague blur of Greek columns, and blotchy marble − the sort of late-Victorian sumptuousness that we've now been taught to regard as decadent vulgarity.

It matched my mood. I felt out of place amongst the audience, a country daisy trying to look like a precious orchid, I thought, and misguidedly planted in a bed of simple evergreens.

The members of the society were largely male − spindly

professors and well-built explorers, with a wealth of sideboards, and small neat spectacles without rims. But there was a scattering of women, too. Mostly young, and confident-looking, with wasp-waisted blouses, and hats drawn tight under their chins with long scarves.

These were the blue-stockings, the vanguard of Stockholm's progressive crowd – the women who were always leaders of opinion rather than followers of fashion. And there was I, aware very sharply of the white sweep of my neck and my bare shoulders. I felt like a woman strayed in from a cheap nightclub, the tawdry companion of a provincial tourist, out for a bit of fun, with his gold-chain, and his meerschaum pipe.

No one we knew was there, and we passed from the padded leather of the hall sofas, and the frowning portraits of great scientists and doctors, into a long hall furnished with twin rows of cushioned benches. At the far end of the room there was a platform, with a white screen hung above it, and half way down, in the aisle between the rows of benches, an impressive brass and oak machine stood on a small table flanked by a box of lantern slides.

We took our seats near to the back, and I waited for Nils to appear.

The lights dimmed, there was a sharp click, and then there ahead of us, larger than life almost it seemed, the white screen was filled with the black outlines of what would form the text for the lecture, the line drawings, done to an exact scale, of the side elevations of the polar balloon.

Perhaps, after all, it was more dramatic than for Nils to have entered in a puff of smoke and flame. Here, floating in the air, on flat silk, I was suddenly confronted by the ghostly presence of what was to rule and direct my life.

By some trick of the light, or some current of wind in the hall, it even billowed for a moment, then sagged, as if already at the mercy of those Arctic winds that would govern its future course.

Out of the darkness in the middle of the room, I heard Nils's voice, drifting above the silence like the eerie keening of some prophet, the acolyte or monstrant of a strange new god, whose coming it was his duty to announce and welcome.

95

I kept my eyes on that screen all the time that he spoke, mesmerized by the diagram. The very abstraction of the balloon's contours, its reduction to a mathematical series of shapes and lines, increased for me its quality of a sinister and numinous presence, a power that could only be apprehended through the uneasy and incomplete measure of human science.

The balloon has been manufactured under the supervision of Per Nordenfelt, a Swedish engineer, said Nils. It is, as you see, somewhat elliptical in form, and has a capacity of 4,800 cubic metres.

The words plunged out into the darkness, echoing and mysterious. I heard them, but without fully understanding. They were the spells of a ritual. As Nils spoke, he would come forward from time to time with a long pointer and gesture from the floor up at some portion of the diagram on the screen. Thus his points were given emphasis and clarity. But the diagram retained, for me at least, its gnomic resonance.

As I write now, I telescope what was a lecture of over an hour's length into a few recalled and pregnant sentences. It was the effect that mattered to me at the time, not the content. I had ample opportunity later to get to know that terrible balloon like part of my own skin. Like a swollen organ. Like a lethal tumour.

For the moment it was a new element in the fantasy of my life, a close rival who had stolen Nils's affections, and whom I obscurely hated, and wanted to destroy. But this was unconscious in me, part of an undefined air of unease, a blinding headache, and an awkward need to go to the lavatory, none of which I could, for the moment, do much about.

So I watched the polar balloon, and I tried to listen. One part of what Nils said did stay in more detail, and it has its importance for what came later. He was up on the platform by then, sliding his pointer across the diagram as he spoke.

If the balloon becomes a little wet, he said, or if it cools some degrees below its normal temperature, it soon grows, as it were, unwilling, and tired. That is, it loses some of its carrying-power. Such diminutions in carrying-power are to be counteracted by drag-lines in such a way that, when the balloon sinks, a great part of the weight of these ropes will be sustained by the ground.

Nils drew his pointer down the lines of the drag-ropes.

Number fifteen, he said, then continued. The sinking of the balloon must cease when a sufficient length of the lines rests on the earth, and the balloon has thus been relieved from a corresponding weight. If, on the other hand, the carrying-power of the balloon is increased, for example by the action of the rays of the sun on the gas, the balloon will not be able to rise to any great height, for, the higher it goes, the greater will be the length of drag-line it has to support.

I remembered how Andrée had used drag-lines in his third voyage in the *Svea*, when he had been carried out across the Baltic Sea. It seemed to me, as I listened, that my poor Nils was a puppet, a sort of lecturing Pinocchio, manipulated at a distance by his dominating master, through the medium of those very drag-lines he was indicating with his pointer.

I shivered, feeling my headache rise to a peak, and lights blaze and quiver in my skull. I felt my bowels churn, and I tightened my clasped hands in my lap to keep control of myself.

Each drag-line, Nils continued, consists of an upper part of hemp, and a lower section of cocoa-nut fibre. Each of the cocoa-nut fibre lines is provided, at a distance of about fifty metres from that end which rests on the earth, with a slenderer part, or neck, intended to make the line weaker just there. The object of this is that, if the line should catch in anything, it will not be able to hold fast, but will break instead.

Nils was wiping sweat from his brow with an immaculate white handkerchief. It outshone the screen in the darkness, as if painted with some kind of phosphorescent paint. He replaced the handkerchief in the top pocket of his black jacket, raised his pointer again, and let it quiver along the ropes.

I saw them billowing up, incurling as round the Medusa's head. The rustle of a woman's dress in the row behind seemed for a moment like the hiss of fangs.

97

Through my headache, and the pangs in my bowels, I felt a sort of premonition, a forehint of doom.

It had happened before, and it would happen again. The fairy blood in me, if that's what it was, chose its own time to give its warnings, and demand its price. And in those days it was still a stranger to me in its power, obscured by the random physiology of my girl's body. What mattered most was to hold on, until the lecture ended.

As, however, each line has not more than one weak point, said Nils, it might happen that the balloon would still be held fast, in consequence of a line, which had already broken at the weak point, once more fastening. To be able, in such a case, to release the balloon without having to cut free the entire line, there has been arranged, at the point of union between the hemp part and the cocoa-nut fibre part, a screwing device, in such a way that it can be unscrewed by means of twisting the rope. This twisting can be brought about with the help of a special mechanism, arranged close by the balloon, provided with a powerful gearing.

There was more to come, about the sail-system, and the two anchors, and the kind of sledges to be carried. But I couldn't wait any longer.

Excuse me, I said to my father, intent and upright with the bowl of his pipe clenched firmly in his hand, and I slid past him and into the aisle, and then swiftly to the back of the hall, and through the double doors onto those chilling tiles.

I breathed more freely there, and felt a moment's relief from the hammer-on-anvil effects in my head. Then I started across the floor and towards the cloakroom.

There I combed my hair, and took a sniff of sal volatile, from a phial I'd been prudent enough to slip in my hand-bag, and I felt much better.

I adjusted the silk shawl round my shoulders, and walked back across the hall, pausing to stare up at the frowning eyes of the cold soldiers and aldermen in their gilt frames. They disapproved of my low-cut dress, I knew. Well, let them. This was 1896, and times were changing. Nils would feel very differently.

I stood for the remainder of the lecture, slipping in

again through those huge mahogany doors, and placing my back against them, as if to prevent any other member of the audience from going out or coming in. It was there, when the gas was turned up, and the ripple of applause ran through the room, and Baron Nordenskjöld spoke from the centre of the platform, praising the lecture for its detail and clarity, that Nils saw me.

He was up beside Nordenskjöld, a plump lively figure beside the small, bearded one. His hands were out, as always a little extravagant, as he acknowledged the limited round of clapping. His eyes went to and fro like fish, nibbling at the faces for any sign of real approval or admiration, or, even, perhaps, veiled contempt.

Then they met mine, and were still. We were thirty metres or more from each other, isolated by a roomful of people. But the thing had happened. I knew it had. The spark had fallen, and the wood kindled.

I thought at first that Nils hadn't recognized me, and I was right. He simply saw, or so it seemed, someone whose whole soul was open to him in the way she stared. Well, it was true. I'd never dared to look into his eyes in that way before.

Our eyes locked, it seemed for hours. Then, the noise broke us apart, the bustle of chairs moving, rustle of clothes, babble of voices. I turned, and walked rapidly away on my own, through that inner portico, and out under the sloping Greek doorway onto the steps.

I was half way down, watching the rain still spit in the puddles under the gas-lights, when I heard quick foot-steps, and looked round, feeling a hand on my shoulder.

Anna, said Nils.

I smiled, brushing hair from my eyes.

You've changed.

Nils was holding me at arm's length.

Totally, he said. You're like a Greek god.

I wasn't. I was like a professional tart, in Stockholm terms, in my tight, outmoded velvet dress, with a shawl over my bare shoulders. I know that now, as I didn't then. I had a voluptuous figure, and a lot of it was on show. There were men in that audience whose trousers must have strained as they looked at me.

But, yes, there were naked boys in niches on the wall on either side of us, and their hair was up in braids, like mine. I wasn't puzzled by what Nils said, at the time. It seemed the spontaneous outpouring of a true emotion, finding what words it could.

I mean, you're beautiful, he said, correcting himself.

I still said nothing. I didn't know what to say. The moment had come, the thing had happened, that was all I knew. It was raining, and I was in love, and Nils was in love, and that was all that seemed to matter.

Come inside, said Nils. You'll get cold.

I shook my head.

No, I said. No.

The rain fell, a low hushing sound in the night, and still no one else came through the doors. We had silence, and, something almost inexplicable in those times, a few moments completely alone with each other.

Anna, said Nils, quickly. Then, helplessly, Anna.

He was standing a little apart, and now he touched me, very gently, on the elbow. I drew away.

Anna, said Nils. We must go in. We must.

I let him take my arm, and lead me back up the steps. At the top, he paused, and drew me aside against the wall. I looked into his eyes, breathing hard. I said nothing.

There was a long silence, and I could feel his heart beating, as he tried to decide what to do. I closed my eyes, trying to help. Then I opened my eyes, and I saw the muscles in Nils's arm tremble, where it was braced against my neck.

Your mother, he said suddenly, blinking. How's your mother.

The moment was passing. I could feel it slowly sliding away, like a ship going out of harbour.

O, I said, shaking myself. She's not well. It's her lungs.

Nils was pacing to and fro, a metre away in the darkness. His movements made a little wind on the steps.

Catarrh, he said. I thought it was just catarrh?

Yes, I said. Well it was. But the doctor says that it seems to have taken a turn for the worse. It's bronchitis now.

Bronchitis.

Yes.

There's a man, said Nils, and he seemed to be gathering strength as he spoke, as if he was coming back to normal after some kind of stroke or seizure. Yes, a man.

He ran his fingers over his face, smoothing the skin, and then brushing down the ends of his moustache.

In England, he said. Sir Hermann Weber. A great authority on all complaints of the nose and throat. It seems to be spores, he says.

I gazed into his eyes, flat on my back against the wall still. I began to play his game.

Spores, I said. What are spores?

Organic matter, I mean, said Nils. It's in the air. We breathe it all the time. Your mother's lungs, my dear Anna, are a jungle of decomposing spores.

I reached out my hand, very gently, and touched his cheek. It felt stiff, rigid.

So what can we do, I asked, softly.

He took my hand, holding it firm. I could feel him breathing faster again.

In a large industrial town, said Nils, and then he paused. Such as Manchester, he suggested. That's where they did the work. In Manchester, it appears that one breathes in three million seven hundred thousand spores every ten hours.

That's a lot, I said, stroking his fingers.

In Klippan, said Nils, it can't be quite so many.

No.

Up in the mountains, you know, said Nils, and his voice sounded very far away, there are no spores at all. Virtually none. You breathe pure air. Air, without matter. Without impurities.

Nils cleared his throat, and the sound seemed very loud on the steps.

It's the same at sea, he said. No spores. That's why they approve of Alpine resorts. And cruises.

A large man with a square beard appeared in the doorway to our right, and Nils gripped me suddenly by the arm and led me into the light.

Your mother needs a cruise, he said, loudly.

Eckholm, he added, with a sweep of his arm. This is Miss Anna Charlier. My pupil and my friend.

Nils Eckholm bowed. I already knew who he was from his pictures in the newspapers. He looked younger in real life, more humorous.

He's a real liar, Eckholm said, smiling at me. I was given to believe that you were a gawky little rabbit in pigtails.

He liked to shock, I knew that already. But Nils was ready for this jibe, more ready than I was.

She has indeed aged, he agreed. The bloom of youth has faded fast. You see before you, my dear Eckholm, a young woman already eighteen years of age.

Eckholm put his head on one side.

I love your dress, he said.

He obviously took me for more sophisticated than I was, and was complimenting me, perhaps rather tactfully, as he might have done a mature woman. I was flattered, and mollified.

Well, I like your beard, I said, rather daring.

Both men laughed, and at this moment my father appeared, looking very angry and a little worried.

There you are, Anna, he said. Then, noticing Strindberg: My congratulations. It went wonderfully.

I'm sorry, father, I said quickly. I felt ill, and came out for some air. Mr Strindberg and Mr Eckholm have been looking after me.

Of course, my father agreed. Of course. How do you do, Eckholm.

They shook hands, and there was a moment's awkward silence. The two younger men sensed that they appeared to have been caught out in mild flirtation, and were at a loss for words.

There's tea and coffee indoors, Eckholm suggested. In the ante-room.

But no one made a move to go.

I've been saying that your wife might profit from a cruise to improve her lungs, Nils put in smoothly. You know, they all recommend the pure sea air in the *British Journal of Tuberculosis*.

My father took his pipe out, and lit it with a match. He stared at Nils.

It's catarrh, he said, a little testily. I don't think it's quite got to be tuberculosis yet, whatever Anna may say.

I breathed heavily, and said nothing.

Ought to be careful, though, said Eckholm. These things get worse. Why doesn't she take a holiday on the *Erling Jarl*, and come up and see us all off at Danes Island?

There was a gust of wind, and rain was blown across my face.

It's a mean little trawler, explained Nils, in his joking way. They do a regular Arctic cruise, from Trondheim up to Spitzbergen, for those who enjoy three weeks of sea sickness, and a distant view of some rather yellowed icebergs.

My father saw that he was being joked with, and he let himself laugh. Then, plucking the stem of the meerschaum from his mouth, and tamping down the tobacco, he turned to Eckholm.

They'll call at Virgo Harbour with mail this year, I suppose, he said.

Eckholm nodded.

For, and I quote, he said, the intrepid aeronauts. It's already promised. The company knows a good advertisement when it sees one.

My father stared at Nils for a moment, a slow smile breaking across his face.

Well, he said.

Then he looked at me, rather more thoughtfully.

Mrs Charlier would no doubt require a chaperone, said Eckholm, rubbing his beard. I know what the ladies are like when they get away from home. No doubt your pretty daughter could double the role of nursing attendant and companion-at-arms.

Nils was digging his toe into the step.

You mark my words, he said. They'll be sick. They'll both be very sick. I take no responsibility at all.

Eckholm took my father by the arm, and we all walked back through the doors into the hall. A press of people was milling to and fro, collecting hats, laying down cups of coffee, bidding farewell to friends.

It would, you know, he said to my father, seriously. It would help her health a great deal. We did months of work on that in Spitzbergen, and there's no doubt at all that the combination of sea air and the cold climate improves the nasal cavities as well as anything can.

Then he nodded to me and Nils, and turned to leave.

Andrée, my father said, looking round. Is Andrée here? I'd like to meet him.

No, said Nils. He hates publicity. He'll be locked away at home working on one of his patents. You could have talked to Nordenskjöld, but I see he's gone. I'm sorry.

My father nodded, and pointed towards the ante-room, where the tea-urns had been placed.

I like your friend Eckholm, he said. He did some good work up there in Spitzbergen. Let's get some tea, Strindberg. And I want to hear much more about that screwing-mechanism.

Later, back at the Hotel Rydberg, as we climbed the stairs together to our rooms, my father reverted to the subject of the *Erling Jarl*. Until then, I hadn't dared to consider the talk about a cruise as any more than a summer evening's jesting.

Mean little trawler, indeed, my father said. It's brand-new. Displaces ten thousand tons, and carries its own doctor. I've read about the *Erling Jarl*. Might suit your mother very well.

You're serious, I said. You're really serious.

My father smiled.

Maybe, he said. We'll see.

4
STRINDBERG
1897

AFTER THE BASKET SETTLED, Fraenkel and Andrée remained on the roof, while the car was dragged for some metres through the snow. I could hear the grinding, and feel the pull, and the slowing, from where I was lying up in the carrying-ring.

Then, when the car had finally come to a stop, and they were sure the ropes and the basket were sufficiently embedded in the ice to prevent the balloon taking off again at the loss of their weight, Andrée and then Fraenkel climbed the rail, and then jumped down to the ground.

I heard their voices receding. Then I got to my feet, rather groggy still, and eased myself down through the trap onto the roof of the car. I stood for a moment looking round.

Visibility was poor, not more than a hundred metres in all directions. There was a light drizzle falling, and it was dank and cold. Andrée and Fraenkel were vague, blurry figures a little distance away on the ice. They were like two furry animals, delighted to be released from their cages for a morning run.

I could hear them laugh, and see them scramble and tumble in the snow. Fraenkel bent, and seemed to be fumbling with his clothes. An arc of water sprang from his middle and arched in the air. He turned round and round, roaring with laughter, and I watched the far liquid leap and seem to sizzle in the air.

A sense of great elation seemed to fill me, too, and I scrambled over the side and onto the ice, almost losing my footing for a moment, and half sliding as I landed. But I recovered my balance and ran to join the others.

It was wonderful to be back on the ground. I felt a ridiculous desire to fling off all my clothes and do a sort of dance beside the balloon.

I suppose that sailors feel the same, when they come out of a narrow boat. But we were the first men ever to have landed after so long in the air. It was a new experience, a new release.

Fraenkel had found a pool of melted snow, and was scooping up the fresh water into his mouth. He lay on his belly, like a lion at a water-hole. I ran over and lay down beside him. The water tasted good, ice-cold, and unutterably pure. It was like drinking diamonds, or so it seemed to me then, in that first euphoria of our landing.

Superb, said Fraenkel, rising to his feet, and giving me a helping hand. Absolutely superb.

We turned and faced the balloon. It lay about fifty metres away, like a huge, slightly sagging Christmas pudding on a plate of white porcelain. The ropes and the car, now dragged over on its side by the loss of all our weights, made a curious kind of appendage, as if the pudding had been cooked in a string bag, or been drawn out of a box, and inflated.

Yes, it was still a balloon. It rose, massive and dome-like, our great cathedral of the air-ways, undaunted still by its fresh, improper contact with the earth. It looked ready enough for a new ascent, if we should choose to make one.

It's covered with ice, Andrée said, as he came up beside us, rubbing his fingers through his woollen gloves. There must be over a ton on the net and the calotte.

That's why it sank, I said, stating the obvious.

Andrée smiled at me.

Yes, he said. But it might still rise. I've closed the valves.

He left us, and walked away towards the balloon. It seemed to billow as he approached, and then sag, as if it was recognizing his comment, and his captaincy. He was dwarfed by the great bag, but he seemed, still, its master.

What does he mean? I whispered to Fraenkel.

I was afraid that sound would travel for ever in this clear air.

Does he mean to try and take off again? I asked.

108

But Fraenkel only shrugged, and walked after Andrée. I watched the pair of them stand together in the shadow of the balloon. Then I took my camera, and I adjusted the distance and the exposure, and I took the first of many photographs of our situation on the ice.

You'll see the photographs when they're developed, Anna. They ought to be the best I've ever done. You remember what I said about Nansen's crew and the *Fram*? Their chance to make the real picture of a masted ship embedded in ice? No one has ever had my chance — to take a photograph of a hydrogen balloon sunk in snow.

So I took several, from all angles. Andrée alone on the car, too, when we had it loose, and he was fastening up the Swedish flag. I had Fraenkel in the foreground, like a sort of great bear standing watching him.

They were good to do. I enjoyed the work. It helped me to get my stomach back to normal before the hard labour of unpacking our stores and erecting the tent. After forty minutes, I was ready for anything.

Fraenkel had lit his pipe, and he was burning and fuming away like a small volcano in the midst of our Arctic wilderness. He looked a more contented man, with that wooden arch in his fist. It seemed to calm his nerves, whatever harm it may have been doing to his lungs.

After the first half hour, we all grew more sober, and the serious business of unloading began. We'd landed at eight o'clock, and it was seven hours later before we were finished, and could take some well-earned sleep.

The first thing we did was to flatten a space of ice near to the car for the tent to be erected on. Then we loosened the ropes, and manhandled the car back to an upright position. This made it easier to get at the baskets of stores which were mostly still packed above the carrying-ring.

Nothing had been damaged. But they were hard to reach, and harder still to unpack with the balloon on its side. We worked with a will, and were shortly sweating, even in the cold.

The tent was soon up, and I spread the expedition's sleeping-bag on the floor inside. Fraenkel arranged a sort of cache of boxes and baskets outside, and I began to unpack what might be required for our immediate needs.

Andrée gave little help. He busied himself mainly with making observations, noting details of the terrain and the condition of the balloon in his log. He was very much the captain now that we were on land, and he seemed anxious to keep a certain distance between himself and Fraenkel and me.

This came out most clearly at three o'clock, when he called a halt to the work, and decided that we should rest, as it were, for the night. I'd made a sort of stew, of meat in soup, and we were all well-enough fed, and anxious to lie down.

I'll take the sleeping-bag in the tent, Andrée said to me. You and Fraenkel can share the bunk in the car. We might as well have as much space as we can before we start to move.

It was spoken like an order, and neither Fraenkel nor I was inclined to object. In effect, it established the principle that the tent was to be a kind of captain's cabin, and the car of the balloon was to be the common quarters for the crew.

So that was the 14th of July. We all slept like logs, I have no doubt. I did, for sure. The next morning we rose late, at about eleven.

It was overcast, with some puffs of wind from the north-west. The fine drizzle was still continuing, but visibility seemed a little improved. The temperature remained at a fraction below zero.

The crucial thing to be decided was where to move, or whether to stay still, and we took our time discussing this, over a long breakfast, with coffee, marmalade, and sardines.

Andrée sat propped on the sleeping-bag in the back of the tent, like a saracen warrior in his palanquin, and Fraenkel and I lay at his feet like his dutiful squires, pouring him more to drink as he needed it, and passing the tins and the plates.

The situation is this, Andrée began, after his third cup of coffee. We are far out at sea. What is below our feet is water, salt water, just as surely as if we were sailing in a merchantman off the coast of Japan, or in the Pacific. If the sun were hotter, we should drown. The ice would melt, and we should be food for sharks and killer whales.

We have a boat, suggested Fraenkel.

Andrée ignored him. He wanted to analyse the situation in his own way, and he wasn't prepared to accept any interruptions.

Before, he said, we were aeronauts. Balloonists. Our element was the air, the empty sky. Now, said Andrée, we are mariners. Men of the sea. We thought before in terms of the winds. Now we must think of the properties of water. Its power to solidify and to flow.

So what do we do, said Fraenkel impatiently. Sit still and allow this frozen water to take us wherever it wants to go? Float on a raft of ice until we're hailed and found by some passing whaler?

That's our first option, said Andrée, leaning forward. I'm against it.

So am I, said Fraenkel. I can't bear doing nothing.

Nor me, I said.

Our second and third options, Andrée continued, involve a choice of routes across the ice. Spitzbergen is about 307 kilometres from where we are. So far as I can judge, that is. Franz Josef Land is about 335. South-west for Spitzbergen, gentlemen. Or south-east for Franz Josef Land.

Andrée paused, like a tour director, offering his customers an attractive choice.

Take your pick, he said.

He let us debate the issue for half an hour. But I knew from the start that we all thought Franz Josef Land was the better bet. It was further, yes. But there's food there, a large cache for us. And Nansen, we know, was able to winter for nine months there in an earth cellar. What Nansen could do, so, at the worst, can we.

There's more to look at in Franz Josef Land, said Fraenkel, finally. They have better trees there. And birds, too, for that matter. Spitzbergen is a barren wilderness in winter. A dreadful bore. There's nothing there for us. I vote for Franz Josef Land.

Andrée nodded.

There's a fourth option, he said, slowly. I think you know what it is, gentlemen.

There was a long silence. Fraenkel and I turned our cups

111

in our hands. I knew what Andrée was going to say, but I said nothing.

We could wait for the wind from the south, said Andrée, inexorably. We could fasten the ropes back on to the net. I think the balloon could be made to rise again.

There's more than a ton of ice by now, I said. You know there is. It would never rise.

It would rise with one man, said Andrée flatly. I know it would.

So there it was, out in the open. He still wanted to try for the Pole. Alone, this time. Like Nansen leaving the *Fram*, he had this crazy idea that he on his own might still drift on to the north.

No, I said. It means certain death for us all. It's a kind of suicide, and I want no part of it. Next year, if we all get home alive, and I know we can, we can build a balloon that's sure to get there and back in safety. That's what matters. Not some sort of madman's bid to push on with a piece of apparatus we all know in our heart of hearts to be faulty. It wouldn't prove a thing, even if you got there. It would just be a fluke.

Fraenkel, said Andrée, looking at him.

Fraenkel lit his pipe. He puffed for a moment, and then he delivered his ultimatum.

There may be a chance, he said. But it means the youngest and strongest man going. That means me.

I looked at him, disbelieving.

Andrée shook his head, violently.

Never, he said.

Look, I said, angry now. You both just want to be the first man to go furthest north. To beat Nansen, if you can. At whatever cost. You know you can't reach the Pole. And you can't hope to get back alone. It's a kind of suicide. And a matter of condemning the other two to a greater chance of death as well. Our best bet is to stay together. You know it is.

I'll draw lots with you, said Fraenkel, staring at Andrée.

No, said Andrée. This chance is my right as captain of the *Eagle*. I order you both to let me try.

Never, I said, in blatant mutiny.

Andrée stared at Fraenkel.

No, said Fraenkel. I won't do it. Either I go, or no one goes.

I got up and walked away across the ice. In the drizzle the surface felt slippery, but easy to walk on, like paving-stones after a storm of rain. I walked a long way, trying to let the tension come out of me, and some calm return. I didn't look where I was going.

When I turned, the car and the balloon and the tent were one strange dark blur in the mist. I stood watching them for a long time, and then I walked back.

Fraenkel and Andrée were still drinking coffee. They looked more at ease, as if they'd both accepted the situation.

So it's Franz Josef Land, said Andrée. And added, that is, when we're ready.

Later in the day, only a few moments before I sat down in the car to write all this down, Anna, we deflated the balloon.

It was a moment with its own touch of tragedy. At first, Andrée opened the valves, but the gas came out too slowly, and he grew tired of waiting. Once he'd decided it had to come down, he wanted the whole thing over as quickly as possible.

We'll use the bursting-apparatus, he said.

So, while Fraenkel and I stood by and watched, he went over and took a grip on the rip-panel rope. You know how it's supposed to work, Anna. In an emergency, you give one quick wrench on the rope, and the panel is torn aside to let more gas escape, and the balloon fall.

Luckily, perhaps, we never had to pull the rope in a hurry in the air. It took all Andrée's strength, until he was red in the face with the effort, to make it work. Fraenkel was about to step forward and give him a hand, when the panel finally gave.

There was a fierce tearing sound, then the strip came away and hung like a fold of skin from a wound. There was a heavy, low gushing sound, and then the gas was flooding out, and the rounded shape of the great balloon started to sag more, and then cave in.

Faster and faster, the gas came out. Andrée stood to attention, facing the balloon. I think he almost wanted to

113

bring his hand to a salute. Above him, the huge mass of silk was losing its life, dwindling from a living, floating thing to a collapsed heap of dead material on the ice.

Fraenkel tipped back a bottle of ale, and swallowed. I shifted my feet. I felt embarrassed. Andrée just stood there, very close, and the great balloon shivered into a mass of trembling jelly at his feet.

When it was all down, he knelt, and put his face in the silk. I turned away. I didn't want to watch.

Dear Anna. Five days have gone by since I wrote, six since we landed. It's Tuesday, July 20th, and a cold, sunny day. Actually, it's the first real day of sun we've had, and we're making the best use of it we can.

I'm sitting outside the tent, wearing my snow-glasses to keep off the glare, and I'm surrounded by what looks like the aftermath of one of your regular Monday wash-days at Klippan. Everything has been spread out to dry: clothes, blankets, books, baskets, whatever suffered, or might have suffered, from the steady drizzle and then the light snow.

The snow started almost as soon as we landed, not big heavy flakes, but a small flickering sort of snow, the kind of burst-pillowcase, feathery snow that seems to drift everywhere, and then melt into moisture and dampness.

It wasn't cold especially, and the wind was quite mild, but the snow left everything drenched through, or, at best, vestigially dank even when it had been packed at the bottom of a box or a basket. So we've emptied everything out. A good way to remember exactly what you've got! I've been making inventories, and discussing the loading of the sledges with Andrée.

After the balloon journey, which seemed so long, and so hectic, the last few days have been very calm, and they seem to have swum by in a kind of slow dream. One or two events are worth recording, but, on the whole, it's been a time of rest, and reclamation, and almost a sort of euphoria.

On the 16th, which was last Friday, the snow started, fairly early. It was quite a change to wake up and push the trap-door open, and see a whirl of tiny white flakes.

114

It reduced visibility, but it wasn't continuous, and there was a clean, soft look to everything when the fall was over.

After breakfast, we began work on assembling the first of the three sledges. They're very easy to fit together, and they run well on the ice, at least when it's flat. Unfortunately, apart from our own immediate vicinity, which is a kind of open square or plain, the ice is normally an incredible hummocky mixture of upright slabs, half fallen blocks, and jagged, sea-water-filled leads, or fjords. It remains to be seen how easily the sledges will move over any distance through that kind of terrain.

Andrée wanted us to break off and assemble the boat next, and we turned our hands to that in the afternoon. It wasn't nearly so easy, and we were still fiddling away to get it exactly right three days later.

Fraenkel and I did most of the work together. It was rather like trying to assemble an enormous jig-saw, with a fear that some of the pieces might be missing, and without an overall picture or key. In fact, the pieces *are* all here, and the boat is finished now, and was tested yesterday, and seems to hold water, and support loads, and in general do all that might be expected of it. But I certainly wouldn't give the manufacturers a medal for creating something easy to build.

Well, those were the first three days, building and resting. Talking and reading. The gradual reduction of the spars and laths and tarpaulins and cross-pieces and jambs and thwarts of the boat into an intelligible pattern. That, and the shooting of our first bear. I'd been reading in the car of the balloon, and suddenly I heard a single report, and then Fraenkel shouting.

I came up through the trap-door, fast, reaching for my Remington, and hoping we still had it loaded. I couldn't remember.

There was Andrée, a hundred metres away, standing staring down at the ground, into a sort of yellowy heap of snow, with his shot-gun at the slope under his arm. Fraenkel was running towards him, fifty metres away.

I clambered over the ring, and dropped into the slush around the car. It was still drizzling, and there were occa-

115

sional sharp puffs of wind. I started to run towards Andrée, clutching the Remington, and slipping off the safety-catch.

But I needn't have worried.

It's dead, said Fraenkel, speaking over his shoulder, from where he knelt by the bear's side.

I stopped, my breath coming in quick gasps. Andrée was leaning on the stock of his gun, the double barrels pointing up in the air. Fraenkel rose, reached round, and deflected them away from Andrée's face.

Be careful, he said. There are two shots, you know. One bear's enough for the day.

Andrée's face broke into a rare smile. He looked younger suddenly, and more vulnerable. He was obviously pleased with himself.

Not bad, eh? he said.

It wasn't a big bear, but it was big enough to reduce even Fraenkel's bulk to something inconsiderable as he turned over the claws, and inspected the pelt. It was a heavy, rather rough-looking skin, quite white still. It was a young bear, perhaps a two-year-old.

It came from the north-east, said Andrée, staring into the distance. There may be more.

Let's cut him up, said Fraenkel, and he got to his feet. There's good sweet meat there, he added.

So we went back to the tent, and got knives, and came back and took the skin off. I've often done the same thing before, up in Norrland, with a deer or a fox, but it was good to get some more practice. It was a poor quality skin, really, so Fraenkel said, and not worth the keeping. The carcase looked very unpalatable uncooked, and uncovered. But we worked hard, and soon had it all reduced to a heap of joints. We kept the best, and left the rest, offal and all, in a pool of slime.

We have plenty of meat, but Andrée pointed out that we ought to try and get used to what we shall certainly have to be eating more of, before we reach land. So we stored away a choice of the best steaks.

Within half an hour, a couple of fulmars were circling the remains. I watched them through my glasses from the roof of the car. They're plump, stocky little birds, when

116

you see them on the ice. Bigger than little auks, which we've also seen, but without the lean, rakish air of other gulls.

They look almost like ducks, on the ice. They have a kind of portly, waddling gait. I watched them tearing at the remains of the bear, drawing long red strips into the wind, and gulping to swallow them down. It was a raw sight.

They're not so different from us, you know, said Fraenkel, lowering his own glasses. We all depend on a good square meal up here in the north.

Fulmars are fair eating themselves, I'll bet, said Andrée. Shall I try a shot?

Fraenkel shook his head.

It's a waste of time, at that distance, he said.

So we let the birds live. They ate their fill, and then rose, circling, and screaming, like a pair of harpies in the silence. They flew off towards the north, and we lost sight of them in the rain.

It's Wednesday, July 21st now. I broke off to start the primus, and cook us our first meal of roast bear's meat, and afterwards, what with over-eating, and drinking ale, and feeling weary, I never got started again.

There's no more sun now. Yesterday was evidently a brief interlude. I'm spending my last night in the car of the balloon. Outside I can hear the wind, flapping the tent. It's rougher tonight.

We tested the boat in the water today, and packed all three of the sledges. Tomorrow, we start. We've already gained almost twenty-four kilometres by the drift of the current. It means that Franz Josef Land is only about 311 kilometres away.

I'm looking forward to being on the move. The enjoyment of resting and preparing has begun to grow stale.

We've all been irritable, touchy about little things. It didn't help when the last pigeon flew away today. Andrée had opened its cage, and was feeding it with some of the last of our peas. We'd meant to keep it for a final message when we were on our way. But it hopped out onto his shoulder, and then flew to the instrument-ring of the car.

Andrée tried — we all three tried — to catch and put it

117

back in the cage. But it dodged away. Hopping a few yards in the slush. Or soaring and then dropping onto a hummock of ice. Once it settled on the pole of the tent, and I reached up and thought I had it.

But, no. It was off again. After nearly an hour, we were very tired, and extremely annoyed. I almost think that Fraenkel would have loaded the Remington, and shot it dead. But it seemed to sense just how far it could go in teasing us, and finally took a long hop, and flew off into the mist.

That was at ten o'clock. So far we haven't seen it again, and I don't think we shall. It may make landfall. I wonder. Even if it does, no one, alas, will know that it was one of ours.

Yesterday we got off to a late start. It was nearly seven in the evening before we were ready to break camp. In some ways, I think our slowness was deliberate. Andrée, in particular, was reluctant, I could see, to leave the landing-site.

There lay the balloon, or the remains of it, and the balloon, for him, was still what seemed to symbolize the point of our journey. I do believe that on his own he might well have stayed where he was, and let the ice drift him, like a faithful hound over the body of his dead master, until he either reached landfall or died of starvation.

Next year, Fraenkel said, as he pulled his glasses down, and smoothed his gloves over his fingers.

Then he led the way. I took one last look at the upright car on the ice, the clustered froth of the calotte, the embedded net. Then I drew the ropes over my shoulders and began to pull.

After a few yards, I paused, and glanced round. Andrée stood at attention, his back to me. He was facing the car, and his right hand was to his forehead in a military salute. Ahead of me, Fraenkel was pulling strongly, and I bent my head, and followed in his tracks.

In the course of the day we had to cross leads in the ice, more than once. They vary in width, and in length, too, but the distance across, towards the south-east, is the measure that we're concerned with.

Fraenkel soon discovered the best way to get across. We'd haul, or push, a number of drifting floes, or bergs, into a solid mass, and then we'd gradually build up a sort of bumpy bridge that would hold until the sledges were drawn over.

The ice-floes move surprisingly easily in the water. You can push one weighing several tons, just like moving a boat away from a harbour wall. They have one useful property, too. When two come close together they tend to suck at each other, and then take a grip, and stick.

So we made our bridges exactly as boys in winter make their snowballs. Letting the icy particles cling to each other like so many burrs or Spanish chestnut cases in an autumn wood.

It was hard work, though, shoving each sledge up onto the bridge. Sometimes we had to hack a sort of ramp with our spades. The way over was normally not too bad, and then on the other side we had to jump down and guide the sledges off with our arms in case they tipped over and burst open.

After a march of three hours, we were all exhausted. Andrée paused, and called to Fraenkel up ahead.

Stop a moment, he said.

I had already stopped, and was leaning back on my baskets. Fraenkel turned, abandoned his sledge, and walked over to us.

They're too heavy, said Andrée, almost breathless I could now see. I want to try a new method. Instead of each pulling our own sledge, and having these frequent rests, I suggest that we each pull one sledge a given distance — five hundred yards, perhaps — and then come back for each of the other sledges in turn.

My back was breaking with fatigue. It sounded like a good idea. Let's try it, I said.

Fraenkel was staring up into the sky, shading his eyes against the sun.

Looks like a fulmar, he said.

Andrée followed his gaze.

The first today, he said. Four little auks, two ivory gulls and one fulmar. Shall we go, gentlemen?

One hour later we pitched camp. I'd been dragging well

119

behind, and I think they took pity on me. Fraenkel, for sure, would have gone on marching for another hour, I know. But it doesn't pay to go too far.

We have to conserve our strength. I may be the weakest of the three of us, in pure point of physical power, but I know how to husband my resources.

Now, for instance. We pitched camp at eleven o'clock, in bright sunshine, just think of it! It's now, I see, nearly half past two. Fraenkel and Andrée have both been asleep for over two hours, and I've managed to stay awake and write up my log-book, and this new letter to you, Anna.

I can't be so weak as they seem to think, after all. I feel tired, yes. I think I should sleep soon. But it's very strange in the tent, with two other people. I've never known what it's like before.

Outside, in the snow, the three sledges, arranged in a triangle, and the remains of the little meal we had before we turned in. I can hear the wind occasionally, and see the flap of the tent stirring. Above my head, there's the canvas rafters, and the two upright poles driven into the ice.

On all sides, the tent. No windows. No chink for wind. Underneath, on the ground, this enormous sleeping-bag, that holds three. I'm sitting upright, as I write to you, Anna, with my jacket on, and a book propped on my knees to support the paper.

It's cosy enough, with the candle sending out a fair light on a box at my elbow. I'm at the left-hand side of the bag, and there's Fraenkel down beside me, flat on his belly, as usual, with his face turned away, and his hair like a brush that needs trimming.

Andrée took first choice of place, and he decided to be on the right outside. I can see the hump of his back, with his face turned away, too. I wonder how I shall sleep?

There are really two choices. I can't bear to be on my back or my belly, so it means either the spoon position, hooped, as it were, into what would be Andrée's back if he were next to me, or the back to back position, butting my spine against what would be Fraenkel's spine if he were to make his body follow the direction of his face.

Lord, Anna, how I'm going on about this! I'd better lie down, and get some rest. I've slept with a man before.

Many times, I could now say. And in a balloon. But with *two* men!

That's really extraordinary. Goodnight, my love.

It's your birthday, Anna. Two days have gone by, almost two days exactly since I last wrote, and I'm in the same position as before in the tent, in the sleeping-bag, with Andrée and Fraenkel asleep, and it's the 25th of July, 1897. Three years until the end of the century.

Things aren't going too well. We make slow progress, only a few hundred metres, allowing for the drift of the ice, which is towards the north, against the direction we're trying to march. I'm beginning to fear that we may have to winter like Nansen did, up here in an earth cellar, and I may not even be home for your next birthday.

The terrain, I'm afraid, has been increasingly difficult. On our second day's march, we made an attempt to start earlier, and cover much more ground. All of us agreed that we ought to be away by the middle of the day, and that we should try to double our marching time of the first day. Four hours had been far too little.

I know we get tired, Andrée said. But it's best to make more stops, and to walk more slowly. That way, we can keep on the move for a longer period. At least, we shall enjoy the feeling that we've put in a full day's work.

Fraenkel smiled, one of those twisted smiles of his.

I agree, he said, hauling the ropes over his shoulders. But remember. It may not mean, in fact, that we cover a greater distance. We have to be flexible. We ought to be ready to try out a different method, if need be, every day.

Let's go, I said. While there's still some sun.

That day, we more than doubled our marching time. It was one o'clock when we broke camp, and ten at night when we pitched the tent. The weather changed in the course of the day, and the sun gave way to mist, and a strongish wind.

The leads we began to encounter were wider, and more awkward to negotiate than on the first day. There seemed to be fewer floes, too, and it was taking us more and more time to build our bridges.

At the third lead, the widest we'd yet reached, we

121

paused. There seemed to be no sign of a floe in either direction, and the lead stretched away indefinitely until it was lost at both ends in the mist. It ran athwart our path, roughly from east to west, and there seemed to be nothing to be done but try to cross it.

Fraenkel pushed his glasses up. I suppose it's his experience as a skier. He always likes to march with his eyes covered against the glare, even when there's no sun, as there wasn't then. I find my eyes get used to the white of the snow, and the dark glass bothers me. Everything looks too gloomy, and unreal.

Besides this, I find that wearing glasses makes a man look undefinably sinister. I don't quite know why. Fraenkel becomes a kind of automaton when he walks. He takes very steady, long strides, and the dark voids in his eye sockets make him look like a giant insect with all-round vision.

We'd better try the boat, he said.

So far we hadn't used the boat at all. It seemed an enormous bother to unpack it from the sledge, and then load all the equipment on top of it, and then repack the sledges again at the end of everything.

I strained my eyes into the mist in each direction.

Must we? I said. Might it not be better to make a check first to see if there are any floes just out of sight?

You try, said Fraenkel, brutally.

He was already untying the straps that held the boat fast on his sledge. I turned away, and walked some distance to my left, glancing back to see the figures of the others grow dim and vague in the fog. I went about a hundred metres, but there was no sign of a floe.

No luck? said Fraenkel, pleasantly, as I came back.

He had the boat on the ice now, and was drawing off its tarpaulin cover. Andrée stood with his hands on his hips, watching. He seemed tired, and glad of the chance to rest.

I set off again to my right, angry now, and determined to prove my method was best. I was lucky. I came on a small group of floes, and managed to shove them together into a solid mass. They stretched three quarters of the way across.

I went on, found another, pushed it back, and locked it

on to the others. My bridge was completed. I set off at a run through the light snow to join the others.

Fraenkel was half way across the lead, working an oar to keep the boat steady, and holding one of the sledges level with his free hand at right angles across the boat. It looked very precarious.

Andrée had a hand up to his brow, watching.

It's fast, he said, judiciously. I think it may be the best way.

Fraenkel was already at the other bank. He leapt out on the ice, drew his sledge ashore, and then climbed back into the boat, and began to oar his way along on the return trip.

But I've built a perfectly good bridge, I said. It's less than a hundred metres away.

Fraenkel was already back on our side of the lead.

How's that? he said, smiling up in triumph from the boat. Rather less work than tugging the sledges uphill onto a bridge, eh?

Andrée bent, and began to unload his sledge.

Let's give it a trial, he said, over his shoulder.

It wasn't exactly an order, and I stood in two minds for a moment. There they were, repacking the load of Andrée's sledge into the boat. They had to get that across, and then Fraenkel's load, and then Andrée's empty sledge. Assuming that one of them stayed on the other side, and pushed the boat across empty, it would still mean three journeys.

In that time, I could haul my own sledge to the bridge, push it up, slide it along the ridge, and then let it slide down on the other side. I could even, perhaps, haul it over to where they were.

I thought for a moment. Yes, I had time. But the effort would almost finish me off for the day.

Look, I called down. If we all work together, it's bound to be quicker to use my bridge. The way we've been doing all the time so far.

Andrée looked up.

Quicker, he said. Yes, maybe. But not easier. We need a way that conserves energy.

Fraenkel grinned at me. He was cock-a-hoop. I felt very angry. I wasn't even sure that Andrée was right. I'm not

123

now. But this endless unloading and loading has become the order of the day so far as negotiating leads is concerned.

I didn't even try to get over my bridge on my own. I helped Andrée unload his sledge, and I didn't say another word, and that was that. At least for the moment.

I'm not sure I can ever think quite the same about Knut Fraenkel, though. From now on, I see him as a rival, a competitor. I want a return match. And I mean to have my revenge.

There are so many sources of irritation. The weight of the loads, for example. We've spent hours discussing the rights and wrongs of these. Fraenkel claims that his is far too heavy, and mine far too light.

We ought to reload, he said this morning.

We'd broken camp again at one o'clock, and we were all ready to start. The temperature had fallen a degree below freezing-point, and it was snowing. The flakes were forming in little white butterflies on Andrée's great moustache.

No, Andrée said. Not yet. It's too soon to know just what we can do without.

There was more discussion, some bickering about food and ammunition, protein versus vegetable food. And then we abandoned the conversation for the moment, and began our third march.

It was a wintry day. For most of the time, we were able to follow the line of a long channel, and there was no trouble about ferrying our things across leads. It made a welcome change.

Well, correction. It would have made a welcome change if we could have made progress, as we did the previous day, over level ice, where the runners could slide easily. But we couldn't.

The banks of the channel were incredibly tortuous. The ice had been thrown up into a constant series of hummocks and piled-up blocks. Imagine trying to move a wheelbarrow across a field. And then just suppose that this field turns suddenly into a builder's yard. A wilderness of rubble.

That's what we had to contend with. It meant a constant process of lifting and steadying. One of us would have to

124

go ahead and brace himself between the blocks. Then the other two would half shove half lift from behind, and the man in front would grip as best he could and ease or pull.

It wasn't just that the work was immensely tiring. It put an impossible strain on the sledges. More than once we feared that the material would smash or tear open. And we hadn't the resources to do more than a patch-up sort of repair job.

Nevertheless, we slaved on for even longer than the previous day. It was half past twelve when Andrée finally called a halt, and we'd been on the move for eleven hours.

Strindberg, he said, beckoning Fraenkel and me over, as he stood with the sledge-ropes over his shoulders. This is the 25th of July. The birthday of your fiancée. Hip, hip.

Hooray, shouted he and Fraenkel together.

Hip, hip, he repeated, and this time we all three shouted hooray. And after the third, and final, hip, hip, our long hooray seemed to hang in the air, and then rise and linger, like a great banner pinned above the masthead of our march.

I felt much better for that, Anna, I can tell you. After dinner, we sat sucking caramels — a special treat for the occasion — and the mood was one of the most relaxed and easy of the whole journey.

It was a mellow night, as I say, and I felt a gentle demon urge me to speak as we all three lounged on our sleeping-bag in the few moments before lying down to sleep.

I think we ought to celebrate, I said. And I think we ought to do so by each making a confession.

Confession? said Andrée, sitting up. We're none of us Catholics, I hope.

I laughed.

I want your advice, gentlemen, I said. As two confirmed bachelors, you must each tell me what vice in yourselves you think a wife would most dislike.

A wife is a luxury, said Andrée. A luxury I shall never have. I'm far too possessive. I should never allow her any life of her own.

You, Fraenkel, I said.

He sucked hard on his caramel.

125

I'm much too uneasy, he said, after a while. I'm restless. I can't keep still. And I smoke a pipe, he added, with a grin.

I think you're both dishonest, I said. The fact of the matter is, that neither of you like women, and any girl would very quickly appreciate this. As I said, you're a pair of confirmed and impossible old bachelors.

Fraenkel punched me in a friendly way on the shoulder.

Get away, he said. What about you? You're just as bad yourself, with your violin and your cameras. You're just as much of a bachelor as that scientific English detective, Sherlock Holmes. No woman would stand for your foibles. You'll have to change, my lad. You mark my words.

We were all very merry, Anna. It's been the best night we've had, after the worst day, I think.

I'm going to drain the last drop of our raspberry syrup and go to sleep.

Fraenkel and Andrée have gone ahead to reconnoitre. I stayed behind with the sledges, and I'm writing this under the shadow of an ice-hummock. I'm wearing two woollen sweaters under my jacket, and leaning back against the frozen block.

It's restful, dangerously so. I sometimes almost nod off to sleep, and I can well understand how Arctic explorers have always emphasized the importance of keeping awake. There's a kind of seductive relaxation about the cold. You start to feel numbed by it, exactly the same way you grow soothed, and lulled into a doze, in a very hot bath.

It sounds ridiculous, I know. But the body's a funny thing. It has the power to turn things topsy-turvy when it wants to. Fortunately, I keep growing stiff, and I get a pain in my back. So I have to rise and flex my limbs. This keeps me alert.

You may be wondering why the others have gone ahead, and left me here.

The idea was to look out for a likely place to camp. We've tended so far to settle on somewhere reasonably suitable whenever we get tired, and feel like stopping.

126

Last night − I think it was last night, or was it the night before? − something happened that made us feel we ought to take more care over where we choose to camp. I was brushing snow aside to settle the primus for making cocoa when I discovered two sets of tracks just outside the tent.

Look at these, I said to Fraenkel.

He bent and studied the broad, clawed impressions, one set fairly deep in the snow, the other, smaller set less firmly incised.

Andrée, Fraenkel called. Look at these.

Andrée came over, buttoning his trousers up.

No doubt at all, he said, looking at the tracks. It looks to me like a she-bear and her cub. The most awkward visitors we could have had.

They must have come and gone while we were all asleep, I said. I heard nothing.

Nor did I, said Fraenkel.

Andrée had got the shot-gun off the sledge, and was loading it with two fresh shells.

We must take more care, he said. From now on, we sleep with a loaded gun beside the sack. And we ought to try and pitch camp in a less exposed position.

I looked round. On all sides, the ice stretched clear and unimpeded. The tent must have been visible for a considerable distance, even in the mist.

We must aim to find a spot sheltered by hummocks, I suggested. Supposing we start to look round for a place each day before we get too tired. It would simply mean taking turns to go without a sledge and look for a place.

No, said Fraenkel. Safer for two to go, and one to stay with the equipment. A single man could have a hundred and one kinds of trouble. And besides, we'd have two men to take responsibility for the choice.

So the bears have given me time on my own to write to you, Anna. Not cooped up in a smelly tent for once, but out in the bracing open air.

Only one thing has happened since the others left, almost an hour ago. I've seen a new kind of gull! It swooped very low, and then spiralled high into the fog. I got the glasses out to examine it more closely. I could see it wasn't a fulmar, or an ivory gull. It had a dull-red belly, with wings blue, both underneath and above, and there was a dark ring around its neck.

There seems no doubt it's one that hasn't been seen before, or at least not outside the Arctic. I'm going to call it Anna's Gull. Alas, it didn't stay to be christened. It circled twice, and I just had time to verify the colours, and the sit of its flight. Then it sailed away into the fog.

Incidentally, I ought to tell you that the local fauna have been much in our minds, and not just the birds. It very nearly led to a mild catastrophe.

Yesterday, we set off with a new method of progress in mind. The plan was to follow the banks of any lead that offered fairly smooth ice, looping and back-tracking, if need be, without bothering to keep a straightforward course. As Fraenkel pointed out, we had trouble whenever we tried to cross water, and we had trouble when we had to negotiate heaps of broken or piled-up ice.

The fallacy in our previous plans had been to suppose that we would make better time by trying, at any cost, to keep going in a straight line. This clearly wasn't so.

We shall go much faster, said Fraenkel, if we simply take the easiest route. We should aim to avoid all obstacles, as our main priority. Going south-east, in the direction of Franz Josef Land, should come second.

Andrée swallowed the last of his cocoa, and got to his feet.

I agree, he said. The main thing is to move.

I'd been doing some calculations.

Since we began, I said, looking up, I'm afraid we've covered less than two kilometres in the direction we want to go. The drift of the current towards the north has pretty well cancelled out all our efforts.

The others were less dispirited by this than I might have expected.

The wind will change direction, said Andrée. Swings and roundabouts. In time, we shall travel twice the distance we march, with the wind's help. We have to wait. In the meanwhile, our journey has begun. We practise the best way to progress.

It doesn't really matter which way we go, said Fraenkel,

getting up. At least, we're alive. And besides, if we hadn't marched at all, we'd be further back than when we started. Our advance would have been a minus distance.

I sluiced out my cocoa cup. All this was true, but it didn't make my statistics any more inspiring. We seemed to be having to run very fast to stay on the same spot.

So we got under way, and were soon making fair progress.

For some reason, our new method of drawing the sledges along the banks of the leads, and over whatever smooth ice there was, seemed to give us a sudden wealth of seal-sightings. Andrée was the first to see one. He paused, and pointed with his gloved hand.

I watched the long sleek shape bulge, and break water. The whiskered head seemed to stare at us in astonishment, as well it might. Then it dived, and I watched the V-ripple fan out and away across the lead.

There was something very cheering about the sweep and the stare of the seal. But Fraenkel didn't see it that way. He unslung his Remington, and took a long shot. The bullet hit the water several feet away.

Don't waste your ammunition, said Andrée. There's more, and better, meat on a bear.

After that, we saw several more seals, always one at a time, and always near the edge of the leads. I began to joke that it was the same seal, following us under the ice.

He means to steal up behind you and bite your calf, I said to Fraenkel.

But Fraenkel didn't see the humour.

They swim well, he said. But I'd like to try and hit one on the move.

Another seal appeared, very close to the brink of the lead we were circumventing, and it seemed, for a moment, as if I could reach over and tap it on the nose.

Like this, Fraenkel? I said, and I reached down and took a swipe at the seal with my glove.

It was a mad thing to do, but there was a mood of frivolity, and a kind of wild abandon, in the air. The seals had infected me with their gaiety. Like the sirens, they nearly had my life in payment.

My foot slipped on the ice, and, before I knew where I

was or what was happening, I had slithered down on my rump, and gone feet first into the water. I kicked wildly, reaching out for a hold on the side. There was nothing.

In a second, I was under water, and plummeting down. I had a moment's pure panic, sure I was drowning. Then I regained some sense of self-preservation, and I kicked again, struggling to rise to the surface.

I broke water, gasping. I didn't know yet how cold it was. My feelings were anaesthetized by the shock.

Sorry, I croaked.

Andrée and Fraenkel were lying flat on the bank. Fraenkel had his arm out over the edge.

Reach up, he said. Hurry.

I made a jerking snatch for his arm, hit his glove, and fell back, splashing. There was a kind of pain now, a sort of creeping cold.

Once again, I struck up for Fraenkel's arm.

Get a rope, he called over his shoulder to Andrée.

I struck again, again missing. The cold-pain was worse now, and the panic was coming back.

Then Andrée was dangling a length of rope down into the water, and I threshed over, and clasped it to my chest. I closed my eyes, shaking what seemed to be ice out of my hair.

Fraenkel and Andrée were on their feet, pulling. I felt myself being drawn bodily through what seemed to be a bath of knives. Then I knocked on ice, and my toe seemed to find some grip. I scrabbled, held firm to the rope, and there I was, flat on my back, on the side.

Fraenkel undid my collar, and slapped my cheeks with the back of his hand. Andrée had a flask of brandy open, and was tipping a quantity of the stuff down my throat. It helped a lot. I choked, spat, and felt revived.

He's very pale, Andrée said, seriously, as if I wasn't there.

I sat up.

Of course, I'm pale, I said. You'd be pale yourself if you'd spent five minutes in that ice-hole.

You'd better change, Fraenkel said.

They were like two nurses, worried, fussy. I felt assaulted by their concern. I got to my feet, indignant, and fell back to my knees. Fraenkel put his arm round me, and helped me over to my sledge.

I lay back against the baskets, closing my eyes. I could see green stars, and they were spinning in a black vortex. Fraenkel was pulling off my boots. Andrée had his arm under my shoulder, and was trying to get my arms out of the sleeves of my jacket.

Stop it, I said angrily. I can do all this for myself.

I kicked Fraenkel away, and shook off Andrée's arm. I managed to stand up, swaying a little, and propping myself on the metal arm of the theodolite.

I'll lay out the sleeping-bag, said Andrée. He can change his clothes in that, and keep warm.

He spoke as if I didn't understand Swedish, or as if I'd become a vital, but inarticulate instrument of his need, like a wounded husky.

Listen, Andrée, I said, irritably. I can hear, and I understand everything you're saying. So please don't talk about me like a racehorse with a broken leg. And yes. Do please lay out the sleeping-bag so that I can change.

I felt very tired by this speech, and I closed my eyes again. For the moment, I didn't want to see the two of them. They were hovering, it seemed to me, like vultures over my ineptitude.

They got the sleeping-bag out, and laid it along the ice. I climbed in, and they brought me fresh clothes from my private bag. It felt ludicrous, and, frankly Anna, quite disgusting.

There they were, two fully-clothed men, fumbling in my private bag, amongst my most treasured possessions, and pawing over my underclothes, my shirts, my woollen jerseys. I didn't like it.

I took everything they brought over with a very bad grace. Under the reindeer-wool of the bag, I slid off my trousers, humping and squirming in the bag, while the two of them watched.

Haven't you anything better to do? I asked.

Fraenkel laughed.

You look as if you're trying to catch a flea, he said. I've never seen a man undressing in bed before.

Andrée knelt beside me. He put the thermometer under

my tongue, and took my temperature. Then he tested my pulse. He seemed very grave, in contrast to Fraenkel's hilarity.

You'll be all right, said Andrée, lifting the lid of my eye. But you must be careful. You might have drowned.

I finished my dressing, and started to climb out of the bag.

I know, I said. And I've said already, I'm sorry. I have no desire to kill you both. Or myself either, for that matter.

That day no more was said, and I soon recovered my strength on the short march before we lay down to sleep. The following morning, however, my accident seemed to have decided Andrée that we had to lighten the loads on our sledges.

They're too heavy, he said. What happened to Strindberg could happen to any one of us. The sledge wasn't exactly to blame, but it might be next time.

There was much discussion about the sort of things we ought to leave, and take. I was anxious not to reduce our stock of meat powder too far, but Fraenkel argued for more bread.

We can shoot our protein, he said. There's plenty of meat here on the hoof.

And the wing, suggested Andrée. We have yet to savour the delights of a roasted ivory gull.

Or a seal, I said to Fraenkel, pointedly. We can't always rely on shooting to kill.

Fraenkel shrugged.

So we take plenty of ammunition, he said. There is plenty.

That settled that. They were killers, in their way, both of them, and they welcomed the opportunity of living off the sea. They each enjoyed the stimulus that hunting for the pot would give them. I let them have their way. I'm a meat-eater, too, after all, and I much prefer a toasted bear-steak to a stew of Rousseau's dried lamb-substitute.

The rest of the discarding was a matter of gradual barter, and gaming. If I agree to this, will you be prepared to sacrifice that? It wasn't so hard as it might sound. The main concession Andrée made was that each of us should be allowed so many kilos in our personal bag. To Fraenkel and me that was what really mattered.

So we got the weight down by nearly half. The sledges looked very sleek and streamlined when we'd finished. Fraenkel took one round and round the tent, at a fast trot, to show how easy it was to pull. Andrée and I stood still, and applauded.

The repacking inevitably meant that we had a vast store of food left over, that was just going to be abandoned. It seemed a great pity to let it waste, or rather revert to fodder for the bears, so we spent a good deal of time, as we worked, simply guzzling whatever we had a taste for.

It was an orgiastic business. We didn't bother much with cooking, simply opened the tins and packets, and ate what we wanted, and then threw the remainer aside. Empty sardine cans. Tins of corned beef. Boxes of biscuits. Tinned fruit. It was a bizarre, and an untidy, feast. No wonder it proved an instant attraction for livestock. We had several sorts of gull circling in no time, and they began to take greater and greater risks in diving for titbits.

At last, as we expected, even the bears were drawn towards our camp.

Here's your chance, Fraenkel said, suddenly, pointing with the shot-gun.

A huge bear was shambling about, only thirty yards away. He couldn't quite pluck up the courage to come closer, but he was hungry. His nostrils were flaring at the odour of sardine.

Fraenkel handed me the loaded gun.

Get him, Strindberg, he said. It's your turn.

I took the shot-gun in my hands, levelled it to my shoulder, and got the bear in the sights. He was only about twenty metres away then. I couldn't miss.

There was a choking report, then another, as I fired the second shot, and the bear dropped like a hunk of snow from a bush. It didn't move. I never realized that killing something that large could be so easy.

It doesn't do to be sentimental. I don't enjoy killing things. I was glad to have shot straight, and I took Fraenkel's congratulations with pleasure. But I felt a pang of sadness to see that great, hungry hump lying dead

133

there on the ice. He would so much have enjoyed a few of our left-over sardines.

The following morning Fraenkel got his bear, too. I knew that he'd thought mine was too easy. He dropped his at forty metres with a single shot from the Remington. It was bigger than mine, a beauty.

We cut the skin off Fraenkel's bear, to help mend the sleeping-sack, if necessary, and we took steaks from both his and mine. It helped confirm the decision not to have too much of that awful meat-powder.

The others are coming back. I can just see them with the glasses as dark blurs in the mist.

Anna, I miss you so much, my dear. Goodbye.

5
ANNA
1896

THE *Erling Jarl* was a small ship, but a comfortable one. There were only five or six cabins, and our fellow-passengers were a sociable, if eccentric, group. On the veranda after dinner, or in the brocaded elegance of the saloon, there was ample opportunity to get to know their charms and their foibles.

But for my mother's illness, which drove us into a frowning seclusion, I should have found the voyage an entertaining, and perhaps enlightening, experience. The little Japanese, for example, who travelled in Scotch whisky, and spent hours by the rail, shredding bread for the gulls, was a fortnight's study in himself.

He used to leer at me, and click his heels, when I led my mother along the deck to a basket-chair in the sun. But it was only a consequence of his badly-fitting false teeth I soon realized, and his few remarks, as we settled ourselves with sewing and rugs, were always kindly and well considered.

I knew nothing of Japan, or of any other country for that matter, and a chance to talk to him at more length about the island of Hokkaido, where he came from, would have been a rare pleasure. Unfortunately, my mother's health forbade such conversation.

As the first week wore on, the voyage became something of a nightmare. At home, my mother had always been demanding, and time and experience of my nature had taught her many tricks to compel attention. Here on shipboard there was no escape from her obsessive needs.

Every day she would see the ship's doctor, in his

137

narrow, ether-smelling cabin below the bridge. He would set his cold stethoscope to her chest, murmur thoughtfully, and then tap his nails on the brass edge of his desk.

Well, he would say. Yes, very well, indeed.

My mother always interpreted this enthusiasm as a kind of terminal evasiveness, and her health would seem at its very worst for a few hours after the visit. She would insist on being half carried back to our cabin, where she would sink down on her bed, and require that the curtains be drawn, and her inhaler brought.

This inhaler was a dreadful contraption of rubber and metal that fitted over her nose and mouth, and allowed a steamy fume from a mixture of foul liquids out of proprietary Stockholm bottles to be sucked noisily into her lungs. It never did her the slightest bit of good, in my opinion, and it filled the cabin with a horrible smell.

Still, it was the one thing that my mother insisted was helping her breathing, and I had to bear with its drawbacks. I would set it out on the neat bedside table the Company had provided, and mingle the required fluids in the right proportions for the steward to have heated in the ship's galley.

This took time, and caused trouble, and enabled my mother to make a great public exhibition of her ailments, which she liked doing, and felt better for. She was an expert at fluttering her eyes, and needing a pillow adjusted, every time the steward arrived at our cabin door with his boiling saucepan and his polite smile. Word of her courage, and her sufferings, thus penetrated to all quarters of the ship, and she could emerge for afternoon tea sure of a sympathetic audience.

The days went by, and we passed Bergen, and Trondheim, and a whole series of indistinguishable fjords. The sun blazed down, and the sea remained a steady calm, and the air was as crisp and chill as the most extreme sufferer from catarrh or consumption could have wished for.

Personally, I found it often cold, and I paraded the even decks in layers of shawls, anxious to cosset my frame with a good reserve of warmth. My mother, on the other hand, felt that a strong exposure to the elements was of benefit to her complaint, and she would throw off scarves and coverings with a fine disregard for the temperature.

This, more than anything, convinced me that there was very little wrong with her, and I put up with her supposed illness in increasing poor humour. Age, I suppose, and the natural adolescent need to be free of restraints, was making me more and more contemptuous of my mother's temperament, and it was only the knowledge that her illness had made this voyage to Spitzbergen possible that kept me going.

On Sundays, my mother would carry a small Bible to her favourite chair in the ship's bows, and there insist that I read to her from the more glamorous books, which she considered to be the *Song of Solomon* and *Ecclesiastes*.

I would lean forward into the biting wind, with my finger in the place, and strive to combine an adequate rendering of the passage about the golden bowl being loosed with keeping my straw hat on. I still remember the feel of that little steel cross in the hard leather, and the wild, dark, icy smell of the sea.

We Swedes have always been seafaring people. The long ships crossed the Atlantic, and the last Vikings died in Greenland, flanked by their barrels of dry grain, and the bones of mice, many centuries before I was born. But the North was always there, and the bitter sea, and I felt a grim drive in my blood knowing the tide running under the keel.

There were no oarsmen on the *Erling Jarl*, no men with flaxen hair and horned helmets clasping spears, no drums beating the slow war speed. It was a well-appointed, modern touring vessel. But I still liked to know the fish and the weeds were under my heel as I walked the decks.

At night, my mother would sometimes retire to bed early, and I could creep out after she was asleep and enjoy a little time on my own in the bright, eternal day of the far North. I would watch the elderly German couple, the Gutmans, pacing arm and arm, with their Baedeker out to identify some remote peak on the shoreline, and their guttural vowels punctuating the low thrum of the engines.

Mr Gutman would raise his hat, and Mrs Gutman would bob and bow, as I passed them by. The lonely

139

Englishman, with the black patch over his eye, and the rolled newspaper, which he carried like a club, never spoke, and only rarely nodded. I was fascinated by his lean frame, and his air of mystery.

I was sure that he was a lord. His voice had a low commanding tone when he ordered a drink or a cigar, and the ship's crew all treated him with a special kind of deference. I knew, from what our steward had once told me, that he spent his evenings playing billiards with the little Japanese in the men's smoking-room, but I never saw him speak or sit with any other passenger on the deck or in the saloon. He ate alone, at a table by the port side, and his face never rose from his plate or his paper.

For the first nine days of the voyage, the ship was hugging the Norwegian coastline. Like a pencil tracing the intricate contours for a map, its prow wove in and out of bay and inlet, round cape and foreland, alongside rocky shores, and under sheer abrupt cliffs.

From the stinking harbour of Tromsö, with its cod heads underfoot as we trod the cobbles during an hour's refuelling stop, and where I tried to visualize the exact spot on the quay the *Virgo* must have sailed from, and from the even worse-smelling bustle of Hammerfest, in the reek of the train-oil factories, and the blubber and hides being unloaded from whalers, on up to the icy grandeur of the North Cape, where I climbed the rock in the company of the Gutmans, leaving my mother wheezing at the quay, and stared out across the wrinkled grey of the Arctic, under the granite column of King Oscar II, it was all a land voyage, a cruise round the jagged perimeter of a known country, our long-standing rival, Norway.

At the North Cape, the Englishman spoke to me as we turned to climb down the rocky pathway and return to the ship.

Look inland, he said, hooking with his thumb across the mountains. It's the last you'll see of land for three days.

He spoke in Swedish, with a heavy accent, but a good grip of idiom.

The mist's coming down, he added, looking up at the sky. There's going to be rough weather.

He was right. The following morning the *Erling Jarl* put

140

out of the harbour at first light, and I heard the sounds of men moving equipment to and fro as I woke and lay listening in my bed. My mother was fast asleep, snoring, with her mouth open.

I dressed quickly and went up on deck. It was bitter cold, and the sailors were all working in big sweaters, and caps. There was a wintry, northerly feel to the morning. A thick mist lay everywhere, and we might already have been far out at sea for all I could see of the shoreline.

The Englishman was leaning against the rail, dressed in an ulster, with a deerstalker's cap over his ears. He looked invigorated, and immensely cheered up, by the bad weather. His manner was communicative.

He greeted me with a touch to the flap of his cap.

There's going to be a high sea, he said. The men are lashing down everything that's moveable.

He glanced at me, with a kind of hangman's look in his eye, as if weighing me up.

Are you a good sailor? he asked.

I had no idea.

I don't know, I said. I've never been out at sea in a storm.

In Scotland, he said, we're used to high seas. I like a good swell.

It was the first time I'd learned that he was Scottish. Indeed, it was many years beyond that date before I fully realized that some Scotsmen are even more English than the most English of Englishmen.

Hume, he said suddenly. John Hume.

We shook hands.

Anna Charlier, I said uncertainly.

I was afraid of my mother appearing and finding me gossiping with a strange man. I made a move to continue my stroll along the deck.

Forgive the shipboard introduction, the Scotsman said, evidently sensing my embarrassment. I've been wanting to ask about your mother.

He strolled beside me, as we passed men fastening deckchairs down with ropes, and carrying small basket-tables into the saloon.

She has trouble with her nose, he said. It's a form of catarrh.

141

I was surprised that he knew this, since my mother had not been seen to inhale or discuss her breathing in public.

We stopped in the prow, watching the bow wave churning as the ship began to move slowly across the harbour and towards the open sea.

Yes, said the Scotsman, with every satisfaction. It's going to be rough.

He turned up the collar of his ulster, and stared down at me, leaning once more on the rail.

She has too much cream in her diet, he said, with great authority. She needs more protein. Beef, and the yolks of eggs. Do her a world of good. You mark my words.

He took a pair of old leather gloves from his coat pocket, and pulled them on.

I'm a doctor, he said. I know.

We watched the bow wave in silence for a moment, feeling the throb of the ship's engines, at low power, under our feet.

I cleared my throat.

Thank you, I said.

There was a sudden pitch, and then a violent roll, that almost threw me off balance. I felt my stomach turn over, and then flatten out again, like a seal in a pool. I put one hand on the rail, and the other up to my neck.

Thought I'd better mention it, the Scotsman continued, snapping the orange clasp of his gloves. In view of the bad weather, it may be our last chance to talk for a while.

It was. I made my way carefully back to the saloon stairs, and then down the swaying flight of steps to our cabin. The *Erling Jarl*, with all her moveables lashed down, emerged into the open sea at about the same time as I collapsed on my bed, and it was three long and desperate days before I was able to get up and walk about again.

I was aware of the steward arriving, and the ship's doctor, with a series of yellow concoctions that I drank down and then very rapidly threw up, and the rest was a lurid dream of uneven surfaces, and heat alternating with cold, and strange voices trying to make me do things.

I was hardly alone in my sufferings. It was the worst crossing to Spitzbergen for several years I heard later, and, apart from the Scots doctor, the little Japanese and, most humiliating to my adolescent sense of fitness, my mother, almost all of the passengers, and several of the crew, were severely affected.

The storm seemed to do my mother's general health as much good as the Scotsman's prescribed diet of eggs and beef was supposed to do, and she spent more time – to my great relief – on deck and out of the cabin than at any earlier period of the voyage.

She did, in fact, strike up quite a friendship with the mysterious Dr Hume, as I discovered on the afternoon of the third day, when, bleary-eyed, and very weak, I at last managed to stagger out of bed, dress, and climb those awful stairs to the deck.

The mist had gone, and the sun was shining on an unbroken expanse of grey, icy sea. The wind was sharp, and the air very clear. The rolling had entirely ceased, and the ship was steaming north at a steady fifteen knots an hour.

Good afternoon, Anna, my mother called, from her favourite basket-chair, where she lay swathed in a tartan rug, with a tray of tea and cakes by her side.

The Scotsman got to his feet, as I approached. He'd evidently been chatting with my mother on a second basket-chair drawn up by her side. I felt an immediate pang of jealousy at this promiscuity in his affections. He was *my* Scotsman, even if I had had to neglect him for three days.

It's lovely weather, he said, making no mention of my health.

I was grateful to him for this reticence. I still felt very shaky, and was sure my face was green.

Tea, I said boldly. May I have a cup, mother?

Dr Hume poured. He handed me a plate of digestive biscuits, and waited as I chose one.

You're looking terrible, Anna, my mother said, inspecting my face critically. You might have combed your hair.

Very bad for the head to comb the hair too often, said Dr Hume, coming to my rescue. I think your daughter has a good sense of what her head requires, Mrs Charlier.

He had clearly acquired the knack of dealing with my mother. He wasn't prepared to let her get away with

143

anything. I began to warm to his charm, and his bluntness.

More tea, I suggested, and the conversation turned again to the weather.

Tomorrow, said Dr Hume, we shall reach the channel between Danes Island and Amsterdam Island. It may be blocked with pack-ice.

He was right. I rose early, the first time since we'd left the North Cape, and there ahead of me, as I came up on deck, stood a small cluster of figures in the bows. Dr Hume was amongst them, wearing a dark-blue sweater today, and carrying a telescope lifted to his good eye.

Look, he said, as I came up to the group.

I took the telescope, and focused through the lens. Yes, there it was. A broken mass of white slices, like winter candy broken and heaped up on a plate.

That's pack-ice, Dr Hume said. We'll have to cut through it. The *Virgo* must have done the same, and it's formed again over the last few weeks. It can't be very firm.

I handed the telescope back to him.

Tell me, Dr Hume, I said. Why are you making this trip?

It was a bold question, but I'd learned very young the advantages of asking straight out what I wanted to know.

You seem so healthy, I said. It's not your health.

I watched him put the telescope to his eye again, appearing to ignore my question.

I'll tell you what they do, he said. They fill the stern tanks with water, and the bows rise. The propeller sinks to a depth of four metres below the surface, and that should allow enough draught for the screws to grip. They'll use the engines at full power, then they'll use them cautiously, more slowly, with the captain keeping his eye on the ice from the bridge. That way, we ought to go through without mishap. At least, I hope so.

He closed the telescope with a snap, and stood slapping it into his open palm, like a police constable making a show of force to a malefactor.

I'm a doctor, he said. I learned my poor Swedish in Uppsala, when I was a student.

Where do you practise? I asked, feeling a need to pull away from my earlier query, as in a small boat rowed too near a whirlpool.

144

The engine's note changed, and there was a sudden flurry of commands. Men ran to and fro, staring over the side and probing with long rods.

In Edinburgh, said Dr Hume, watching me.

The ship lurched, and then surged forward again. I looked over the rail, and saw the yellow-grey blocks of the ice thrown up and folded back on each other as the keel drove its way into the field. There seemed to be little resistance.

You approach by the port of Leith, said Dr Hume. Many Swedish people come to Scotland on holiday, and to seek their fortune. You may do so yourself one day.

It was a prophetic remark, although it seemed an idle one, at the time. I was fascinated by Dr Hume, and I pushed my queries forward as the ship drove through the ice.

You're a surgeon, I guessed. You have a surgeon's hands.

No, said Dr Hume, confirming my guess. I've retired.

The ship was now in the midst of the field, a moving black shape in a great uneven plain of broken triangles. The air felt made of a frosty kind of tissue, like a drink of acid lemon, fresh from snow.

Everyone here, said Dr Hume, gesturing round the deck, has an aim below the aim they show. The North draws us like a great magnet. Some come for health, as your mother has. One or two to meet a friend, like you.

I saw now as he looked at me that his eyes were green, a very intense wavering green, like the light on a marsh at night. His breath hung, cold in the air, as he pinned me down.

You'll meet your friend, said Dr Hume, turning to look out at the clear water approaching. But remember, he won't be alone. He has things to do. Men to know.

Then, he put his hand on my shoulder and led me away towards the veranda, where we sat down alone in a pair of deckchairs. A steward went by, and Dr Hume ordered a glass of orange juice for us both.

As you see, he said. I'm a dietician now.

He looked down at his hands. They were trembling slightly in his leather gloves.

145

They won't keep still any more, he said.

I watched the Gutmans go by, guttural as always over their Baedeker. The air was warming a little, as the sun moved higher.

You see, said Dr Hume, slowly, I'm very ill. That's why I'm here. Only the North, I think, and the Scandinavian gods, can save me.

But they didn't save him, any more than they saved me. When I went to Edinburgh five years later, he was already dead. Whatever had made his hands tremble had travelled up his arms, and down to his heart.

I got the story piecemeal, from a nurse at the hospital in the Canongate, and an old specialist who lived in Morningside. I was interested by Dr Hume, and I learned the truth. But it took a long time.

That day the *Erling Jarl* broke free of the pack-ice as we drank our orange juice, and then my mother joined us, and cracked the mood. We dropped anchor off Danes Island at noon, a hundred metres from the brittle masts of the *Virgo*, and the bleak shore with the flopping sides of the balloon-house. Here my own destiny took over, and Dr Hume and his tragedy stood back once more into the wings.

But it was his remembered kindness, years later, that brought me to Scotland. I thought that all Scotsmen would have the same sober thoughtfulness. I was wrong. But by then, when I'd learned the disappointing truth − that there are good people and bad people in all countries − I'd burned my boats.

Eckholm, the perennially jaunty Eckholm, was there to greet us on the shore.

You'll meet Strindberg tonight, he confided to me, as he led the party from the *Erling Jarl* on a rapid tour. He's three kilometres away today at a freshwater lagoon we found, collecting specimens. The man's a marvel. Most of us have all our attention taken up by the balloon, but Nils finds time for his magnetism − over there, in a little black tent he erects, like a knight's palanquin.

What's magnetism? I asked.

I have no idea, said Eckholm, scratching his beard. And

I doubt if Strindberg does either. But without it there to pull us back, we'd all roll off the edge and be into Uranus in no time. You look very pretty, by the way. Did I ever tell you that?

I blushed. The other tourists were a little way behind, but I feared they would overhear, particularly Dr Hume.

No, I didn't, said Eckholm. Nils is potty about you, you know, and I'm not surprised. He'll be as jealous as a mother-cat without a kitten when he sees your new beau.

Don't be silly, I said. He's just a friend we met on the ship.

Eckholm had paused to let the others catch up. He stood with his hands on his broad hips, a comfortable, healthy man in the prime of life. He scuffed a pile of snow with his boots.

A friend from the ship, he emphasized, lifting his finger. Yes. I know what you mean.

Then, before I had time to contradict the outrageous implication in this, he added in a louder tone for the others: Ahead of you, is the most important erection on the site. Erection, yes. We had to build it from scratch, to the designs of one Ivar Svedberg, an engineer at the Billesholm coal mine at Hoganas. Down there, he added, and this chiefly for my own benefit, I supposed, is the place we call Svedberg's Crag, so named, and mapped, by my colleague Nils Strindberg, our cartographer, photographer, and violinist.

I was surprised by this.

I never knew Nils played the violin, I said.

Always has, you know, said Eckholm. But he keeps it, like so many of his accomplishments, a dark dark secret. A deep one is our canny Nils. Very deep, like a pool in a Scottish glen.

Dr Hume smiled at this, with a thin-lipped smile. He was able to take in all of what Eckholm said, whereas the Gutmans, the little Japanese, and the rest of the party, had to make do with the occasional, and rather arbitrary, translations into German or French. Eckholm was a fine linguist, but he was contemptuous of those who knew no Swedish, and he took no trouble. Unfortunately, said Eckholm, gesturing up at the flimsy bulk of the balloon-

147

house, we must delay our inspection of the balloon itself until later. The leader of the expedition, our lord and master, is currently examining the condition of the gas-valves, which have been giving some trouble.

There was an odd note in Eckholm's voice, a touch of scorn, or perhaps fear. It was hard to place. The others turned away, and began to walk back along the path towards the sea. But Eckholm put his hand on my shoulder.

Go in, he said, nodding at the balloon-house. Make him a surprise visit. Meet the great panjandrum in person, before he knows who you are. He'll be horrified.

I daren't, I said.

Yes, you dare, said Eckholm.

With a sweep of his arm, he opened a flap in the side of the building, and I stepped through, alone, into the innermost sanctum of the dream.

Dream, yes. It was always a dream. Never real, in the common everyday sense of that strange word. It had the psychological reality of nightmare.

I stepped through from that naked beach, and the jaunty conversation of Eckholm, into a sort of shrine to the power of flight, the echoing mystery of an obsession. There should have been incense, the swinging of unseen censers by priestly hands. The thin, faraway keening of some choir, or muezzin.

Instead, there was silence, broken only by the slight flapping of silk in the wind. Silence, and the heavy, greasy smell of tallow, rubbed into ropes.

The balloon-house was high, narrowing at the top like a medieval kitchen with a hole to let smoke out from the central fire. But here there was no friendly hearth, no crossed heap of sticks for the pots or the roast.

There was the wicker drum of the car, and then, to one side and sometimes half billowing above it, in each gust of wind, was the half-inflated body, restless and miserable as it seemed to me, of the captive spirit that ruled this whole active island, the soul of the polar balloon.

I stood for a moment, not sure what to do. The space was dwarfed, reduced to a tight narrowness by the giant size of the shrugging monster. It was never still. It seemed

148

almost to boil, as I watched, a cauldron of slippery patch-work, oiled as if for a terrible wrestling-match with the Nordic gods who were anxious to hold their lonely Pole inviolate from the foot of man.

I cleared my throat. It seemed to make a sharp, explosive report in the enclosed space. I felt suddenly afraid. I could see no sign of a human presence in this weird room. For a moment, I felt convinced that the balloon had shaken free of its bonds, and consumed its own creator, on the brink of his flight to fame.

He had drowned in silk, slithered into that shaking womb of black and golden worm-sheddings, as surely as if his corpse had been burned in flame, or embalmed, like a mummy's, in Egyptian wax.

Then I gasped. A head suddenly appeared, like some-thing struggling to escape from a native's cooking-pot, above the brass rail, from which rods and ropes extended out to the surface of the balloon itself. The head grimaced, and then a whole torso reared, hands gripping the rail, as if to drag up some unimaginable nether limb, or tail, from the seething interior of the car.

Skirted by the protective tarpaulin, which draped inwards from the rail to the roof of the car, the torso took on the air of some capped warrior, a mighty clansman from Scotland, unearthing himself from a primeval bog to do battle for the honour of his kind.

Then reality took over, and the man at the rail of the balloon pulled off his cap, and bowed slightly.

Good afternoon, madam, he said.

I took a step forward, searching the face for some sign of his mood. It was a hard face, marked by the high bridge of an aquiline nose, a Roman eagle's, if ever there was one. But there was a Roman sensuality, too, in those drooping, supercilious eyes. They were eyes that seemed to have sucked the world dry of its pleasures, and thrown them down in contempt.

I'm sorry, I said. Have I disturbed you?

Well, yes, the man said. Of course. But then, I don't disturb easily. And so, no. I'm not really disturbed, no.

He put up a hand, and stroked down the ends of an enormous moustache, the sort that became famous later in the war, when you saw it everywhere above Kitchener's pointing finger. Andrée, I sometimes thought, was the model for all that.

I know your name, the man said. You're Anna Charlier. You have to be.

Why do I have to be? I asked.

You have to be, he repeated, watching my face.

I felt his eyes go in through my ears, and up to my brain, and then out through the twin holes of my nose, cleaning my head of all its impurities. I felt, afterwards, that something of Andrée's was always there in my skull, holding the fort for his principles. I was frightened, but a little angry, too.

Then you have to be Salomon August Andrée, I said.

Of course, Andrée agreed, with a sudden, wolfish smile. Who else could I be?

He pointed down at a small rope ladder on the side of the car, and I came forward, and set my foot on it. He reached his arm down, and I caught the sleeve of his coat. For a moment we hung, thus, and I stared hard into his eyes.

You must never tell anyone, he said, very seriously, that I have allowed you to enter the polar balloon. They would consider it most unsuitable.

He grunted, lifting me almost bodily up the ladder, and then helping me over the brass rail, averting his gaze as he did so. It was no more indecent than throwing a leg across a man's bicycle, but then that was something no self-respecting girl would have done in the nineteenth century.

I landed, smoothing my dress down, flustered, and with my heart beating a thousand a minute. I had no idea why I was letting this happen.

I was in a little half-tent, waist-high. Only a metre away, Andrée lolled back on the rail, crossing his legs at the ankles, and staring at me.

Well, he said.

It seemed to be a sort of question.

I ran my gloved hand along the rail, fingering the beads at my neck with the other hand.

Unsuitable, I murmured. Why unsuitable?

150

Andrée grunted again, more of a snort this time, like the trapped gas exploding in a pipe.

They're superstitious fools, he said. That's why.

Then he leaned back, and moved his head to and fro, as if studying something inside the bag of the balloon.

Women, he said. I loathe women.

I had no idea how to deal with anything quite so overt as this, and I went as red as a ripe young tomato. I said nothing, and then, seeing that Andrée wasn't going to say any more either, I changed the subject.

What's this? I asked, laying my hand on the brass rail.

Andrée glanced round.

It keeps things still, he said. It leaves both hands free, he added, slipping his own into his trouser pockets, and jingling something, a bunch of keys perhaps.

Then he took his hands out, and spread his fingers along the rail.

He's well equipped, he said.

He? I asked. Why do you call the balloon he? It has an anchor, and a sail, just like a ship. You ought to call it she.

Andrée said nothing.

I felt the atmosphere charged with something, contempt perhaps. I let my tongue run on before I could stop myself, or show my awkwardness.

What's this? I asked, I suppose for the sake of something to say.

I had turned, and was facing away from Andrée. I felt him come up behind me, laying his hand over what I'd found.

My dear girl, he said, very testily. You know what that is. It's a book.

I admired the little flat stand, arranged on a swing, with a bar across it, to keep the book open at any required page.

I tried to push his fingers apart so that I could see the page. I was irritated, scarcely aware of my effrontery.

This isn't written in Swedish, I said.

I twisted my neck, and looked up under Andrée's chin. His eyes were turned on the print, shown through the narrow gate between our fingers, mine clothed in grey suede, his hairy and blunt.

I got it from a friend in London, said Andrée,

apparently a little disconcerted. Count Stenbock. It's written in English.

I felt a surge of wind sweep through the balloon-house, and I watched the envelope lift and swell, then droop and flatten again behind Andrée's head. I thought how small the space was, here on the roof of the car, for three men to live in.

Eckholm said you were busy, I said slyly. Something to do with the gas-valves. But you weren't busy. You were just reading.

Andrée laughed, and stepped away. I turned to face him.

Weren't you? I persisted.

Andrée looked at me, an odd look.

I can be alone in here, he said. It's the only way to learn.

About gas-valves? I asked.

About gas-valves, agreed Andrée. And other things.

I fiddled with my gloves. I was consumed by now with curiosity.

Has Nils seen your book? I asked.

O, I expect so, said Andrée, coolly. But he doesn't read English, alas. I learned the language pushing a broom, in the United States, at the Philadelphia World Fair, in 1876.

Please read me some, I said.

Andrée reached forward, easing the book out of its clamp, and shutting the pages.

No, he said evenly. I don't think I will.

Spoilsport, I said. Why not?

He smiled again, as he took the book up and moved to see me out.

You wouldn't understand, he said.

Then he undid a section of the balloon's skirt, and held it back, so that I could more easily set foot on the rope ladder and descend to the ground. I did so, with a bad grace. I felt very wilful, and hard done by.

Tell me, I said, looking up. What's the book's title? I may learn English and read it one day for myself.

He looked down at me, with a queer grin.

I doubt that, he said. It's a very rare book. There are only three hundred copies in print.

He stood, tapping the volume on the brass rail.

I'll see you at dinner, he added. I gather we're to celebrate your birthday.

I read the title then, incised in curving silver letters on
the yellow of the spine. A single word, a name perhaps,
and then a phrase that meant nothing to me, but which I
remembered for thirty-four years. *The Reverse of the Medal.*

All right, I said. I'll see you at dinner. But I think you're
horrible.

Tell me about him, Nils, I said, as I cut my lamb into
smaller, more ladylike pieces on my plate.

The dinner to celebrate my birthday had begun with
champagne on the deck of the *Erling Jarl*, and a toast to
myself and my mother proposed by Eckholm.

The meal was being served in the dining-saloon, and
the long tables were heavy with food.

The expedition had saved several joints from the two
lambs they'd brought from Sweden for Midsummer's Eve.
Together with green beans, freshly-baked rye bread, salt
herring, and a wealth of other delicacies, these had been
roasted, basted and served by our ship's cook, a man with
a tongue, as it were, for every occasion.

At the table of honour, headed by Andrée himself, with
my mother on his right and the ship's captain to his left, I
had managed to nudge myself in next to Nils, at the far
end, and I was trying to supply myself with some background about Andrée's earlier life. I was still smarting
from his treatment of me in the balloon-house, and it
annoyed me that Nils wasn't more sympathetic.

You know so much already, said Nils, laying his knife
and fork aside. But here goes. He is forty-two years old.
He learned English as he said, yes, when employed as a
sweeper at the Philadelphia World's Exposition in 1876. In
1882, he went with Eckholm, as you know, to do aero-
electrical work at Cape Thordsen in Isfjorden.

I know, I said, impatiently. But that's what he's done. I
want to know what he's like. As a man, I mean.

There was a burst of laughter from the other end of the
table, and I saw my mother looking primly down at her
hands.

Anna, called Eckholm, raising his glass. Andrée has

153

quite annoyed your mother. He says he will never marry. And why? Because he could never bring himself to let another individual occupy the same place in his life that he himself occupies.

I found myself staring into the cut glass of the wall mirrors behind Eckholm's head. The saloon was very much a room of the period, all carved mahogany, and reflections. A real old gin palace, in fact. I could see tiny flecks of dandruff on the back of Eckholm's collar.

Indeed so, said Andrée, with a curt nod. No two objects can occupy the same space. It's a scientific law.

There was a clink of glasses, and a murmur of amused agreement.

Perhaps, I said suddenly, in the silence. But people aren't objects. They're immortal souls.

I could see that my mother approved of this comment, but she said nothing. She was overawed by the confidence of Andrée. I watched those drooping eyes of his flicker down the table towards me.

How many angels can dance on the head of a pin? he said, rhetorically. How many spirits float in the narrow cage of a basket? A straight line contains an infinite number of points. But the line governs the points as the father his children.

Andrée drank, and reached out for a flask of white wine. He poured, sipped, and grunted.

In marriage, Miss Charlier, he said slowly, the wife could never be considered, morally, as a child. The conscience revolts at such an idea. Nor could the husband sacrifice his freedom of action. It follows, therefore, that for Salomon Andrée no marriage is possible.

The plates were being cleared, and a general buzz of conversation broke out before I could think of any reply to this. I swivelled my fixed chair in a mood of irritation. It was like being in a barber's shop, or worse, at a dentist's, and not being able to open your mouth to speak.

You see, said Nils, at my ear. That's how he is. A puritan, and an idealist. It all comes out sounding a bit absurd, but it makes a kind of sense.

Rubbish, I said.

I'd read my Ibsen in the last year, and my head was full

of ideas about the liberty of women.

My Uncle Johan, said Nils, would entirely agree with Andrée. He regards all womankind as conspiring to have him certified.

I leaned back to allow a steward to lay a fork and spoon for dessert in front of me.

Are Andrée's parents alive? I asked.

His father died, said Nils, when he was sixteen. He dotes now on his old mother, and she, I suspect, on him. There was quite a tearful farewell at Gothenburg. A great deal of embracing and wiping of eyes with handkerchiefs. He isn't just an iceberg, you know, as far as emotion goes.

I helped myself to a measure of cloudberries from a silver bowl the steward was holding to my left. There was cream in a tall jug, and a dish of sugar.

Mmm, said Nils. These are good. Really good.

He wiped his mouth with a napkin.

I'll tell you a story about our great leader, he said. There used to be some doubt about whether the polar darkness really affected the face, or if the yellowish-green tinge it tends to display at daylight resulted from the eyes of the investigators being dazzled by the light. A classic sort of problem in Arctic studies, and, indeed, in scientific experiments in general. Is it the instrument, or is it the thing itself, that creates the phenomenon?

I ate my cloudberries.

Well, anyway, said Nils, clearing the last scraps from his plate. Andrée volunteered to be shut up in a house for a whole month, away from light. At the end of the month when he came out, it was proved that his face really was yellowish-green.

I made a bored, clicking noise with my teeth.

It isn't green now, I said.

No, said Nils. Well, it wore off.

Coffee cups were being laid on the table.

Anna, said Nils, a little sadly. Do you really have to be quite so sceptical?

You taught me, I said.

He laughed then, and squeezed my knee. I pretended to be annoyed, and he laughed again, and the mood was back to the friendly tomboy style that he still seemed to

155

want from me. It was only at intervals, still, that Nils seemed to remember that I was no longer a little girl. He would gaze then, with a kind of surprised wonder, at the marvel of my body.

But he didn't seem to suspect that a grown-up spirit had come to inhabit its fleshy recesses, as demanding and quirky, in its way, as those pouter pigeons that we saw strutting and cooing all day in the attic of Pike's House at the end of the beach. For Nils I was still a clockwork mouse in a gilded cage. He would wind me up, and then I said what he wanted.

Sugar? the steward asked, and I helped myself from the bowl.

Liqueurs were being served, and I watched the brilliant greens and golds as they poured from their rounded containers into the tiny upright or bulbous vessels, as mysterious and unreal as the waters for a chemist's shop.

Cigars came, too, in their fragrant long boxes, and the men leaned back with cutters, accepting lights from held matches, puffing and pronouncing the tobacco good. In Sweden it had become the progressive thing for men to smoke in the presence of ladies, but neither my mother, nor Andrée it appeared, altogether approved of this licence.

There was a scraping of chairs, and my mother rose to go. She walked along the table towards me. Andrée was making a brief speech of farewell.

I shall take a turn on the deck, he said, and then perhaps a walk on the shore.

We mustn't let the balloon feel lonely, said Eckholm, sarcastically.

Andrée put one hand on his shoulder. It was a gesture that seemed at once dominating, and kindly.

Tomorrow, he said, we'll check the gas-tightness of the cloth again. Goodnight, Eckholm.

I could sense, even down the length of the table, that something was wrong between him and Eckholm. There was a kind of irony, an exaggerated politeness, in the way Andrée spoke, and perhaps something else, a veiled mistrust.

Eckholm nodded, as my mother bent at my side and whispered to me.

156

Now don't stay up too long, Anna. I'm sure that Mr Strindberg has a long day tomorrow.

I felt mulish, and angry. I didn't want, as she obviously expected, to get up and make an excuse, and escort her to our cabin.

It *is* my birthday, mother, I said.

The steward was pouring brandy into a huge balloon at my side, and my mother yielded. She had her moments of knowing when it was best to wait.

Well, don't be too late, she said again.

Dr Hume, who had been a quiet presence in the middle of the table, rose and took her arm. He smiled at me.

One brandy only, he said. Two are bad for the heart.

Who is that man? asked Nils, twisting in his chair to watch them go.

He seemed a little drunk, and on the edge of being belligerent with it. He leaned on the table, with the long tube of a full Corona between his fingers. He seemed more plump tonight, and as dandified as when I had first met him.

Dr Hume, I said. I told you. A friend from the ship.

O, yes, Nils said. A friend from the ship. You told me. So did Eckholm.

I kicked him hard under the table, rose from my chair, and ran quickly upstairs to the deck. It was very bright, and I walked to the rail. The air felt crisp and still.

A boat was pulling away to the shore, with Andrée sitting in the stern. He looked back up, and waved to me. I raised my eyes and saw again the hump of the mountain, and the strange biscuit tin of the balloon-house.

He was like the keeper of a lion, I felt, rowing in to feed his pet for the night; or no, perhaps more like Franken-stein, on the way down to his laboratory to check the condition of his monster.

I heard a step behind me, and Nils was there, very red, and like a little boy in the extreme of his discomfiture.

O, Anna, he said.

I let him take me into his arms. It was the first time. I smelled the tobacco, and the alcohol on his breath.

Jealousy, said Nils, is the last infirmity of a noble spirit.

I pulled away.

No, it isn't, I said. It's natural.

Nils leaned beside me on the rail. He watched the boat reach the shore, and the sailor ship his oars, and Andrée step out into the water, and then stride ashore.

It's like a Norse saga, he said. We have to follow him. To the ends of the earth. Quite literally.

I turned away, and started to walk along the deck. Nils called after me.

Where are you going?

To the ends of the earth, I said, over my shoulder. Follow me.

It isn't that, he said, as he paced beside me. It isn't that at all. There's no choice.

There is a choice, I said, halting. Him or me.

For a long time, Nils looked at me. Then he took me into his arms once again, and led me to the rail. Andrée was a tiny figure now, at the door of the balloon-house, and then he opened a flap, and was gone inside. It felt like the sun setting, or perhaps the return of Count Dracula to his coffin in the morning.

I could not love thee, dear, so much, said Nils, very quietly. Loved I not honour more. An English poet, Richard Lovelace, wrote that to his mistress before he went to fight for his king in the Civil War. It's exactly how I feel.

Honour, I said, Civil War. King. What kind of words are these? You're going on a balloon journey to the North Pole. To satisfy some thirst for knowledge. And to please that madman down there on Danes Island. I don't want any talk about honour and kings. And as for civil wars, the only issue at stake is some petty rivalry between Norway and Sweden that ought to have been settled centuries ago.

I put my head on Nils's shoulder.

Nils, I said. I want to tell you something. That Dr Hume.

Then I told my lie.

He asked me to marry him.

I felt Nils's body grow rigid.

O, he said. Then again, O.

I drew away and leaned back on the rail.

He's dying, I said. He wants me to go and spend the last

year of his life with him in Edinburgh. That's where he used to practise, as a heart surgeon.

You said no, said Nils. I know, you said no.

I said nothing, I said.

Then he turned away, and drove his fists into his cheeks, rocking his head to and fro. It was cold now, getting colder, and I was glad of the shawl around my back.

Look, Nils said. I have to go. I have to. I've promised. I can't betray him now.

No, I said. No, of course.

Nils blinked, shaking his head, as if he was coming out of water.

Eckholm's worried, he said morosely. He thinks the balloon won't hold the gas.

My stomach turned over. I felt my mouth dry with fear.

Won't it? I asked.

Of course it will, said Nils. Then again, as if to convince both of us, of course it will.

Several other people had come out on deck, and were standing in a group, chatting, some distance away.

Anna, said Nils, making, it seemed, a great effort. Anna. I love you. I know that. When I come back.

He paused.

If you come back, I stressed.

Nils, called Eckholm, from the other group. Let's go ashore and drink some brandy on Danes Island.

Yes, Nils said, waving. Yes. All right. In a minute.

I feel cold, I said, moving away. I'm going in.

But Nils put his hand on my arm.

Forget this Dr Hume, he said. You can't waste your life on a man dying.

Well, I said, should I waste my life on a man dead?

Then he followed me to the top of the stairs.

Anna, he said. We may not go, you know. Wait and see.

Goodbye, Nils, I said.

In the morning we weighed anchor, and sailed for Trondheim.

It was the beginning of September, a month after we got home, that the parcel arrived. I cut the string, and tore

159

open the brown paper. Inside there was a plain cardboard box, with a letter folded over something wrapped in tissue.

My dear Anna, the letter began. The silk will tell its own story. I thought your mother might use it as a table-cover. The polar flight, you see, has been aborted. We cut the balloon open on August 16th. On August 30th we sailed for Tromsö, with the emptied envelope and all our equipment stowed in the hold. We were all in very low spirits. You may by now have read in the papers about the achievements of Nansen. He and Johanssen reached the Norwegian mainland on August 13th, and I gather the news was instantly wired around the world.

You'll have heard how they spent the Arctic winter alone together, two men in an earth cellar for nine months. They left the *Fram* with their thirty dogs and made a bid for the Pole. An incredible thing. You know, they reached 86 degrees North, the furthest yet. I can hardly believe it's true.

But for us the most poignant touch was the *Fram* coming. They put in to Virgo Harbour on August 14th. Otto Sverdrup had brought the ship right across the polar sea, drifting frozen into the pack-ice exactly as Nansen had said he could. We recognized the ship immediately.

I was the one who had to tell Andrée. He came up on deck, and took the glasses. I wouldn't like to interpret what was in his face. Of course, he was glad. We all were. They'd made one of the greatest voyages in polar history, and without a single loss of life.

But they were Norwegians. And this was the 14th of August. The very day Andrée had to decide we couldn't fly. We were too late. We'd failed. And they'd succeeded. Nansen and Sverdrup would have all the glory, and we'd go home with our Swedish tails between our legs.

That was what Andrée was thinking, I know, when he gave me the glasses back, and went down again to his cabin. The following day we ground the scissors.

Anna, this letter is all news, bare news. But it tells you what I feel, I hope. I haven't seen you, or heard from you for twenty-nine days. But I've thought about you every one of those, night and morning.

I've been thinking about that Dr Hume, with his shaking hands, and his long lantern Scottish jaw. You couldn't marry a man like that. He has no humour, no style, only his craggy bones, and his doom. His need for you.

Anna, you have to do what you must. It's up to you, of course. But I feel more sure now of exactly what I want. Next year the balloon will fly to the North Pole. Nothing can stand in its way. And I shall ride in the car with Andrée, if necessary alone. We shall reach the Pole, and return as heroes. The first men to set foot on the world's tip.

I know we shall. But Anna, I want to make that flight with the firm knowledge that I shall return, not just as a famous man for my own sake. But also for the sake of my future wife, and the children I shall one day have by her. I want her to think of her husband, and they to think of their father, as the man who flew to the North Pole with Salomon Andrée.

I need that knowledge in my head before I fly. I need to know that I shall be undertaking the voyage for your sake, Anna, and for the unborn family we shall one day have.

There. The words are out, in dry ink here on the page. Today I'm writing this letter in Tromsö, at a little bar on the quay. I can see the *Virgo* riding at anchor, and men working on the rigging. There's a dim sun, and a heavy smell of stale fish. It's hardly the place for a declaration of love. But that's what this letter is, Anna. And this piece of silk, sawn with my own hands from what most mattered to me, is a pledge of love. Receive it in that spirit, I beg you.

We sail tonight for Trondheim, and then on down the coast until we reach Sweden, and put in at Gothenburg. I shall come at once to see your father.

Anna, is this what you want? I hope with all my soul that it is. You have my love. You take my life in your hands. I mean to make you a good husband. One who is kind. But one who is famous, too. With all my heart, your loving Nils.

I laid the letter aside, and lifted, and unfolded, the rectangle of varnished silk. It was frayed a little, and smelled of candle-wax. It wasn't very attractive, and I

161

didn't suppose that my mother would think it at all suitable for a table-cover.

I felt my hands begin to tremble, and suddenly I could bear the touch of the silk no longer. It was as if the balloon, with all its evil associations, and its magnetic power, had entered the room, and was intruding itself once again, even in death and deflation, between me and the man I loved.

I stood up and walked to the stove, opened the gate in the front, and threw the parcel of silk onto the flames. In a second, it was a ball of fire.

After that, it was just a matter of waiting, and counting the days. It was a cold October afternoon when Nils arrived. The leaves were all stripped off the birches, and a bitter wind was howling through every crack and cranny of our little wooden house. Even at three o'clock, when Nils paid off the carriage, and rang the bell at our front door, it was already dark as if for a thunderstorm.

Lamps were burning downstairs in the kitchen, where my mother and I were preparing for dinner, and up in the dining-room, where my father was waiting alone for his interview.

Your father will let him in today, my mother said, laying a restraining hand on my arm, as I rose to answer the door. You bide your time, my girl, and peel your potatoes.

Half an hour went by, in the creaking silence of the kitchen, with the wind making the cups rattle on the dresser, and the dog stirring and shivering in his doze beside the stove, before we heard the bell from upstairs, and I knew that my fate, one way or another, had been decided.

You go up, my mother said, unusually kindly for her.

The voyage to Spitzbergen had done her catarrh a world of good, and seemed in the process to have acted favourably on her temper as well, so that the last month or so had been a period of untroubled happiness in our household. I had small hopes of it lasting, knowing my mother's moods of old, but I took the moment's calm for what it was, and enjoyed it.

I knocked on the dining-room door, and waited, like a servant girl applying for a new post, and anxious not to make the wrong impression. But, of course, my father never called come in, and I simply smoothed my dress down, and walked through.

The lamp was dim, and I went over to turn the screw, and give us more light. The wind swept past the window as I did so, and the shutters creaked in their frames. I stood by the central table, bowed over the dome of the glass.

The wick needs trimming, my father said, from the sideboard, where he was fondling the curved handle of his tantalus. I should leave it for now, Anna.

The tantalus was a splendid example of its kind and period, an oak and brass affair, with seats for three decanters, and a strong lock to prevent servants from pilfering the liquor. My father was taking the little silver key from his waistcoat pocket, and unlocking the door that dropped in the front.

Sherry, Nils, he said, over his shoulder. There's port, or whisky, if you prefer them.

I took in Nils then for the first time. He was dressed in a dark three-piece suit, and a bunch of roses he'd brought, no doubt for my mother, lay on the settle beside him. He was leaning forward, his hands clasped in his lap. I couldn't see his face in the dim light. I went over and took a hard seat by the window.

The pelargoniums needed watering, and I lifted the copper can and turned to pour some water over the soil. It helped my nerves to do something with my hands.

I think you know why Nils is here, my father said, as he lifted the cut-glass decanter, and poured a measure of sherry.

The metal label clinked on its chain, a faint skeletal sound. Everything seemed to be making sharp, clear noises today, from the wood falling in the stove to the Swiss clock chiming. I crossed my legs, hearing my silk stockings hiss.

He's been telling me something about his plans, my father continued, handing a glass to Nils. Port, my dear?

He knew that I always preferred port, and this confirmation of his memory put me more at my ease. I nodded.

There is no doubt in my mind, my father said, as he

lifted the deep red liquid in its crystal cylinder, that Nils is able to support a wife. He has entirely convinced me of his prospects. He has money now, a post at the university, and the certainty of inheriting more than a competence from his family in the fullness of time.

I took the rounded globe of port my father was handing to me. In the shadowy light, it seemed to glow, and almost whirl, like a tiny lake of blood, in a witch's cave. I sipped quickly, and felt my sense of unreality recede a little.

On that score, my father said, weighing his words, there is no difficulty. I am also convinced, he continued, that Nils is honest, sober, and reliable. After all, these things do matter.

I could see, across the room, that Nils was nodding. He gulped at his sherry. The wind whined, and the flame flickered in the lamp. Our shadows danced on the wooden walls.

I am also quite convinced, my father added, as he seated himself in an armchair at the table, and took a sip from his own glass, that Nils is sure of his own feelings, and has a deep and considered affection for you, Anna. That ought to go without saying in these cases, but it doesn't always, and I do say it, and it matters to me.

My father stroked the fluted stem of his glass. His bulk seemed to fill the room, dwarfing Nils and me. He was like a great rock, as true and clear as a hill out in the rain.

No, Anna, he said quietly. I know that Nils loves you, and has the means and the character to take care of you. That isn't the difficulty.

I felt the whalebone of my stays pressing into my waist. I sat straighter, clutching my glass in my lap.

The difficulty is this, my father said.

He got up, and helped himself to more whisky, adding water from a blue jug to the glistening gold. Then he came and sat down again, without offering either of us any more.

Nils is going away next May, my father said. He will spend next summer, as this one, on Danes Island. In July, or at latest in August, he will take off in the polar balloon with Andrée, and probably another aeronaut, and will navigate in the Arctic.

The room was very still now. The wind had dropped,

164

and only the wood in the stove occasionally fell with a subdued crash. Outside, I could see the shapes of the houses across the road, vague and menacing in the gathering darkness.

Nils will either return, my father said, as a famous man. The Conqueror of the Pole.

He paused.

Or he will die, he said slowly. And never be heard of again. You both have to face that possibility. We all do.

There was a long silence after that, and the wind seemed to draw courage from it, and start again. It made a long low howl round the skirting-boards, and then curled up, like a cat springing, and landed on the table, and made the shield of the lamp clatter on the metal.

Now, Anna, my father said. I've asked you before, and I know your answer. You love Nils, and you want to be his wife. But it worries you, I know it does, that he may be lost for ever up there in the snow. So Nils.

My father turned, with a creak, in his chair.

I have to ask you this again, he said. And this time in the presence of Anna. Whatever happens here today, and think carefully before you answer this, do you still mean to go on the polar flight?

It was very dark in the room now. The lamp seemed to have grown very dim, and I could only see Nils as a humped shape on the wooden settle, a bag of bones in a skin of clothes. The wind rose, whining as if it were there at the Pole itself, begging like one of Nansen's dogs for food. And then,

I mean to go, I heard Nils say. And then,

But I love Anna. And I want to marry her.

My father shifted his bulk again, and this time I sensed, rather than saw, his deep eyes boring through the darkness at me. I sat very still on my stiff chair by the window. The whalebone was into my guts, driving its horn through, from the Arctic sea.

Anna, my father said, and I could feel his fingers taking the hook out of my throat. I know that you don't know what to say.

No, I said. I do know what to say. I love Nils, father. And I want to marry him.

The polar wind was there in the roof now, whirling up everything in the room to a fine swirl of snow. I seemed to be in a glass ball, like one of those Christmas toys you shake, and the false flakes fly and then settle, on a little safe house, on children playing. But this wasn't a safe house, not any more, and we weren't children.

O, no, my father said, rising to his feet. O, no. O, no.

He was like an avalanche moving now, pacing with easy control in the tight space, clasping his whisky like a sacred chalice, the voice of divine judgement made physical, a huge man laying down the law for his daughter, where she might go, what she might do. I felt small near him, felt Nils small, as if we were toys, or dolls, clogging his feet.

Listen, my father said, pausing by the stove. I'll tell you what I agree to. And about this there is to be absolutely no argument. I forbid an immediate marriage.

The cuckoo sounded, and the little man in his gaiters came out on the wooden slide, and looked at the sky. Then the clock chimed, and it was four o'clock.

If, my father said, lifting his bad hand, and looking from one of us to the other. If, he repeated, you disobey me in this, then that is the end. You will no longer be my daughter, Anna.

I knew what he meant. It wasn't money. He had little enough of that to spare, or deprive me of. It was pride, the old yeoman's pride of Scania, of a man whose family had owned their own land for seven centuries, and thought no one, not even the King, their superior in blood.

It was pride he could take away. The pride in being part of that family, however low and small a part. The pride in knowing that one day I would wear the ring my great-grandfather had worn in the presence of Gustavus III, that one day my neck would chill to the jet necklace my great-great-grandmother had worn at a ball for the English ambassador.

He could take away that pride. He could make quite sure that no one in that wide ramifying family would ever speak or write to me again. Or even think of my name except as the name of a stranger, some local girl who ran away to marry a young blood in Stockholm.

It was that close in our family. I knew what he meant.

166

And I felt the cold wind of its force, under and even beyond, that other, physical wind that rattled the three decanters now in their seats, making the metal labels chink like the bite of gold in a dead man's teeth.

I said nothing. I waited. Across the room, I saw Nils appear to wilt, and shrivel into his clothes. He had billowed large for a while, like that awful polar balloon in its wooden cage, and now he seemed much smaller, as if the gas had been drained from him, scissored out for another year.

My father was walking to and fro, charging our glasses now, replacing crystal stoppers as he spoke again.

There will be no marriage, my father said. Not yet. But I consent to an immediate engagement, if that is what you both desire. Should your feelings remain the same, then the marriage will take place if, and when, Nils comes back home in safety from the polar flight.

There was an instant sense of relaxation in the room. I heard Nils change his position, and clear his throat.

Of course, he said, in the darkness. That's very fair. That's really very fair, indeed.

Anna, my father said.

It was a question.

I waited as long as I could. Neither of them saw my two hands bending the copper spout of the watering can into a vicious hoop. Neither of them knew I was trembling. Neither of them had wakened, night after night, with the sheet twisted between their legs, not knowing what to do, soaking with sheer frustrated lust.

All right, I said at last. I agree.

So my father rang the bell again, and my mother came up and took a glass of sherry, and Nils embraced me like a happy brother, and I drew away and trimmed the wick, and the flame sprang higher, and the room was full of cheerful faces, like trolls in a Christmas painting.

Later, before he left, I had some time alone with Nils. There were two matters I wanted to discuss with him. They'd been on my mind since the day in Spitzbergen I'd first met Andrée.

We were in the garden, pacing under the darkened trees in a last stroll before his carriage came to take him back to

167

Malmö for the train. Branches would brush our faces as we walked, and I stopped for a moment, under the overhanging bough of a beech.

Nils, I said. I've been wondering. Are you superstitious?

My dear girl, he said. What a funny question. You know I'm not. I am a man of reason, pure and simple.

I leaned back on the trunk.

I know, I said thoughtfully. But Andrée said you were superstitious fools. All of you. All ballooning people.

Not me, said Nils. Be sure of that.

I plucked a twig down in the darkness, and broke it in two.

There's something I didn't tell you, I said slowly. When Andrée and I first met, in the balloon-house on Danes Island, he invited me into the car of the balloon. I stood there with him, on the roof of the car. That's when he said you were superstitious. He said you would all think it was wrong — unsuitable, I think he said — for a woman to be in the car of a balloon.

Unsuitable, yes, agreed Nils. But not unlucky. It's a matter of common propriety. Long skirts and ladies' bloomers, they don't look right in the air. It's like a poem.

I laughed.

Yes, I see, I said. So you don't think I put some kind of curse on the balloon by going into the car.

Nils took my chin in his hand. He looked closely into my eyes.

What rubbish, he said. What utter, utter rubbish.

I started to walk on, lashing at flowers on either side with my twig. It was a cold night, and I felt the need to keep moving to fend off the chill.

I'm glad, I said. I'd been wondering.

Nils fell into step beside me.

Anna, he said seriously. It was the weather, and the time. Wind and insurance. Nothing more supernatural than that. You can rest assured you had no influence on the flight of the polar balloon being postponed.

We walked in silence for a moment.

There's another thing, I said, after a while. I didn't tell you before. Andrée was reading a book in the balloon. He wouldn't tell me what it was. I asked him to read me some, but he wouldn't.

Well, said Nils, diplomatically. I don't exactly see why he should have done. Why did you mind?

We had reached the gate now, and I leaned over it, looking across the road into a lighted room. Someone was drawing curtains.

The book was in English, I said.

English, said Nils, in amusement. How did you know?

He told me so.

I turned and faced him, with my back to the fence.

Do you understand English? I asked.

Nils laughed.

A bit, he said. A little bit. Why?

I looked down at my hands.

Andrée said you didn't, I said, then: I remembered the title. I don't know if I've got it right.

Recite, O English girl, said Nils, striking an attitude.

I looked hard at him.

It went something like this, I said, and I quoted the words that had stayed in my mind. *The Reverse of the Medal.* Do you know the book?

There was a long silence before Nils spoke.

No, I don't, he said. I think you must have got it wrong. It doesn't sound like English to me.

But I knew I hadn't got it wrong, and I knew he was lying. Then we heard the sound of the carriage wheels, and the snort of horses, and the rattle of wood coming over the bridge, and the time had come for Nils to leave. He went in to say goodbye to my mother and father, without kissing me.

Then he came out, and we shook hands. And then he was gone. And that was all that was ever said about that book that Andrée had been reading in the polar balloon.

169

6
STRINDBERG
1897

A GREAT DEAL OF TIME has gone by. Every day Andrée writes up his diary, Fraenkel makes his meteorological notes, and I keep my almanac. I know from all this that the date is now August 14th, and that means about fourteen days have gone by since I last wrote to you.

I suppose I realized suddenly just how similar each of our days was starting to be. There seemed no point — there *seems* no point — in repeating time after time the minutiae of our regular life.

Tonight we've eaten well for the first time in over a week. Yesterday morning we were down to our last pound of bear's meat. I'd got into the habit of cutting the pieces very small so that at least they would look a lot.

We were all rather morose. Not exactly hungry, but knowing that we very soon would be. Then God seemed to take a hand. We decided to spend the day hunting, that's to say, trying to find food, rather than attempting to make progress.

Andrée set the style, by discovering a minute fish and slaughtering it with a shovel. It was only three inches long but it seemed, somehow, to be a symbol of good fortune. It had a green, prickly back, violet side, and white belly. We saw a seal next, and Fraenkel took a shot. But he missed.

Then, just as we were skirting a sort of copse of ice hummocks, I sighted a group of three bears, a female and two cubs.

Bears, I shouted, and Andrée, who was nearest, swung and took a shot with his Remington.

173

It took him three shots to drop the mother, and with his fourth he got one cub. The other fell to me, after Fraenkel had wounded him.

Did I ever tell you which parts of the bear we eat? We find the meat on the ribs excellent, but also the heart, brain, kidneys, and tongue. I've eaten more parts of a bear than I'd ever eaten parts of a cow or a sheep before. Innards appeal.

Enough meat for twenty-three days. That's what it means. Not to be blunt about it, our death sentence repealed for the best part of a month.

You've no idea what it's like to feel well fed after days of fearing starvation. Nothing equals the sense of repleteness. All the other irritations of life recede into the background, if only for a moment.

Mind you, there are plenty of these. Let me try and set out things in some kind of order.

My hands, first. They're warm enough, as I say. In the daytime, the weather has been so hot that we've sometimes had to draw the sledges with our jackets off, and at night, the temperature in the tent is high enough, still, to make sleeping outside the bag seem a real possibility.

My hands, though. I washed them three days ago, for the first time since we rose in the balloon. Think what that means, Anna. The ingrained air-filth of nearly a month without soap or water!

Why? Every time we need hot water, it means heating a little tray on top of the primus stove. When I washed my hands I used an old sock to scrub the dirt with. The end result was that I had a stretch of skin the colour of light walnut instead of mahogany.

But that's the least of it. My clothes tonight are soaked in bear's blood, and slime of guts. Of course, I've brushed off what I could with snow, but there's plenty still rubbed in. And the same goes for Andrée and Fraenkel.

One or other of us goes out from time to time to get a breath of fresh air. Even one third less impregnated bear's blood helps a little.

This isn't the worst, though. Tonight the meat has given me energy to write, and a kind of extra sensitivity, too. I'm bound to say that in earlier nights my sense of smell has grown to be rather dulled.

It's had to be. On two occasions, Fraenkel has been suffering from bouts of acute diarrhoea, and Andrée has had to dose him with opium. It seems to be helping a little, but we can't tell yet how much.

It's not clear what exactly has caused Fraenkel's trouble, but I have my ideas. I can only hope the same complaint won't affect Andrée and me. The bowels are funny things. They need regular clearing, and it isn't only the diet that seems to disturb their working.

Poor old Fraenkel. He had an attack of snow-blindness a few days earlier. I suppose I shouldn't have chivvied him so much about always wearing those dark glasses. He took them off for an hour or two one bright morning, and the sun seems to have had its revenge.

As the days go by, our respective roles are becoming rather more standardized. Outdoors, when we're pulling the sledges, Fraenkel is very much our work horse. He can drag twice the weight that Andrée and I do, and he positively enjoys the punishing marches we set ourselves. I let him take the larger brunt of the work. I have to.

Andrée marches conserving his strength. He keeps his eyes open, and I think he's the only one of us who behaves, even now, as if we're out on a scientific expedition, and not a trek to land for our lives.

Mind you, he's the one who's always up on a hummock staring out through his binoculars for a sight of land. There isn't any. But he still tries.

A week ago, we took time to climb a huge ice pyramid, over twelve metres high, with a view through the sunny air of many kilometres. We all stood there on the top like the first men on the Matterhorn, breathless, and dazzled.

Far below, there were the three sledges, minute in the snow, like children's toys. On all sides we could see the spread of the pack-ice, broken and hillocky, and pierced by leads, exactly as it looked from ground level.

I remember Andrée turning to all four points of the compass. He couldn't seem to believe that there wouldn't be something − some tiny fragment of sea or land − some jagged sky-line of coast or mountain to give us hope and a

175

sense of direction. But there wasn't even an outcrop of rock or the crest of a wave. Just the pack-ice, and the zigzag leads.

Nothing, he said.

Then he sat down, as if tired out, on a block of ice, and took a biscuit out of his pocket. We sat down beside him, three fagged-out climbers there in the endless sun, and it was over an hour before we could summon up the energy to climb down to the sledges again, and try to press on.

That night I made an astronomical observation, and it became clear that we'd drifted further west than we'd marched east. The evening of July 31st. It was a bad moment.

I won't go into all the discussions. They took us the better part of three days, in the intervals of keeping alive. But the end of it all was that we made a decision. We had to change course.

On the morning of August 4th, we cancelled our plan to march east. We struck out for the Seven Islands. Ever since then, our aim has been to abandon our march towards Franz Josef Land, and make for Spitzbergen.

How are we progressing? How can I say? None of us has the courage to make the observations every day. It's too depressing. But the force of the current's drift is bound to be often against us. One day, it will change. But it may not be soon.

How can I give you the variety of our journeys? Most of the time our labour is appalling, and poor Fraenkel is getting worse and worse. Today Andrée had to massage his foot. The knee seemed to have gone out of joint, from putting pressure on it the wrong way. As I say, he's a titan for work. But he seems almost to court disaster. He undertakes more than he knows is possible.

I, too, have had trouble. A pain in my toe, cause unknown. But alas, Andrée pays less attention to my ailments than he does to Fraenkel's. I represent a much smaller amount of horsepower between the shafts of the sledges.

I do my bit, though. More than Andrée does himself. I cut my hand on the 5th August, when my sledge nearly

176

capsized at the edge of a floe, and I had to have the wrist in bandages. That same day, a boil opened up on my lip, and I could hardly swallow for the pain.

Our bodies are showing the strain. Both Andrée and I have now come down with diarrhoea, and I'm sure it can't be long before Fraenkel has another dose. Fortunately, the complaint seems to come and go, and we're left able to recover, and eat again.

The food may well be the trouble. I'm still not sure. But we had one outbreak after a night of trying bear's meat raw.

It was Andrée who insisted on the experiment.

Raw bear with salt, he suggested. It ought to be rather piquant.

So we prepared some slices of steak, and laid them out on plates. Fraenkel was the first to try. He chewed for a few moments, and then went through a parody of pretending to vomit. Andrée laughed. Then he became serious.

Tell me, though, he said, not reaching out himself to the plate. What's it like?

Fraenkel savoured a morsel on his palate.

Well, he said. I think it tastes like oysters. Rather bad oysters.

Later, we made blood-pancake, and Fraenkel served it with fried meat. It seemed to work like a sort of bread-substitute, and we all quite enjoyed the flavour.

Most of what we eat now is based on bear. We have bear broth for breakfast. Fillet of bear at night. Sandwiches made of bear fragments for lunch. The best of our dishes, in my opinion, is the bear-ham when it's several days old. It takes on a high salty flavour, like a well-hung pheasant.

The bear has become our pork, our lamb, and our poultry. He offers us all we have that keeps us going. Hail to thee, polar bear! Thou art our walking butcher's shop.

Sometimes, despite their power, and their dangerous vindictiveness, I feel quite sorry for the bears. They get so hungry themselves. They come right up to the door of the tent. The other day, we were attacked by three cubs. They must have tracked us after we shot their old father. He was the biggest and the best bear we've had so far. A truly magnificent skin.

We've all learned to hold our fire, and to aim for the heart or the brain. The bears don't really have much of a chance. But they're very brave. And they don't always die easily. The she-bear we shot on August 13th had bitten right through her tongue.

So much for bears, and the diarrhoea that comes from bears. I wanted to tell you about the variety of our journeys. There are two extremes. Normally, about nine days out of ten are solid slogging. Leads, pack-ice, bridges. Boats and floes. Intolerable labour for a gain of a thousand metres. Cancelled out by the drift.

But just once in a while, on that tenth day, everything changes. We hit a stretch of what Andrée calls 'parade-ice', or paradise. The sledges glide along for hundreds of metres over absolutely even ground, with no obstacles. Exactly like wheeled artillery moving over a parade-square.

Then we rejoice. But it's never for long, alas. The hummocky masses close in and we're back where we started. Today, for instance. We were negotiating what I can only describe as a mountainous landscape fissured with lakes and precipices.

It was necessary to thread a passage along narrow tracks, hacked out with axe and spade, and then followed on a slender brink, with a sheer drop towards a glittering pool of water. Fraenkel was leading the way, with Andrée bringing up the rear, and I myself in the middle.

More than once, one of us would lose his balance, and slither over the edge. We had ropes lashing each of us to the sledge we were pulling, so that no one could fall far. But it meant several horrific moments, when someone was dangling in air, needing to grope for a foothold to haul himself back to the track.

Lie still, Fraenkel called, when Andrée fell, and we both turned, and edged back until we could reach over and help our leader – yes, it feels like that, still, even when he's leading from behind – help our leader up to safety.

Once I fell myself, and I was hanging upside down, my head and shoulders banging against the ice-wall to my left, while I yelled out for the others to run and get me back. The blood all rushed into my brain, and a moment's curious delirium came. I had hallucinations.

178

Angels with great wings were flapping and squawking round my feet. One of them bit my ankle, another slipped its hand under my legs. Then I was turning a somersault, like a catherine wheel at a firework display, and then I was on my feet and the angels were only Fraenkel and Andrée.

I saw them for a moment as they really were, as they'd come to be.

No more tidy hair, and neat moustaches. Clean skins and hairless cheeks. I was facing two long- and lank-haired Viking warriors, each with a face dark brown from dirt and sun and wind, one with a wiry flaxen beard, the other a tangled, grizzled one. They looked a terrible pair of rough and tumble fellows. Beggars. Tramps. Men you would turn away from your door until they'd had a wash and a shave. The sort of visitors you wouldn't trust your daughter or your chickens near.

Thank you, I said, sweeping snow off my coat. I thought I was gone that time.

Andrée drew back his lips, showing his blackened teeth. I realized that he was smiling, and that this was what passed with us now for a smile.

You nearly were, he said.

Anna. I've had a shock. This is written later. I don't know what the date is, but it doesn't matter. The time is noon, and we've been up for about an hour. Breakfast is over, and Fraenkel and Andrée have gone out together to reconnoitre our route for the day's march.

I was waiting for the chance. I know that now. The need to do what I've done has been growing for weeks. You can't imagine how strange one gets to feel out here. Normal standards of morality just don't seem to apply.

Of course, we pretend they do. We try. But we watch each other. We get suspicious.

Anyway. I had to do it. I've watched Andrée night after night, day after day, endlessly writing away in that little buff diary of his. I had to find out what he thought of me. What he was doing.

Well. I waited for ten minutes, until they were both out of sight, then I went over to Andrée's sledge, and pulled open the laces of his private bag.

There it was, closed on top, with an elastic band round

179

the covers. He doesn't use a code. It was all in plain Swedish.

Not much. Pages about the snow, and the temperature. And some wonderful stuff about the cries of the ivory gull. The piyyyrrr of the mother, the warning cry. The pyot, pyot of the little ones. Exactly right. He has an ear.

He has an eye, too. Very good stretches about the consistency of the ice. All that. And, of course, there isn't much about Fraenkel and me. No, not much. But enough.

Just enough to confirm a little of what I thought. For last night, for instance, he's written 'we shall see if he can become a man again'.

Poor Fraenkel. I wonder if he can. I think that I know what Andrée means. I fear I do.

You see, there was something else under the diary, something I couldn't help seeing. A little folder of photographs. No, not women, Anna. Not the sort of Folies Bergère stuff I've been shown by men who've had a holiday in Paris, and got snaps of thick-thighed girls lifting their frilly knickers in return for their kroner. No, not those.

Those I could understand. Fraenkel, even. He might have some of those. But these were different. Very tasteful. Very elegant. Studies of young boys. Very slim, and with vine leaves around their temples, and words in what looks like Italian written underneath.

And naked. All naked. Showing what isn't normally shown. Nothing rude, or suggestive. No, not that. Rather more as if they were meant to arouse an emotion of pity, or affection. It makes me think. It makes me think very hard, Anna.

It's getting colder. During the day, while we pull the sledges, it's still quite warm, but at night the tent is now always covered with ice inside. You know what it's like to find a window frosted with crystals in an old house. Imagine the curtains round your bed caked with frost. It's that kind of difference.

Andrée no longer even talks about sleeping outside the bag in a single blanket. The few days that he did I now think he must have been suffering from a fever. It's hard

180

to distinguish sometimes between symptoms of illness and evidence of intended stoicism.

Andrée likes to think of himself as a bit of a tough character, certainly. He wants to make us realize that he can endure the cold and the privation just as easily as we younger men.

It came out for a time over the drugs. Let me give you the latest news, Anna, on the diarrhoea story. Not very elevating, I'm afraid, but for the last ten days it hasn't ever been very far from our thoughts.

To begin with, the good news. My own one bout soon came to an end, I'm completely clean, as one might say, with a suitable pun. So it looks, after all, as if it may not be entirely the food to blame.

We don't all eat exactly the same amount, of course. And naturally, one cut may contain more or less of what's giving the trouble. But over a period of several days, one would expect these variations to even out.

They haven't. I remain unaffected, whatever I eat. And poor Fraenkel gets worse and worse. At first, Andrée seemed to be immune, too, but that hasn't lasted. For the past week or so, he's been neck and neck — or should I say, rectum to rectum? — with poor Fraenkel.

It's a sordid business. Andrée tried hard at first to avoid taking any medicine. But he's had to give way. On the 31st of August, he dosed himself with both morphine and opium. I hope it's going to have some effect.

Fraenkel has had regular doses for nearly ten days. On the 28th of August, he had a tablet against the diarrhoea, and then some morphine for the pains in his stomach. He'd kept Andrée and me awake all the previous night with his groaning while he slept.

This is the trouble. You can be a real old stoic, like Fraenkel is, when he's awake. But once the eyes close, and the will drifts, you start wheezing away like a steam engine that needs a bucket of water to cool it down.

It's more and more clear to me that strength is a complicated thing. Here's Fraenkel with his iron muscles and his eagle eye. A crack shot, and a glutton for hard work. But when it comes to the inside of his body, his guts, if you like, it's not the same.

181

The man with the real guts is me. I don't need to swallow morphine to keep going. My bowels are working normally. The consistency of my faeces is an even thickness, just as it was in Stockholm. I husband my resources, and I don't make a song and dance about being so grand and brave, but I seem to be managing better than either of them.

Surprisingly, scientific investigation still takes place. In spite of all our troubles, Andrée continues to put together his collection of samples.

I don't think I've mentioned these before. What he's been doing is to gather and classify any section of ice which seems to contain extraneous, non-meltable matter. It's as if he's like a starling, flying to and fro to seek out the materials for a durable nest. In Andrée's case, a nest that will hold the precious, breakable eggs of his reputation.

Every day as we trek over the ice, he'll dart aside to alight on something glittering or unusual that's caught his beady eye. Fraenkel and I pause and rest, and then he'll come back to the sledge for the axe or the spade, and dig or hack until he's verified what's there.

Sometimes it's nothing, or nothing that interests him. Once or twice, it seems worth digging out, and he'll take more time, and hack away until he has a little block or bundle in his hands. Another twig or scrap of mud to intertwine with the other twenty.

Actually, he got to number twenty a few days ago, on August 26th. They're a funny set of little packages, each like a small Christmas parcel, loosely wrapped round with string.

Most of the time, it's a bit of clay, or a fragment of moss he finds. But number twenty had leaves, bits of driftwood, and shells. A treasure trove. They were all there in a clod of clay under snow near to where we pitched our tent.

Andrée was like a child with a new toy. He stood there hefting the clay in his fist, a smile like a slice of melon cracking his face.

I can understand his joy. Collecting things isn't my own interest. I'm more concerned with the lunar distances. I find the abstraction of calculating helps to keep my mind away from the more banal terrors of our everyday lives.

Whenever I measure a halo, and note down the mathematics in my almanac, I have a sense of keeping control of my destiny. Andrée must feel the same when he ties his frosted lengths of string round each of those little parcels.

Fraenkel? Well, it's more and more a twilight world of drugs for him. Or so I think. I doubt if he's able to bend his mind to the process of scientific investigation any more.

September 3rd. I'm in the boat. Well, nothing unusual in that, you say. But there is. This is the first day of the journey when we've been able to sail for more than a few minutes on end, and still keep in the right general direction.

The sledges are all stowed in place, and all three of us are crouched on the thwarts. We've been taking turns to row for the last two hours, and at the moment it's Fraenkel's stint. I'm sitting beside Andrée, and watching Fraenkel's shoulders bend as he pulls.

We set off this morning at about eleven-fifteen, and we were soon in an area broken with many water-channels. It rapidly became clear that for the first time we were likely to be able to spend a whole day, or very nearly, in the boat.

Andrée turned to us on the banks of an enormous lead. His face was happy.

Load the boat, he said. We can row, gentlemen.

Now, after two hours, we're still rowing, and in the right direction. South-west, for the Seven Islands. The sun still shines, and the weather is crisp and very sharp and invigorating. It's much colder than usual, of course. I realize now how much the temperature is affected by how hard we have to strain to pull the sledges.

Here I could freeze. My fingers are numb in my gloves, and I can hardly hold the pencil. I rather welcome the change when it comes to be my turn to row. We've had to make the alterations more frequent to keep the men resting from growing more cold than they can stand.

We're not alone out on the water. There are plenty of seals, dipping and plunging like so many porpoises. Once or twice they come up right beside the boat, and I could even reach out, I think, and stroke a whisker sometimes if I chose.

We're not shooting today. It would be too much of a

danger to rock the boat. I've seen Fraenkel look up sadly once or twice at the gulls. I know he'd like to take a pot shot and bring one down as we move. But it wouldn't be worth the risk of tipping everything into the water.

To right and left, the great banks of ice-cliff rear up into the sky. You know what it's like in summer, in Norrland, Anna. Lying back in a punt with the sun in your eyes, and the clouds purling through everlasting blue. On either hand the wooded hills, a wonderland of green and brown.

Imagine it all struck to white. A series of moving photographs, turned solid and rolled out in series from a magic lantern. Only the voice of the lecturer, commenting on the incidental beauties, is absent.

I've tried to take photographs myself. But somehow the scene is too much for my imagination. After the third or fourth, I grew tired. It needs a more subtle reincarnation than the cold frame of the shutter and the dark-room.

September 4th. I wasn't alone, it seems, in being so moved by the row on the lake. It's the following morning, and once again I've had a chance to look into Andrée's diary.

I don't always like what I read, but I need to know. For the moment I just want to add one thing. In case his own diary gets lost.

'Only the shriek of ivory gulls and the splashing of the seals when they dived and the short orders of the steersman broke the silence. We knew that we were moving onwards more quickly than usual and at every turn of the leads we asked ourselves in silence if we might not possibly journey on in this glorious way to the end.'

Yes. In silence. The silence. No wonder that he repeats the word. There was nothing more wonderful than that. One day, perhaps the silence will be all that remains.

The snow falling. And the ice glittering. And our own bones white for ever, like the fur of the bears and the wings of the gulls and the drift of the clouds in the empty sky.

In the silence. The last silence that covers all.

September 5th, 1897. Yesterday was my birthday, Anna, and I'm twenty-five years old. Andrée has agreed for once to give Fraenkel a hand in preparing breakfast, and I'm being allowed to be a sluggard.

It's not just in honour of my advancing years. I had a very bad spill in the soup yesterday, and Andrée fears that I may catch pneumonia. I've told him I won't, and I'm quite all right, but he's growing quite obsessive about our health.

So I've let him have his way. It's a rare luxury to be lying here abed, and hearing the other two shifting the boxes to and fro, and rearranging the things on the sledges. I'm so used to doing all that myself at this time of day.

Not that it's early. I see from my chronometer that it's nearly noon, and I don't suppose we'll be ready to break camp much before the evening. So I ought to have time to finish all I have to tell you.

The spill, first of all. Somehow it always seems to be my misfortune to have the falls. Fraenkel gets his ankle or his knee dislocated, Andrée suffers from depression. Strindberg is the man to tip himself into the water.

That's the mythology of our expedition. To some extent we do all run quite true to form. Yesterday was my worst immersion so far. Let me tell you about this greasy, slippery, yellow-brown, mushy viscosity we call the soup.

It's not soup, of course. Although much of the stuff we drink has a very similar consistency. Did I mention that we'd been experimenting with algae? I don't think I did.

It helps the flavour. We shred or slice in the strips of algae, and then add Stauffer's pease-soup mixture, with a variable dosage of bear's fat, or bear's beef, to give it body. The final product is a hot, steamy, fairly tasteless version of what we have to plough through in our snow-boots whenever we reach the edge of a lead.

It's terribly treacherous. We reach the brink of the lead, and the boat suddenly sloughs in through a thick – sometimes almost a metre thick – soggy margin of sludge. One of us has to leap out and haul it the last few centimetres to the hard ice on the shore.

This is the awkward part. You never know quite how deep it is, or where to find a firm foothold. Imagine yourself nearly waist deep in a sort of marmalade of freezing snow-melt. It isn't pleasant, I can tell you.

185

Yesterday, it got the better of me. We were loading the sledges into the boat for a short crossing, and I lost my footing. I went in over my head, dragging the whole sledge, contents and all, down and over with me.

A good thing it's your birthday, Andrée said, as they helped me out. I'll bet our whole stock of bread and biscuits is ruined.

Alas, Anna, he was right. I'd been carrying the dry food — not just the bread and biscuits, as Andrée said, but the sugar, too, and a fair amount of powdered stuff in packets — and it was all soaked and damaged.

We laid it out on the snow, and examined the limp containers. There wasn't much to be done, except try and dry what we could, and reserve the remainder to eat wet. Wet sugar, wet soup-mixture. It's a grim thought.

We had some of the bread fried for my birthday dinner, with goose-liver paste, and then Stauffer-cake with syrup sauce. There was a bear-steak first, thin slabs kept warm and unfrozen all day under our leather waistcoats as we marched.

The body is a fine de-froster. We still work up quite a sweat as we pull the sledges. The meat feels like a loose extra heart under the leather. It sometimes moves to and fro, or slips down, and we joke about each other's guts coming out, with the strain.

September 9th. Four days gone since I wrote. How much our moods alter, Anna! Today Andrée went into the sludge, thus breaking the pattern. He lay there on his back, spreadeagled like a polecat nailed by a gamekeeper on a wall, until we threw him out an oar, and he got to land.

Sic transit gloria mundi. It's hard to play the great leader when you're dragging down your breeches, and hopping about on one leg to keep warm. But I envy Andrée his good fortune. At least he managed to go in without spilling the things on his sledge.

For my part I seem to have become the depressed one. Even the little comedies of the journey no longer much amuse. I couldn't even raise a smile this morning when we solved the problem of the sea-serpent.

Yes, sea-serpent. Several times one or other of us had

186

been seeing a monster with two humps and a long neck finishing in a whiskered snout. It used to surface and then disappear in a lead. Moving very fast. Sleek and grey-black.

None of us knew what it was. Well, now we do know. It's a walrus. Nothing more esoteric or dangerous than that. The point is that a pair of them — mother and baby, maybe — can sometimes be seen swimming in partnership, the one behind the other. This makes for the double hump, the dromedary effect, as Fraenkel calls it.

Look, he said today, pointing across a lead.

We followed his raised arm, and there, out in the middle of the water, was the characteristic double-back.

Watch, said Fraenkel, and he bent and picked up a loose fragment of ice. With a long lobbing motion, he tossed it towards the monster, and there was a sudden flurry, and grunting in the water.

Two astonished whiskered heads turned and stared at us, honking plaintively, where only a sweep of snaky tail had been evident before.

As I say, Andrée and Fraenkel were much amused, but I couldn't find the energy to laugh. A dark cloud seems to have settled over my spirits again.

One reason may be what's happening between Andrée and Fraenkel. More and more I feel that they've come to behave as a couple. I almost find myself writing a married couple, but I draw the line at believing that.

At first, Fraenkel and I were thrown together a good deal, and Andrée tried to maintain his *de haut en bas* manner towards the two of us. We were very much what he once, in an unguarded moment, said that we were. His handmaidens.

Of course, he's older. And it was a joke. But he seemed to derive a lot of pleasure from being waited on, hand and foot, as it were. And by two strapping men, who might have been his grown-up sons.

He seemed to want to look after us, and at the same time to be attended to by us, and treated with a proper deference. It might be, well I don't know, just because he never married, and had children of his own.

Anyway, that's all changed. Not suddenly, but grad-

187

ually, he's come to behave towards Fraenkel as if towards a favourite child. His first-born, and his heir. And I don't like the change.

I was Andrée's partner before ever Fraenkel appeared on the scene. We were never close, but I was always the senior, and the more expert, member of the crew. Now it seems that this curious affinity he has for Fraenkel has caused Andrée to make me feel left out of things.

I've read before about snow-jealousy, of course. This tendency to feel slighted by some member of the crew is common amongst sailors on long voyages, and many Arctic explorers have written passages explaining its effects. I'm making allowances.

But there are details hard to swallow. Fraenkel's foot, for instance, is getting worse and worse. Today it was so swollen and raw that he could only help our progress by pushing. Andrée and I had to take it in turns to go back and bring up his sledge.

I don't mind this. I accept that the foot is very sore. But Andrée seems to go overboard in his worry and sympathy. Night after night, he'll sit here in the tent massaging Fraenkel's foot in his lap, and rubbing it with a liniment.

I suppose it helps. But he's never offered to do the same for me when I have a pain. He's much more likely to grumble about the trouble I'm causing.

Besides, this isn't all. It's always Fraenkel who gets a word of praise when he downs an ivory gull with his rifle or finds a particularly interesting sample for Andrée's specimen collection.

However. This isn't really the worst. I'm skirting round what happened last night.

I was awakened in the small hours by what I thought at first was the sound of a large animal snuffling round the outside of the tent. I lay for a moment in a half doze, wondering where the shot-gun was. Then I came fully awake, and lay very still.

I realized that the noises I'd heard were coming from my right-hand side, and that they were being produced by movements inside the tent. Indeed, inside the sleeping-bag.

Andrée had been sleeping more or less regularly in the middle, and Fraenkel was on the far outside position. When I turned my head, I could see Andrée raised up, apparently on his elbow, half bending over Fraenkel, who was prone in his usual face down on the pillow position.

Fraenkel was grunting, and seemed to be trying to thresh to and fro, while Andrée held him still. Andrée's hands were pressed down onto Fraenkel's shoulder blades. The upper part of his body was outside the bag, his dark bearded face shadowy, but gazing down on Fraenkel.

Fraenkel's face was turned towards me, on the pillow, his eyes closed, and his features oddly contorted, as if he was in the throes of a nightmare. He was evidently groaning and muttering in his sleep.

It's all right, I heard Andrée murmur, his mouth close to Fraenkel's ear. It'll soon be over.

Then Fraenkel seemed to arch his back, almost throwing Andrée aside. He seemed to sigh, and then he was still.

Andrée rolled back, and then slid down under the covers again. I lay very still, and I don't think he realized that I was awake.

This is all that happened, Anna, and I suppose, yes, let's suppose, that Fraenkel was feverish, and groaning in his dreams, and that Andrée, awakened as I had been, was trying to calm him down. That's all it was.

Perhaps. But even so, I don't imagine that Andrée would have taken so much trouble if the man experiencing the nightmare had been his old comrade, Nils Strindberg.

One last word. I had a chance to read a bit of his diary again. Let me quote you how he sums up yesterday.

'On such a journey as this there is developed a sense both of the great and the little. The great nature and the little food and other details.'

The great nature. If that's what he and Fraenkel are busy with, I want no part of their strange affairs.

Goodnight, Anna. I really do feel most low today. I shall try to be more cheerful when I write again.

We have decided to winter on the ice. No more daily journeys. No more falling in the soup, or hanging down

189

crevasses. From now on we're going to drift with the tides.

It may surprise you, Anna, I know. This was precisely the option we rejected at the very beginning. None of us was prepared to contemplate the inaction. We thought that we had to move by our own efforts, or else grow lethargic, and lose hope.

That all changed on the night of September 12th. We rose as usual, then, quite late in the day, and it was evening before we were ready to break camp. There was some snow falling, and it was very cold.

But we had no reason to suppose that anything would delay our march. Until the wind rose. At first it was only a light breeze, lifting the new-fallen snow in white flurries, and drawing sweeps along the ice.

Each of us wore our snow-glasses, and muffled up well at the neck, as we loaded the sledges, and arranged our harness. There was a brief discussion about our method of progress, as often, before we struck out.

Fraenkel's foot by then was a little better, but it still had a long way to go. Unfortunately, my own feet had started to hurt, and the strain of drawing Fraenkel's sledge as well as our own was telling rather badly on both Andrée and me.

I'll try pulling for a while again today, Fraenkel offered, but he didn't sound keen.

Andrée turned to me.

How's your foot, Nils, he asked.

It ached whenever I leaned on it. I flexed my toes in my shoe, and said nothing. By now, the wind was starting to howl, and the snow was coming up in whirling gusts. Our clothes were already powdered with fresh white, and we hadn't moved a yard.

It'll be on our backs, Andrée said, his words partly muffled as he stared round into the wind. We could give it a try.

But the wind was increasing in force every minute. I fumbled in the instrument box on my sledge and got out the wind-gauge. The velocity was twelve metres per second. The most severe we'd had. And it was still rising.

I almost fell over as I walked back to the box and put the wind-gauge away. Andrée was holding his hat on, and Fraenkel sat hunched up against the runners of his sledge.

190

None of us wanted to say what seemed to be inevitable.

Let's go, Andrée said, and he led the way, drawing his own sledge with firm, steady steps.

Fraenkel and I watched him recede into the swirl of drifting flakes. The wind was hard north-east, absolutely in the right direction for our march towards the base at Spitzbergen. But this wasn't the point. The force of the blast was going to throw us off balance.

I looked at Fraenkel and shrugged my shoulders. Then I followed Andrée into the tunnel of the storm. The wind hit me like a swung spade between the shoulder blades, and I found it hard to maintain an even step. Ahead of me, the flakes of snow streaked forward like icy motes of dust in the slipstream of a fast carriage.

I paused, and turned. There was no sign of Fraenkel. The snow in my face was bitter-cold. My cheeks felt instantly raw and chapped. We hadn't tried to march before in this kind of storm.

I could just see Andrée ahead of me, a vague blur in the driving snow. As I watched, the direction of the wind seemed to veer a fraction, and I saw him stumble, and almost fall. I unharnessed myself, and ran forward towards him, the great force of the wind shoving me on like a giant hand.

Andrée, I called, and I saw him stop and turn.

Look, I said, as I came up to him, panting. I think we'll have to camp until this is over.

Andrée said nothing. He stared into the snow, his lips compressed.

It's too hard, I said.

Andrée lifted his hands, then let them fall.

We'll rest for an hour, and see if the storm abates, he said.

So I trudged back, and found Fraenkel, and helped him push his sledge forward to where mine stood beside Andrée's. Then we spent a laborious hour unpacking everything we'd just so carefully packed, and getting the tent up in the blizzard.

It wasn't easy. It took all our strength to hold the canvas firm, and drive in the stakes. The wind was like a mad schoolboy, everywhere at once, getting in the way, and howling with laughter.

191

The snow beat in our faces. Wherever we were, it seemed to be driving straight at us. The direction of the wind hadn't changed. It was still dead north-east, but we had to keep moving to and fro, and there was always a point where it met us head on.

I checked the velocity again before we all got back into the tent. I checked it twice to make sure. It was fifteen by then. The kind of wind I hadn't known before.

Inside the tent, we all sat huddled together shoulder to shoulder on top of the sleeping-bag. We weren't tired, and we were all bad-tempered over the change of plan.

I won't bore you with the details of our conversation, Anna. You can guess the drift. This was the first day we'd had to cancel any advance because of weather conditions. Before we'd always managed a march of an hour or two, at worst.

Seven minutes, Andrée muttered, bitterly. We marched for seven minutes today.

You did, I said. And so did I. Fraenkel never moved.

Fraenkel was rubbing his ankle with his hands.

Strindberg, he said, savagely. If you'd been pulling your fair share of the weight, I'd never have had this bad foot. So keep your hoity-toity little sneers to yourself.

It's all right, Fraenkel, said Andrée, putting his hand out to touch Fraenkel's leg. We're all a little jumpy today, that's all.

I'm not jumpy, I said. I'm just tired of this waste of time.

Be quiet, Nils, said Andrée, then: That's an order.

Then he reached over and began to help Fraenkel massage his foot, rubbing liniment in, and unwinding his sock for him, while I sat back and nursed my own feet as best I could on my own.

That night, the night of September 12th, we stayed in the tent, and heard the wind howl, and went round and round our troubles. But we came to no conclusion. We went to sleep at dawn, and woke the next day thinking we might be able to break camp and march forward as before.

But the snow was still falling thickly, and the wind held a steady twelve metres per second. Worst of all, the direction had changed a point or two, and it was now blowing from the east. If we moved, we'd have it full on the sides

192

of the sledges, with every chance of them being tipped over the first time we encountered a hummock.

It means another day wasted, Andrée said, and we had to agree with him.

I spent the time reading, and Fraenkel engrossed himself with one of his awful poems. Andrée? Andrée went out and in like a jack-in-the-box, like those two little figures on your mother's Swiss clock, Anna. Telling the hours, and collecting his specimens, and making drawings of the formation of the ice.

So the hours passed. But the worst news came when I took our position with the universal instrument, and it became clear that, despite the wind, we had actually drifted away from the coast of Spitzbergen. There no longer seemed any hope that the current was going to let us get there, however hard we marched, or whatever luck we had with the wind.

This was a bitter pill to swallow. We seemed likely to be carried by the current somewhere to the west of Spitzbergen. So we had only one strategy left, it seemed.

We must dig in, said Andrée, as we sat with cups of our precious coffee, after midnight on the morning of September 14th. Build a shelter here on the floe.

We lay down with the wind still howling, and the snow piling up outside the tent. It was cold, and I felt very lonely. I didn't want to think about Andrée and Fraenkel, and I took two aspirin tablets, and went to sleep.

September 15th. Several things have happened. Three of them really rather good. I'm in fresh spirits.

First of all, we've moved to a new floe. The one we were on seemed too small, and we made a big effort, and got everything into the boat, and ferried ourselves and all our possessions over to a larger floe.

The work seemed to help our mood. It's not so much, I think, that we need to be marching on, it's more that we need to be engaged in some obviously profitable or productive activity. Crossing to the new floe gave us a sense of purpose.

Once we were settled, we looked round for a suitable area, and I at once organized a plan to build a snow-hut. There's a reasonable dip in one area of the ice, and we've made that the building-site. Each day we heap up blocks of ice and snow, and pour water over them. When it freezes up at night, the water forms a kind of frozen mortar, and we have a solid, durable wall for our dwelling-place. It will take time to finish, but we've made a good start.

I shall say more about the hut later. I have to mention the second good thing that's happened. Andrée shot a seal!

Amazingly enough, it's the first time we've hit one, and it offers an attractive prospect for our future diet, if we can continue to bring them in. One seal will provide enough meat to feed us all for three weeks.

We eat the lot, except for the skin and bones. Even the stomach and the intestines and the liver are reasonably palatable when boiled up in the soup, and seasoned with Mellin's food. The steaks and the blubber are both excellent fried. We are all great seal gourmets, and Fraenkel talks of opening a seal restaurant when we return to Stockholm.

So much for seals. The third thing that has happened is perhaps the best of the lot, although its immediate advantages are few. Yesterday morning, for the first time since July 11th, when we left Danes Island, we saw land.

Andrée again, of course, was the first man to get the sighting. Every day he's climbed a block of ice on some occasion to scan the horizon. I have a lovely photograph of him balancing awkwardly on the car of the balloon, staring into nowhere with his binoculars glued to his eyes. At least, I hope it will be lovely, if it comes out. I sometimes wish I'd brought the materials for developing film with me. It would relieve the tedium.

Anyway, yesterday morning at eleven o'clock, Salomon August Andrée sighted the coastline of White Island – or so we think it is – from a vantage point on our floating island. We all agreed with him that the position made it likely that we are indeed at last somewhere just to the north-east of Spitzbergen. So White Island it probably is.

Alas, we're a long way from the main island, and our cache of stores. And this particular outlying suburb of Spitzbergen doesn't look at all inviting through the

194

glasses. It's just a long low hoop of a mountain, an unbroken arch, like the back of a low-lying whale, or a slightly bent longbow under the sea. And it's all ice. Just one solid block as far as we can see, with a glacier border.

I don't think there's any chance of our attempting to go ashore. It looks entirely inaccessible, except just possibly on the east and west limits. I thought I saw a bear there in the lens.

But there wouldn't be much point in going ashore, anyway. There would be no direct access to the main island, and our food supplies, and so long as this floe we're on keeps drifting, there is now clearly an outside chance that it may take us near to somewhere else more habitable for the winter.

So we're staying put. In good spirits, and with plenty to do for the moment to keep us busy in building the hut and looking out for more seals to shoot. Life doesn't seem so bad after all today.

7
ANNA
1897

IT WAS IN UNCLE JOHAN'S ROOM that I first heard the name of Knut Fraenkel, and learned of his passion for Charles XII. Christmas had been a lonely festival for me, with Nils penned in Stockholm at some family celebration I wasn't bidden to, and the great spruce our Yuletide baubles had swung and glittered from was already sliced in logs, and burned and blackened in the grate for fuel, before I heard from my elusive fiancé again.

He was coming up to Lund later in the month, with a birthday present for his Uncle Johan, who had taken up residence in lodgings near the University, and was reputed to be settled now for good. In Sweden. We must both seize this opportunity, said Nils, to go and see him, before death or final insanity snatched his genius away for ever. So the bouncy letter, arriving on a hard-frozen January 7th, suggested.

I was by no means loath to see Uncle Johan, who had long since taken on the stature of a private myth. He was famous too, now, though more by way of having some *succès de scandale* than for any more solid sort of reputation. My father viewed the journey with some misgivings, and my mother with real distaste.

He's an atheist, she insisted, and a woman-hater. You'll get nothing but scorn and cold potatoes from that quarter. Mark my words.

This was true enough, and I made no objection to my mother's analysis. But I pointed out that Nils was a busy man, and I hadn't seen him for three months. A journey to Stockholm was a long and expensive business, whereas

199

Lund was only a few miles away. Here was an opportunity not to be missed.

Then invite Nils here, my father said. He can see the mad Strindberg over at Lund, and come over to us for a few days before he goes home.

No, I said firmly. I mean to go. But I will ask Nils to come back with me here. Be reasonable, father. It's surely part of my education to meet such a noted man of the theatre.

Notorious, rather, my father said, rather grudgingly, but at last he agreed.

A place was booked for me in the diligence, and I met Nils, as arranged, at the Blue Ribbon Café, surrounded by the malicious faces and the grubby scarves of student artists, drinking imported Pernod, and blackening each other's reputations, exactly as if they were in Paris.

The University of Lund was a narrow, provincial spot in those days, but it had its pretensions to an international style, and its grey stone buildings nursed some small awareness of what was going on in the world of *art nouveau*. There were young men with long hair, and even one with a green carnation, commemorating the dreadful fate of Oscar Wilde.

The finer points of this artificial milieu were lost on me, but I quite enjoyed being eyed by the crowd, as I sat over a glass of tea in a corner, with my hands demurely in my muff, and my veil over my face. I must have looked a fit enough bride for the devil, I suppose, in my tight stays and my sheeny black.

There was more than one young blood there who must have seen me as Uncle Johan did, when we climbed his tortuous stairs, and stooped through the Gothic arch into his alchemist's cell.

Aha, he said, shy but prompt, as he bent to kiss my hand. The fatal woman in person. The Medusa without her snakes.

I coloured at that, and drew my fingers away. My hand crept back like a dubious mouse into the furry recess of my muff, and I stepped aside, nearer to the light from the oriel window.

It was a dim, low room, medieval in character, if not in

200

origin. There was an odd mixture of elements to its make-up. The stone lintel over the fire was topped by a rack of test-tubes, gleaming and sinister with a range of mysterious bright liquids. On the stolid, old-fashioned writing-table under the window, near to where I was standing, there were half-burned candles propped in silver sconces, and another mass of candles, dripping wax, and contorted by flame and wind into weird, fairy-tale shapes, flourished from a huge candelabra hung in the ceiling.

An aspidistra wilted in a very conventional jardinière, and other plants loomed, stooped, and brushed at arms and clothes from every corner where there was space for an urn or a vase.

A large photograph of Strindberg as a young man, fierce and neat in wing collar and brushed hair, surmounted a knurled dagger, forced into a sheath, and looped over a nail in the wall by a leather thong. In the midst of all this, and as it were washing through and half drowning it all, there were books and papers, bound books in tottering racks of shelves, crumpled sheets and finished sheets of manuscripts scattered over the floor, the sofa and the handful of occasional tables.

It was a place of paper, wax and blossom. Dark, full of strange odours, punctuated by rustling and hissing noises. And cold. Icy cold. The window was open, admitting the sound of University clocks in their many steeples chiming hours, and the winter ice laid its hand, from without, on whatever attempted to keep warm within.

I shivered, and moved closer to the fireplace, where a few criss-crossed logs were smoking and smouldering in the grate. There were more, though not many more, in a copper scoop, though no sign of shovel or tongs. I bent, and threw a log onto the thin blaze.

You must be frozen, I said, warming my hands. Living here like this without a stove.

Strindberg said nothing to this, but, with a sudden leap, sprang to the wall, seized the dagger from its sheath, and stabbed ferociously at the air, in several directions.

Astalamancha, he intoned in a low mutter. *Contarme sidarthe. Bewaila miday.*

201

There was more in the same tone, and then he seemed satisfied, calmed down, and replaced the dagger in its sheath. He turned to Nils, and smiled ruefully.

It's the only way, he said, apologetically. The spirits follow me at all times. The Dalmatian dagger thrust is the one thing they fear.

Nils was leaning beneath the test-tubes, amused, it seemed, by all this.

Isn't that blasphemous, he suggested. I thought you'd become a good Catholic now. You said in your letter –

Letters! exclaimed Strindberg. Letters describe yesterday.

Then he picked up one of the silver candlesticks from the writing-table, and approached my seat by the fire. He held the sconce close to my face, and the flame cast shadows up from below.

Delacroix, lac de sang, hanté des mauvaises anges, he murmured slowly. That's Baudelaire on the worst painter of the nineteenth century. But you might well have been one of the bad angels. The wings of hell beat in your very pupils.

Rubbish, Uncle, said Nils equably. That's going too far. Apologize.

But Strindberg had already moved to another tack. He was laying aside the candlestick, making the flame gutter in the breeze from his monkish cloak as he turned. He had picked up a bottle – wine, I thought, from the colour – and was tipping a quantity down his throat. There was a steady gulping noise.

Bats' guts, he said. It cools the spleen.

I saw his face now, for the first time, as he lowered the bottle. The square head, short greying hair, wild in an undergrowth of curl on top. The dark moustache like a sunburst above his lips. And the eyes. The crazy Strindberg eyes. There was no way of describing those.

You see this cane, he said.

He had thrust a black stick, surmounted by the bust of a dog, long-eared and Egyptian-looking, into my lap.

That's gold, he said, reverently, stroking the top of the dog's head. I made it this morning. *Hail the world's soul, and mine, more glad than is/The teeming earth to see the*

202

*long'd-for sun/Peep through the horns of the celestial Ram,/Am I,
to view thy splendour.*

Volpone, murmured Nils.

The very best of the British dramatists, agreed Strindberg, closing one eye, and staring up at me. You haven't an idea of what we're talking about now have you, my little Dolores? It's real gold. That's all you need to know.

I rubbed the dull yellowish stuff with my thumb.

Why are you never still? I asked.

Strindberg got up from his knees, wheezing, and I realized that he wasn't at all well. He was weak, as well as drunk.

Stillness is death, said Strindberg quietly. We each have two guardian angels. Good angels. And while they watch us, we move. And live. That's what I believe. It's from Swedenborg.

Nils took a small, thin blue book from the pocket of his coat.

I brought you this, he said. For your birthday. It's the first English translation.

Strindberg had pulled a pair of round rimless spectacles from some pouch under his robe, and was peering through these, looped over his ears, at the cover of the book.

De Commercio Animae Et Corporis, he said. Originally published in London, in 1769. Thank you, nephew. Where did you get it?

From Swedenborg, said Nils, with a smile.

But Strindberg was not so easily surprised.

I know, he said, slyly. Your fourth man. I read the papers. Lieutenant Swedenborg, who is married to the daughter of Baron Nordenskjöld. He will sail to Danes Island this year as your first reserve. His father-in-law insisted on that, you can bet your boots. And this young lieutenant, who is following in his great ancestor's footsteps, has provided me, through you, with this apt and lovely birthday present.

He threw the little blue volume up in the air, caught it in one hand, and pretended to take a worrying bite, like a bear catching a fish, out of the gilded spine.

Thank you, he said, sincerely. Thank you both.

203

He darted forward, and put his hands on my knees.

Hello, he said. Would you like some wine?

I stared up into the shifting grey depths of his eyes, watching the lights move in them, like clouds over the empty perspectives of sky. There seemed no end to these eyes, no bottom, only layer over layer of agony and playfulness, interleaving, like meat and bread in a sandwich.

Women have souls, I said.

Strindberg laughed.

Souls! he said. Women have arse-holes, like cattle do. And men, like bulls, drop weights down them.

I blushed, not liking this coarse language.

Uncle, said Nils, uncertainly. She's only eighteen.

She is the mistress of Lucifer, said Strindberg, slapping his hands together. Like all her kind. I know about women. They are muck in paddy fields.

A shudder seemed to run through his body, and he stood up, washing his hands in invisible soap, as if they had acquired some taint of pollution by touching my dress.

You're mad, I said calmly.

But Strindberg's mind was off again, on another tangent of its own. He reached for his wine bottle, poured a glassful, and laid it near me on a small side table. Then he tipped the neck to his lips, and began to swallow. After a while, he passed the bottle to Nils, who shook his head.

You want to kiss me, I said suddenly. That's your trouble.

Then I picked up the wine-glass, and stared at him over the rim.

Anna, said Nils, very shocked.

Strindberg pushed his hands through his hair, striding to and fro in the room.

There's a young Norwegian artist, he said. His name is Edvard Munch. I met him last year in Paris, when he did a drawing of me. He has a lithograph I was very much taken by. It's called 'The Vampire'. It shows a young woman, with long black hair, and a thin straight nose, with her mouth dug in a man's neck for blood. That lithograph, I now realize, reminds me of you, Anna. The long hair, and the nose, and the taste for blood. You're a vampire, that's what you are.

204

Nils had taken his watch out, and was making a show of seeming to snap open the case, and inspect the time. He could feel the charge in the air. The flicker of blunted foils had become the clash of iron sabres.

I like your girl, said Strindberg. She's a good whore. I like her spunk.

I lay back, with my hands in my muff, shivering.

No, I said. You don't like me. You just want to — well, you know what you want to do.

Strindberg stood above me, opening the top of his monkish habit to scratch the hairs on his chest. It was a gesture of calculated rudeness.

No, he said simply. I don't know what I want to do. Women make me angry. They make me frightened. I get jealous. I want to be clear and straightforward, like Charles XII. Make war on all the world. Sleep on the ground with my men.

That sounds like Fraenkel, said Nils, trying hard.

Fraenkel, said Strindberg. I despise all classical scholars.

No, said Nils, recovering quickly. Not him. Our third man. Knut Fraenkel is an engineer and poet. He is also a fine athlete and an excellent shot. He was chosen by Andrée from an application list of several hundreds. And he admires Charles XII as the greatest man that Sweden has ever produced.

I'm sorry, I said. I went too far.

But the atmosphere had cooled, and Strindberg ignored me. Swedenborg in his youth was also a soldier, he said. He did some mining work for Charles XII.

Who, after all, was in one respect very like yourself, said Nils, boldly. He abhorred women.

We all laughed. The dagger was back in its sheath, and there was only the flutter of butterflies' wings.

Later, we sat in the Blue Ribbon Café again, Nils and I, and the waiter brought us open sandwiches, and a bottle of cold beer.

You were very flirtatious, Nils said.

You're exactly like your uncle, I replied. He was very rude, and I gave him a piece of my mind. That's all.

Nils turned his glass round and round on the tabletop.

205

Anna, he said. There's something I want to tell you about.

You want to quarrel, I said, wrapping my scarf round my neck.

No, said Nils humbly. I don't. I really don't, Anna.

So what did you want to tell me about? I asked.

The room was crowded, and a group of students in red scarves, and caps, were lifting huge flagons of beer, and singing a bawdy song. One waved to me, and beckoned. I let my eyes drop.

I have a confession to make, said Nils.

I felt my lips tightening, and I looked up, and the student was still watching, and I let my mouth open, and moistened the tips of my teeth with my tongue. The student looked away, and then back. Then he beckoned again.

After his debate with Andrée at the Physics Society, said Nils, choosing his words, and speaking slowly, Eckholm asked me if I would resign from the expedition with him. I nearly did. He was right about the guide-ropes, and the gas-tightness. The balloon won't float for five weeks without sinking.

No, I said gently. But it won't need to.

Then I reached over and stroked his cheek.

I know, I said. Andrée exaggerated. But it doesn't matter.

You see, said Nils. He's right about the main things. We can get there. And back, too. There's no doubt of that.

Eckholm was in the wrong, I said soothingly. I know that. You mean to go, Nils, whatever happens. I've known that's true for months.

The student at the other table got up to go. I felt his eyes on me, but I didn't look up.

Nils, I said. There's something I'm puzzled about. Why has Andrée chosen Fraenkel? He sounds like an ordinary country boy. Someone who shoots and runs well, and writes a bit of poetry on the side.

He's a good engineer, said Nils.

I'd like some more beer, I said, and then, as Nils was signalling to the waiter. Just an engineer? That isn't much of a qualification, surely? He could have had anyone he

206

asked for, after all this publicity you've been having. Nansen, even. After all, Eckholm was a real Arctic expert.

More beer, please, said Nils to the waiter, and then: Well, you'll have to judge what qualities Knut Fraenkel has for yourself. We'll meet him next month in Stockholm, before he goes to Paris. He's to spend time there with Swedenborg, learning to fly balloons with Lachambre, as I did last year.

And that was all that was said on the subject of Knut Fraenkel, until my first meeting with him at the Royal Opera House in Stockholm, at the Première of *A Masked Ball* on February 1st.

All theatres are much the same, I suppose, on a grand occasion, but the Royal Stockholm Opera House was somewhere I'd never been before. It was unique, and dazzling, to my provincial eyes.

Nowadays, up here in Glasgow, and I imagine even down in London, theatre-going has become a rather subdued business. There isn't the same sense of style and display that there used to be before the war. In the 90s, and in Europe, that style and display were often carried near to extremes.

For the first performance of the new season, with a star soprano singing the leading role in *Un Ballo in Maschera*, there wasn't a man to be seen without a tail-coat and a high collar. As for the women, they positively dripped with diamonds and pearls. Our Scandinavian taste in ornament was a florid one in those days, and excess was the rule.

My mother was very pleased to have seen me invited by Nils to this grand occasion, and she had me decked out in a splendid ball dress in light buff satin, with a wasp waist to do credit to a queen, and an ivory fan, painted with Chinese mandarins, that had belonged to my grandmother.

Everywhere there was the glitter of crystal, the heavy scent of musk and saffron, the low buzz of conversation, and the clink of glass and metal. We stood, Nils and I, near to the bar, clasping our thin vials of champagne, and nibbling caviar from crisp English biscuits. The First Act was over, and the main business of the evening, the parade with fan and conning-glass, the gossip over wine and canapé, had already begun.

There's Fraenkel, said Nils suddenly, touching my arm. I thought he might be here.

I followed the direction of his gaze to where a small group of young men, mostly in military dress, were laughing and smoking at a corner table. One of them caught Nils's eye, exclaimed, and rose to his feet. Nils beckoned, and he excused himself from his friends, and came over.

Fraenkel, said Nils. You look as fit as a fiddle. I want you to meet my fiancée, Miss Anna Charlier.

Fraenkel stooped, lifted my hand in his gloved hand, and lightly brushed the suede with his lips. Then he looked up, and I had a chance to study his face.

He was very tall and broad, much like my father in build, and his features were firmly moulded in a rather square, defended-looking head. His eyes glared out with a kind of abused intensity from deep hollows under his brows. The whole effect was of cannon blazing away from a castle under siege.

Well, he said, you're aptly named. Do you know that the early hydrogen balloons were called charliers – after Charles, the Frenchman, who invented them?

Nils laughed.

I never knew that myself, he said. So I shall be under Anna's protection, even above the Arctic sea. Have a drink, Fraenkel.

But Fraenkel shook his head.

I'm in training, he said. No alcohol except simple beer, and none at all at night. It affects the breathing, and then the heart.

My dear Fraenkel, said Nils, filling his own glass and mine from a bottle wrapped in a white napkin that stood near by on a marble table. Be advised by a younger man. You don't go down to Paris for over a month, and, whatever you do with Lachambre there, you won't be high enough to be short of air. So have some champagne.

He waved the bottle, but Fraenkel shook his head.

No, he said. I've been reading about Glaisher and

208

Coxwell. I'm not taking any risks. Who knows? I might get a chance to beat their height record.

Nils compressed his lips.

Now, now, Fraenkel, he said, evenly. You'll frighten Anna.

But Fraenkel had already fixed me with his glaring eye. His short hair seemed to bristle like the quills on an angry porcupine. He spoke with a savage, deliberate jerkiness.

In 1882, he said, they made their famous ascent from Wolverhampton, in England. Their last recorded observation was made at 9,000 metres, when Glaisher became unconscious. We have no record of the height at which Coxwell, who was almost paralysed, opened the valve with his teeth.

But they were higher than the summit of Mount Everest, I said, remembering my school geography. Don't worry, Nils. It's not the height I'm worried about. It's the distance you'll be from land.

The second bell was ringing, and the crowd was beginning to disperse for the Second Act. I drained my glass, and set it on the counter.

Land, said Fraenkel, baring his teeth in a grin. We'll walk on ice, we'll shoot bears. We'll eat like kings. I'll treat you both in the next interval.

Then he was gone back to his friends, loping through the tables like a prowling tiger, and Nils and I made our way to our box. In the next interval, Fraenkel was as good as his word. He beckoned us over to a table where he was sitting on his own, a silver bucket at his elbow.

Champagne on me this time, he said, with a flourish of his hand. Forgive me, Miss Charlier. I'm so wrapped up in the expedition, I think of nothing else but balloons.

Of course, I said, as we settled on cane chairs. By the way, I added, pronouncing my name in the Swedish way, it's Charlier. Not Charlier.

Charles is my favourite name, said Fraenkel.

Yes, I said, after Charles XII.

He threw his head back, roaring aloud with laughter. It was like a forest being shaken by a great gale. He seemed to explode with energy in all directions.

Nils, he said, shaking his finger. You've been talking

209

about me. Yes, I do admire the great King, Anna. We must go together and do homage at the statue in Kungstradgarden Park.

He was pouring champagne for us, the plump bottle reduced to a strangled goose in his powerful hands. I had a fleeting thought of what it must be like to be gripped and held by those hands. Then Nils was objecting.

Great King, indeed, Fraenkel, he said. He was no more than a mad dog. He had all Europe about his heels before he died. His own officers had to put a ball through his brain.

Fraenkel shook his head, as if he were a beaver coming out of water.

Stop teasing, Strindberg, he said, with a frown. It's a serious charge. You know as well as I do that old story is long discredited. The last time they took the skull out, the experts were quite sure he was shot by a musket ball, fired from a considerable distance. He was not betrayed, and he was not assassinated. He was shot by an enemy sniper, leaning with his arms on the rampart.

At Frederikshall, in 1716, I put in.

But Fraenkel was half on his feet, staring through the crush of people.

Swedenborg! he called, in a deep bellow, that made several heads turn in disapproval. Then, sitting down again, and reaching the bottle out of its bucket: Let's drink to the two of them. The great King, and the man who got his boats across the water that day, Emanuel Swedenborg. Here in the presence of the noble grandson himself. And what a way to have your family ennobled!

A neat, handsome young man in the uniform of an officer in an Artillery Regiment was clicking his heels at our table, his hand on the pommel of a dress sword. He looked every inch what he was, a soldier and an aristocrat.

Not exactly the grandson, he said with a smile. But certainly, a direct descendant. How are you, Strindberg?

The better for seeing you fit and ready to take my place, said Nils, joking. But there was an undercurrent of resentment, I thought, in how he spoke. He felt that he was being forced from his shoes by this well-connected young soldier.

210

Let me introduce my fiancée, said Nils, and Swedenborg bowed, and then smiled politely to me.

Good news, indeed, he said. I'm married myself, Miss Charlier, and I recommend the condition. All good balloonists require some guide-rope, to tie them down to the earth. What do you say, Fraenkel?

Fraenkel frowned.

A balloon is no place for a woman, he said seriously. You both know my views, and they won't change. I think we're all going on a dangerous mission, and one only fit for men. It won't be a birthday party up there at the Pole, you know.

What will it be? I asked, furious and worried.

Honour or death, said Fraenkel, tapping his fingers on the table. A chance to make a name, or to lie for ever forgotten in the snow.

Yes, I suggested, very angry. Like Paktul, when your precious King broke him on the wheel. You men are all the same. Desperate for fame. Always wanting to *do* something. Why can't you simply *be* something for a change? Doesn't that matter, too?

But Fraenkel wasn't listening. There was a faraway glaze in his eyes, and he seemed to be tapping on the table like someone signalling out of an earth-hole, to someone remote in the past, or in the future.

Family commitments, he said. They're a drag on that, either way.

Once again, the bell was ringing, and women were bending to pick up gloves and programmes, men to secure their canes.

You must excuse me, said Swedenborg smoothly, clicking his heels again. I ought to go back to my wife and my father-in-law. Will you join us all for a last glass of champagne when the show is over, Strindberg? I should like Miss Charlier to meet my wife, and I know the baron will be enchanted.

He gestured across the room, to where an elderly man with a monocle was deep in conversation with a pretty, dark-haired girl. There was a curious resemblance, even at a distance. I recognized the elderly man from seeing him in the chair at Nils's lecture.

211

With much pleasure, said Nils, bobbing.

He was clearly delighted at the opportunity to be seen drinking after the show with the great Baron Nordens-kjöld. There were still very few men in Sweden more famous.

That's all arranged then, said Swedenborg, affably. I'll see you in a moment, Fraenkel.

He bowed to me, and was away, threading the crowd like so many beads on a string. He had that kind of inevitable confidence.

Fraenkel watched him go, on his feet now, and hulking over the silver bucket, his fingers clenched on the rim. He managed to seem awkward and intense, whatever he was doing. It was as if some pressure of emotion in him was always just about to come to boiling point, and issue in anger, or violence.

That style, he said, in frank admiration. I would have given my right hand to be a soldier.

Then why aren't you? I asked, as we all three walked towards the stairs.

I was thinking of my father, and how he had given his right hand, and had nothing back in return. It seemed to me that no one should talk of giving his right hand for anything. But I watched Fraenkel's face as he spoke, and I knew that here was one of the few men who meant what he said. He admired soldiers, above all mankind, and he would readily have paid whatever price was asked, for the right to wear the uniform.

What was the difficulty? I asked, when he said nothing.

We had reached the first landing now, and Fraenkel was about to part company with us, and follow Swedenborg to the box he was sharing with Nordens-kjöld.

I had an operation, he said slowly. For a nervous complaint.

Then, with a sort of gruff, brutal imitation of Swedenborg's bow and nod, he turned and walked away, a tiger still, but a tiger, I now saw, bleeding inside from a terrible wound, a wound that no time or fortune could ever heal.

tion that music can bring, we drifted down the long flights of marble stairs. All round us, the audience hissed and murmured like a great sea, absorbed in what it had heard, flowing back into the nets of the plot, seething forward into the frozen night.

Outside the cloakroom, we met Swedenborg, helping his pretty wife into her mink stole. Beside him stood Nordenskjöld, a grey cape over one shoulder, a thin, gold-headed stick in his gloved hand.

His eyes, quick and alert over the precise goatee beard, roved up and down the powdery white and pink of my bare shoulders.

For the third time that evening, I heard my name spoken, and enjoyed a man bowing over my hand. Then we were all gathering coats and capes, and carriages were arriving, and I was being handed up to a seat beside the baron, and the wheels were rattling over cobbles, and along avenues where the pines were thick with clouds of snow.

Opposite to me in the landau sat Nils, deferential and yet elegant, as he slumped over his cane against the window. At his left, throbbing and contained like some great volcano, hunched the uneasy bulk of Fraenkel, a frown on his face, and his eyes fixed through the glass out into the winter night, as if he was already probing it for some secret that would aid or obstruct the polar flight.

I felt the gentle pressure of the old baron's shoulder against my breast, knowing that he was exploiting the licence of the landau's restricted space to ease himself just a fraction closer than necessary. I listened, we all listened, as he talked of how the idea for the polar balloon flight had been born.

It was after a meeting of the S.A.G.S., said Nordens-kjöld. On the evening of 16th March, 1894, I remember I invited Andrée to walk some distance home with me. It was a misty night, and we strolled together up the Drott-ninggatan. I wanted to speak to him about the use of balloons on Arctic expeditions. In fact, my own interest at that time was in a possible voyage to the Antarctic, using a captive balloon.

Nordenskjöld stroked his beard, thinking.

213

Then Andrée plucked up his courage, he said, with a smile. He mentioned his idea of making a voyage across the North Pole in a free balloon.

Outside, I could see a group of children, up very late for some outing, no doubt, slapping their gloved hands on their sides, as they waited tiredly in the snow for some vehicle that was to take them home to bed. I saw Nordens-kjöld follow my eyes, and nod, appreciatively. Then his eyes came back into the landau, and he fixed them on my face.

I told Andrée, he said, that, when he was ready with a firm plan, he could count on my full support.

Nils leaned forward.

We owe you everything, sir, he said.

Nordenskjöld laughed, slapping me lightly on the knee with his gloves.

Not everything, Strindberg, he said. You found this little minx here for yourself. You're a lucky man.

Before Nils could answer, Fraenkel spoke from his corner, where he had evidently been brooding his question for some time. It came out with a long wheeze, like a gush of air from the spout of a sounding whale.

Baron Nordenskjöld, he said, humping over towards the old man, his hands on his two knees. We have just seen a three-act opera about the assassination of a Swedish monarch. I want to ask you. What is your honest opinion of Gustavus III? Do you think that he was a man in any way of the calibre of Charles XII?

But I was never to know the baron's views on this momentous topic. The carriage had already slowed, and stopped, and the door was being opened by a liveried servant. Through the open doorway, I could see Swedenborg and his pretty wife, who had arrived before us in their two-in-hand. I saw Swedenborg reaching up to fasten the long whip on the hook beside the carriage.

Then the baron was down on the pavement, reaching up to offer me his arm, and far more interested in my own chatter about our house in Klippan, and my thoughts about the opera, than in anything Knut Fraenkel might wish to argue or dispute with him on the subject of Swedish kings, or Nils Strindberg, I fear, either, on the

214

subject of polar voyages. At any rate, it was to me, and largely to me only, that the baron devoted the rest of his evening until the last cup of coffee was drunk, and the last cigar stubbed out in its crystal ashtray.

Goodnight, my dear, he said finally, kissing my hand. We shall meet again.

But we didn't meet again, alas, not ever. It was Fraenkel that I met again, more awkward and domineering than before, when he came back from his balloon training in Paris, and the expedition had sailed again for Danes Island. There from the decks of the *Lofoten*, I looked down again on the balloon-house, and the hydrogen gas apparatus, and a single solitary figure, standing with a rifle under its arm. The figure of Knut Fraenkel.

I've been shooting gulls, Fraenkel said, when I met him on the beach. For practice.

It was June 27th, and the sun was burning down as if it was a summer's day in Italy. Fraenkel was wearing only a thin shirt, open at the neck, and his sleeves were rolled up to the elbows. He rolled them down as I approached, evidently feeling that there might be some impropriety in talking to me, as it were, half-dressed.

Look, he said, laying the body of a gull out for me against a rock.

It was all white, wings and underparts, but the tail and wing-tips were flecked with black. It lay spread out on the black of the rock, almost as if alive, but resting like an ermine moth against a window.

These are what we shall eat, he said, if we come down in the snow. These, and bears.

I turned away, and looked out across the bay, to where the steamer lay at anchor. Some distance from it was the *Virgo*, and beyond that, the gunboat the Swedish government had loaned Andrée this year, the *Svenskund*. A second pinnace was leaving the *Lofoten*, and I saw the light sparkle from glass and metal as the passengers made themselves comfortable for the short row to shore.

Strindberg is developing film, said Fraenkel. He has a little dark-room in the bowels of the ship.

He said this, it seemed to me, as if he thought that all

215

decent men ought to be out in the fresh air, getting some healthy exercise. He made a picture of fitness himself, like a prize fighter, with his muscles bulging under the cotton of the shirt.

You don't like him much, I suggested.

The other passengers from the first pinnace had walked towards the balloon-house, chaperoned this year by Andrée, who was doing the guided tour in person. I watched my mother, once again brisk and lively after the convalescent voyage, deep in conversation with the expedition's leader. As always, she was anxious to buttonhole the most important man present, and to be seen to be well-connected.

No, said Fraenkel, grounding his rifle. I don't dislike Strindberg. But, then, I don't much like him, either. On this kind of expedition, liking is unimportant, even dangerous. It could be a distraction. The important thing is loyalty. And you can be sure, he added, straightening his shoulders, that I shall be loyal to Nils Strindberg to the death.

You're not swearing an oath, I said. Relax. I'm sure you're loyal to Nils. And, anyway, let's hope it won't come to the death.

Fraenkel rubbed his thumb around the muzzle of the rifle. Then he laid it down beside the gull against the rock.

It might, he said, almost hopefully. But the better prepared we are, the more chance we shall have of coming through. Let Nansen be our example.

Nansen and Charles XII, I murmured.

But Fraenkel wasn't going to rise to this. He only grinned, and shrugged his big shoulders.

Tell me something, I said. I suppose, if all goes well, you'll over-fly the Pole and then land somewhere in Russia.

We shall land at the Pole, said Fraenkel, proudly. And plant the Swedish flag in the ice. Or on the ground. Whichever it is.

The sun was beginning to burn my neck, and I wished I'd brought my parasol. I eased the shawl off my shoulders, and fastened it round my waist. The action strained the material of the dress over my bust, and I was sharply aware, under the watery silk, of its divided outline. But Fraenkel showed no interest.

216

Shall we stroll? I suggested.

For a time we walked in silence, past the hydrogen gas apparatus, and past Pike's House, where the pigeons were dully cooing and purling from their loft, and then out along the headland to where Nils had erected his ingenious weather-cock.

Yes, I said. But after the Pole. Where will you go?

We shall drift, said Fraenkel, circling his hand in the air. Drift South. Wherever the wind takes us. With a favourable breeze we could sail right round the world, and land again here at Danes Island.

He grinned at me, enjoying his joke.

In eighty days, I said, staring back along the shore to where the balloon-house reared under its little mountain. And to win a bet, I added, which I am now going to make, that you and Nils will never return from the polar voyage alive.

A cloud had come over the sun, and the Arctic chill struck, sharp as a razor. I shivered, and put my shawl back over my shoulders. Fraenkel looked quite impervious to the cold, as if his shirt were made of thick fur.

No, Miss Verne, he said, solemnly. I make no bets about our lives. That's not the point. The point is whether or not we can reach the North Pole.

I turned and faced him.

Andrée, I said suddenly. Isn't he rather old?

He's forty-two, said Fraenkel, imperturbably. He's as strong as a horse. And besides, he has the will.

Does Nils? I asked. Does Nils, Fraenkel?

He looked at me with that great fire blazing out of his eyes. They seemed to have sunk further into his head than when I saw him last, and now it was as if the very substance of his brain was being exposed, the burning chemicals at the core of the man.

He'd better have, said Fraenkel briefly. Or we'll all die.

I laid my hand on his wrist, there on the icy headland, feeling the slow pulse throbbing through the skin.

What does Andrée want? I asked. You ought to know.

Andrée? he said, with a gruff laugh. He wants to go further up than any man has gone before.

He paused, jerking with his head.

217

Further North, he said. As far as the very Pole.

And you, Fraenkel, I pressed him. What do *you* want?

I want to die famous, he said quickly. I don't much care how. But that means being faithful to whatever I undertake to do. And that means getting Andrée to the North Pole.

And Nils? I asked.

Strindberg, too, he said, misunderstanding me. If that's what he wants. I told you before, they can count on my loyalty to the death.

I released his wrist, and started to walk back along the shore towards Pike's House. He fell into step beside me.

What *does* Nils want? I asked, after a time.

You ought to know, said Fraenkel. Who else could say?

What do *you* think he wants?

I think, said Fraenkel, swinging his arms as he walked, that he wants to discover something that no one has ever discovered before.

Yes, I said, that's what you all want. For you, it's the meaning of death. For Andrée, it's what's there at the end of the world. For Nils, it's whatever there is. Whatever there is. He has to bear the curse of not knowing what he wants until he's found it. You and Andrée have your clear-cut goals. The posts driven into the ground at the end of the race.

Fraenkel stopped. We were outside Pike's House, and he leaned his arm on the wooden veranda.

You're quite a philosopher, he said. You ought to have been a man.

You don't like girls, do you? I asked.

Not much, he answered, roughly. But I like you.

I watched him, framed in the doorway of the house, his legs crooked, and the long tight lines of twill going down into the fur of his boots. The hair on his chest furled up like wire out of the V in his low shirt.

I wonder, I said.

I put my hands over my breasts, then ran them both down, very slowly, until they rested on my hips. I stood there, staring at Fraenkel, easily within his reach, out of sight of the ships, and the balloon-house. Fraenkel watched me.

218

Swedenborg may come instead of Strindberg, he said, unexpectedly, and then the moment had passed.

No, I said, starting to walk on. I don't think he will. Nils will make the flight, whatever happens. I've known that now for months.

Fraenkel took my arm, a light, awkward touch, helping me over obstacles in the path.

I hope he will, he said, after a time. He's had much more experience than Swedenborg or I. But he has his doubts about the balloon. I'm sure he has. That villain Eckholm has a lot to answer for. He put the worm into Strindberg's confidence.

Rubbish, I said. Eckholm had his feet on the ground. Not like the rest of you. He wanted to get there, yes. But he also wanted to come back alive to tell the tale. To my mind, that's a far nobler ambition. And likely to make a bigger contribution to science, too.

Fraenkel halted, his features drawn and intense with feeling. He held his palms out to me, face up.

Look, he said. They're swollen and flayed. I've spent days and days rubbing vaseline into guide-ropes and treating each seam with oil and linseed.

I touched the skin of his hands. It was cracked and sore. He drew the hands back, thrusting them both in his trouser pockets.

It's not the same balloon, he said. We've dealt with every defect. We've made it impervious to leaks. Eckholm knew that we could. He just lost his nerve. The trouble was that he didn't want to die.

Who does? I asked, waiting.

But this time it was Fraenkel who made the first move to walk on.

On Midsummer's Day, he said, waving his hand along the shore, we had a great feast on the beach. They brought out trestles, and benches. There were two lambs and a suckling pig roasted there on spits over burning logs.

Fraenkel's eyes were looking into the past. He could see what he was describing rising out of the empty scrub and snow as he spoke. I felt, for the first time, drawn into his vision. There was something sympathetic about him, after all.

219

The smoke went up into the clear air, said Fraenkel. It was warm, and windless. There was a rich, peaty smell, and the crackle of sparks from the fire. The men were dressed in their best uniforms, and the three of us came out of the pinnace down a lane of honour to the board.

He sniffed the air, like an old war-horse, scenting blood.

I've never eaten so well, he said, simply. I realized for the first time that we were all Norsemen. Part of the same blood that led the way across the Atlantic, and made a colony in Greenland, and may have discovered America. That meal was more than any ritual I've had in church. It harmonized the world. For a few hours we were one community, feasting on the shore beside our ships, before a Viking voyage to the West. Only this time it wasn't the West, it was the North.

Fraenkel drew a deep breath. He seemed to come back, partly, from where he'd been. Leaving half-behind that fairy world of the longships, and the red gold.

Andrée made a speech, he said, ruefully. But I don't remember what he said. I just remember the food, and the feeling.

He's here now, I said, and indeed he was. Our walk had brought us past the hydrogen gas apparatus, and almost to the doorway of the balloon-house, outside which Andrée was standing with my mother, and a group of tourists, answering their final questions. He saw us approach, and excused himself, and came over.

Miss Charlier, he said politely. I gather from your excellent mother that I have to congratulate you. On your engagement to my senior colleague. Eh, Fraenkel?

He clapped Fraenkel on the back, then stood with his arm round his shoulder, squeezing the muscle for a moment before letting go.

Thank you, I said. I look forward to my marriage.

Andrée's lips twisted in one of those fastidious smiles of his.

Well, yes, he said primly. In the fullness of time, of course. When we come back. The names of Strindberg and Fraenkel, he added, will then be household words. Household words.

And *your* name? I asked.

220

My name is unpronounceable, said Andrée. No self-respecting Swede is able to wrap his tongue around it. After all, he said, smiling at Fraenkel. It may be the name of the balloon that comes to be best remembered. Like Nansen's ship. The *Fram*.

What name have you chosen? I asked.

There had been a newspaper competition to decide what name would be suitable for the balloon, and every possible alternative had been suggested from *Rosebud* to the *King of Sweden*. Several had been facetious, and more than one, I have no doubt, obscene.

I shall give the balloon his name the day we sail, said Andrée. Until then, it must remain a secret. Even from you, my dear. Even from Strindberg. Even from Fraenkel here.

I shall wait to know, I said, and I turned away to join my mother beside the balloon-house. When I reached her, and looked round, I saw Andrée and Fraenkel deep in conversation. They seemed a united pair, dedicated and at one.

That night Nils and I went together into the loft of Pike's House, and sat down amidst the pigeons. There had been another dinner, on board the *Lofoten*, with Otto Sverdrup and Andrée making competitive speeches afterwards.

Sverdrup had been the captain of Nansen's ship, the *Fram*, and he made a point of saying that he probably knew more than any man alive about navigating a vessel through the polar winter. Andrée had agreed, but pointed out that he probably knew more than any man alive about navigating a balloon in the Arctic.

I'd been bored by the speeches, and the false gaiety of farewells, with bouquets of flowers, and messages of greeting from German newspapers, and I'd asked Nils to take me away somewhere where we could be alone for a few hours.

It wasn't easy. Since I'd arrived, we'd only spent a few minutes on our own. There was always a photograph in the developer, or a fault in the hydrogen gas apparatus, or a last-minute conference with the engineers. It seemed as if all the problems of the expedition, or all the scientific ones, at least, were capable of solution only by Nils.

He was everywhere at once, checking meteorological

221

details with Fraenkel, discussing when to take down the north wall of the balloon-house with Andrée, busy with a hundred and one experiments and calculations and projects of his own.

You're working yourself to death, I said, in one of our few spells together, when he was taking photographs of me up in the rocks.

Keep still, he said, waving his hands. No, that's good. That's good.

Nils, I said, sitting up.

I'd been leaning back, holding my hat on with one hand in a sharp wind. My skirts kept fluttering up, and I'd had to reach down and pull them under my legs, but Nils didn't seem to notice. He was too absorbed in the general view, the black of my small figure against the curving bulk of the snowy mountain.

Amazing shadows, he said, more than once. You're a bad model, my dear. But at least you're dressed in the right colours.

Now I stood up, brushing snow from my lap, and adjusting the fit of the dress at my shoulders.

Nils, I said, for the second time. Why are you working so hard? Surely the others could do more?

He busied himself with tins of film, rolling the glossy strips into their waterproof cases.

They do their share, he murmured, as he worked. We all have our tasks. Besides, work helps me to forget. In a few days you'll be gone.

Then he reached up and kissed me on the cheek.

I'm scarcely even here, I said, moving away. I might as well never have come.

But Anna, said Nils. I love you. You're what this is all for.

I wondered, though, as he gestured round the island, and the balloon-house, and the waiting boats. He was far too preoccupied. He had moved into his man's world of action and ideas, and I had to work harder and harder to pull him back.

I know you do, I said gently. I know you do.

So I let him take more pictures, the sort he wanted, the abstract, remote patterns of black against white, where I was no more than a small shape in the lens, an element in the pattern no more significant than a rock or a seal. The sort I wanted were close, laughing ones, where I parted my lips at the very orifice of the camera, and the froth of shawl and petticoat made a rumpus of flowers on the white linen of a wedding-breakfast tablecloth. But these were never taken. Not by Nils, not then or ever.

So it had been a frustrating two days, even in these rare moments alone together, and I confided to my diary the first evening, as I lay with my hair undone on my hard bunk in the *Lofoten*, with my mother already asleep, and the faint sound of waves lapping the keel below me, that I must have a final, committed meeting with Nils before I went.

There was something I wanted, and I meant to have it. The last night would have to be the time. So we went up into the loft of the pigeon house, and I said what I had to say.

Nils, I began. You can see the *Lofoten* from here.

The loft was a small dusty attic, with a network of creosoted beams and rafters, exposed without plaster or paint. At the base of these, little hooped windows had been scooped out for the doves to go in and out of. The wooden floor, littered with straw and old boxes, had been stained and discoloured by their droppings.

There was room for two people to sit quite comfortably, and a pair of half barrels had been arranged on either side of the one window, a narrow skylight, from which a view of the bay could be obtained. It needed a bit of craning, though, and there was a better position at one side than the other. This was what had occasioned my remark. I knew that Nils couldn't see the bay from where he was. He would have to come over and bend beside me, under the rafters, or on the floor, to see the *Lofoten*.

It was all part of my plan. I'd worn a very tight, wide-swinging green dress, with a cameo at my neck, and my hair up in swathes under a curving hat, scarved below my chin. It was hardly the wear for a walk on the beach, or a climb up into a pigeon loft, though it had seemed admirable for a formal dinner aboard ship, and had drawn many an admiring comment.

223

Nils, of course, had been solicitous in helping me over obstacles as we walked on the shore, taking my arm, and at times putting an arm around my waist to lift me over a piece of driftwood, or a pile of dirty ice. It had all helped.

By the time we reached Pike's House, I was ready. I'd drunk enough champagne on the ship to feel light-headed, and a little giddy, and I knew that Nils, too, under my guidance had been led beyond his usual capacity. He was hardly drunk, he was never that. But he was merry.

The house had never really been occupied as a dwelling, and the expedition had come to use it mainly for stores. Downstairs, the door from the veranda led directly into a large bright room with a stove, a heavy table and one or two ship's basket-chairs. There was a bookcase, with some volumes of naval history, and some rolls of charts.

But most of the room was now filled with baskets of spare silk for the balloon, cans of oil, instruments, boxes of ammunition and tins of food. It was a storehouse, pure and simple.

One flight of stairs went up to a landing, from which doors led to two upstairs rooms. One was always kept locked, and I never did find out what was held in there. It may have been Pike's own secret bedroom, lined with satin, and carpeted with Persian rugs. Or it may, more likely, just have been empty. The other room was packed from floor to ceiling with whaling equipment, harpoons, grease, oil, winching gear, baskets of old, worn jerseys and long thigh boots. It was never used by the expedition.

The second floor was reached by a steep flight of wooden steps from the landing. It consisted entirely of the pigeon loft, and was, in fact, no more than a conversion of the space under the rafters.

Let's go in and take a look at Pike's House, I'd suggested first, on our walk along the shore. I'm feeling cold.

So Nils had pushed the door open, and we'd gone in, over the musty threshold into the large downstairs room.

Why it's much too crowded, I'd said, capriciously, with a toss of my hair. Let's go upstairs.

I don't think Nils had ever been upstairs. He only hesitated a moment, though, and then spread his arm for me to precede him. On the landing, I'd tried the doors, and feasted my eyes on the whaling stores. There was no space there, either.

Then I'd heard the deep cooing, and the rustle and clustery sound of a large number of doves moving.

O, Nils, I said. Let's go up and see them. There must be a lovely view.

So I'd put my shoe on the first step, and my gloved fingers on the rail.

Help me, Nils, I'd said. I'll lead the way.

It was most improper, and, in normal circumstances, I wouldn't have dared. The gradient was very steep, and the steps were quite open. They led towards a closed trap-door in the ceiling.

You'll get very dirty, said Nils, anxiously. Do be careful, Anna.

I looked back over my shoulder. It was further down than I'd thought, and I felt a momentary shudder of fear. But it was quite borne over by another feeling, a more subtle and pleasurable one.

I knew that Nils was standing now well below me. His face was turned up to mine. He had only to drop his gaze a foot or two to see exactly what I wanted him to see.

O, Nils, I cried suddenly, and I let my left foot slip off the rung. Help me, I'm falling.

He was on the ladder then, climbing fast behind me, and I waited, watching until the very moment when his hand was beside my ankle. Then I swung my skirt wide, and stepped one rung down, and let my free leg, in its white silk stocking and lace bloomer, slide off and over Nils's shoulder.

He struggled, freed himself, and then took a firm grip on my ankle.

Now come down, he said. Let me put your foot each time on the rung.

So we reached the landing, I flushed and excited, Nils angry and rather bewildered, it seemed. There was evidently still some way to go.

You go first, I said. Then you can help me up.

I don't think we really ought to, said Nils. You very nearly slipped and fell. You might have broken your leg.

Nonsense, I said, holding his arm. I want to go up and see the doves, and enjoy the view.

He could see I meant to have my way, and by now I think he may have half wanted to go himself. I don't know. At any rate, he turned and took the rail firmly in both hands and rapidly shinned up the ladder to the trapdoor. I watched the lithe, swift movement of his thighs as he climbed.

Is it stuck? I asked. Give it a hard shove.

I found it exciting to say this, and I clasped my arms round my sides, shivering a little but not, I think, with cold. I stood looking up, working my toes to and fro inside the flexible leather of my lace-up boots.

It'll come, said Nils, and then there was a sharp crack, a shower of dust, and the trap was open, with Nils climbing through into darkness above. He turned, and stared down at me, reaching an arm through the gap.

Now don't look down, he said, and take very great care as you climb.

This time I did, and I was soon rising towards him, my face turned up, and my gloved arms following each other in a steady rhythm along the rail. As I reached the top, he reached his arm to clasp me, and I paused a moment, with his hand under the pit of my sleeve, my heart beating hard against his fingers. I moved forward, and my head was between his opened legs.

Then I was tumbling over the edge, grazing my knee, and safely inside the loft, all in one piece, and on my own now on the floor, with Nils on his feet, handing me up and setting me onto a half barrel, and asking if I was all right.

I was flushed and flustered, yes, but I was all right. I was more than all right, I was rather far gone, and I hoped that Nils was, too. After all this, he ought to be, for sure. I knew enough about men to know that.

I'm fine, I said, and then I dusted myself down, and pretended to straighten a stocking seam, and pull my petticoats round and settle my dress over my knees. It was a good performance, and it showed me off well, I knew.

Then I looked through the skylight, and the *Lofoten* was there, a fairy palace in the bay beside the two smaller

226

ships, and it really was a lovely view, and I spoke, and said what I said, knowing what Nils would have to do.

Nils, I began, you can see the *Lofoten* from here.

Then he rose, and stepped over, and knelt in front of me, straining up from the waist to see through the skylight. I put one hand on his shoulder, pointing out with the other one. Then I brought my pointing hand back, and, with a deft movement, slid both hands under the tails of his coat and up to rest on his waist. He looked round and up, startled.

Kiss me, Nils, I said.

Then he swivelled round on his heels and was facing me, I sitting a little above him on the half barrel, leaning forward with my hands on his hips. I let myself fall forward, into his lap, and he put his arms round me, and lost his balance, and we were on the floor, his back on the boards, and my whole trembling length groping and twisting to fit itself to each niche of him. It was beyond a game now, I wanted the rough and tumble, the feel of his body, at any cost.

He rolled away, though, and laid me aside, by main strength. He was still trying to pretend we were both a little off balance, and that nothing was happening to compromise our reputations.

I'm so sorry, he said, laughing. I lost my balance. Are you all right?

There were doves everywhere, posturing and cooing, annoyed, no doubt, by this human intervention into their arena of courtship. Out of the corner of my eye, as I lay on the dirty floor, I saw the remains of an old mattress, stained with droppings, and torn into holes, with handfuls of burst ticking and springs coming out, like a horse gored by a fighting bull. It was a terrible, ramshackle place for the event I now knew I must engineer, but it was at least a little softer than the wooden floor. I squirmed over, and lay flat on my back, one arm under my neck, the hat awry on my head, the dress rumpled and dusty. I looked up at Nils.

I want you, Nils, I said. I want you now.

A pouter pigeon came over, rearing and puffing up his pouch beside me, and I lifted him off onto the floor.

227

Another followed him, and then another, until there were half a dozen billing and cooing round me.

You see, Nils, I said. They all want me.

I lifted one leg, drawing the dress back, so that it fell away into my lap. Nils came over, and knelt beside me, putting one hand on my upraised knee. He was as white as a field of snow.

Anna, he whispered. Not here. It's wrong.

Wrong, I said, softly. We're engaged, aren't we? But for your polar flight, we'd have been married long since. And besides, Nils, it's naughtier when it's wrong, isn't it?

I loosened the scarf, and took my hat off. Then I reached back, and removed a tortoiseshell pin and bow, and my long hair came tumbling down over my forehead, and into my mouth.

Nils, I said. I'm a girl. Don't you want me? I'm your wife, Anna, and you can have me whenever you want me now.

I shook my hair back, and raised myself, and drew his face down, and kissed him directly on the mouth. He let himself fall onto me, and I lay back, and I felt the full stretch of his body, and it was lax and loose, and then, suddenly, trembling. And I thought the time had come.

Then his mouth twisted, and he pulled away from me, and stood up, and walked away, and then knelt, vomiting, below the skylight. I lay very still for a long time. The doves cooed, and I felt them pressing and stumbling all round me. I began to smooth my dress.

I'm so sorry, Nils said, wiping his face. It was the champagne. I had far too much to drink.

He looked at me, like a little boy who's been caught doing something very wrong, and my heart turned over and I knew then, for sure, that I was doomed. I loved him as much as ever, and nothing was ever going to happen about it.

Yes, I said, it must have been the champagne.

Before we returned to the ship, Nils took me into the balloon-house, and I saw the polar balloon fully inflated for the first time.

We both stood in silence, gazing at the great, flopping bag of gas as it strained at its mooring-ropes. There was a windy, sailing-ship sort of noise, as if we were out at sea on the deck of some fast cutter, heeling into the breeze.

But the balloon stood firm. It was like a huge egg, I thought, an ostrich one, perhaps, of the sort my Uncle Knut had had framed and kept in a silver carriage on his writing-table. White, but a little dirty and speckled with imperfections.

It seemed fertile, too, as an egg is fertile. The repository of what future adventures and terrors, who could tell? It billowed and swayed there in the shed, as if it were the mobile rounded tip of some underground growth, as large below as is an iceberg below the waves, compared to the jagged, dangerous tip we see above water.

Let's go, Nils said, after a while.

He spoke in a whisper, as one might speak in church, so as not to disturb another worshipper. And, indeed, for a moment I felt like that. As if I, too, had fallen, albeit briefly, under the sinister spell of this monster. It was exactly the same as when I had first seen the balloon, with Andrée.

I took his arm, and he led me away. Once, by the door, I turned to look back, and I was reminded in a far spurt of recollection, that crossed the years, of that awful boy in the barn, and the pinkish tip of the rubbery thing he'd held in his fingers and jabbed me with, and of what he'd said, that lost day in my adolescence.

Right up, he'd said. You can go right up in one of these.

I went out with Nils back onto the beach, and I felt more frustrated and isolated than I'd ever done before.

8
STRINDBERG
1897

SOMETHING ABOMINABLE has happened. I don't really know how to talk about it. Half an hour has gone by, and I still feel absolutely revolted. I'm sitting here under the ice-wall of the hut we're building, with my back against the frozen blocks, and the book on my knees.

It's four o'clock in the afternoon, and the weather isn't too bad. There's a lot of sun, in intermittent bursts, and I could almost feel it was on the edge of being warm.

But it's not the sun I want to write about. I'm shaking all over − you'll be able to grasp that from the state of my hand-writing when you see this − and I find my mouth keeps twisting, as if I want to spit something out.

What happened was this. I'd better start at the beginning. After the seal the other day, our food problem seemed to be solved, at least for a few weeks. But Andrée wasn't satisfied. He felt that we needed a surplus.

So, while Fraenkel and I got on with our own jobs, which for Fraenkel seemed to mean sitting and moping, and for me meant building the snow-hut, Andrée walked along the rim of the floe with his gun, stalking for seals. He's been incredibly lucky.

First, a small one, yesterday. He got that with a small-shot cartridge in the back, but the wound wasn't deadly. The poor beast had to be clubbed to death. After we'd dissected the seal, Andrée found that the bones of the skull are as thin as egg-shell.

That means I can get more with small shot in the head, he said. They're as fragile as dry sticks.

He crumbled the skull in his fist.

233

Try again, I said. You obviously enjoy the business.

Today he did try again, and, believe it or not, he shot no less than three. The first two fell to a small-shot cartridge in the head, exactly as anticipated, and then Andrée got the third, a real monster, with a ball in the heart.

This means that we now have enough meat to see us through until the end of February. So the whole of this morning – Andrée shot the seals just after breakfast – has been spent in the now familiar butchery.

Slicing down the carcases. Cutting the meat and blubber into steaks. Running off the blood into tins. These are coarse jobs, and I can't say that I've ever come to like them. But they do need doing, and they do keep us warm.

Fraenkel has found a way of making very good blood-pancakes, out of seal-blood mixed with fat, flour, salt and yeast, and they don't seem to lose much weight in the cooking. We all ate several with enjoyment last night.

So now keeping the blood matters as much as storing the guts, and the lights. Dear, wonderful seal! You've almost come to replace the polar bear in my affections. Indeed, if the seal were covered with a thick, fleecy pelt, I'm sure he would have no rival.

I can feel my stomach turning again. Writing about the seal distracted me for a moment, Anna. I have to get back to the point.

You have to imagine the scene. Andrée, as usual, when some really hard work needs to be done, has gone off on his own pursuits. In this case that means poling round the floe in our boat, to look for water samples.

Fraenkel and I are left outside the rising walls of the snow-hut, surrounded by the remains of the three seals. We have them sorted into piles. Offal. Meat. Skins, and other waste. Not very much, in that pile.

There's a bit of bickering.

Watch out, I say once, when Fraenkel almost trips, and sends a chunk of blubber flying into my stomach. If your feet are hurting, why not sit down and take a rest? I can manage without you.

I see Fraenkel's face redden through the dirt. His lips tighten, the way they do when he's fighting hard to control his rage.

You don't need strong feet for this work, he says, pausing with his knife in a long steak. It's arms that matter, and willpower.

Then get on, I say, provokingly, as I bend over a skin, scraping the last of the blubber off. Use your arms.

That's when it happened, Anna. I suddenly felt a crushing pressure round my ribs, and I had to slacken my knees and then squirm round to relax the pain. Fraenkel had come up behind me, and taken my whole body in a great bear-hug.

I felt the pressure lessen as I faced him, breathing hard with my sudden effort. He still had his hands laced in the small of my spine, but his grip was looser. He was grinning at me through his matted beard.

Use my arms? he said mockingly. They're stronger than yours are, little Strindberg.

I'd left my knife in the skin, luckily I now think. I might have cut his throat. So I put out the flats of my hands and thrust at him, to put more distance between us, and break the hold of his hands. But I couldn't. He was too strong.

Why not sit down and take a rest? he said, imitating me.

Then he tightened his hands, and simply drew me hard against his chest. I felt as if my ribs were going to break. I jammed one leg between his thighs, and tried to trip him up.

No, you don't, he said. You little, and he used a word I won't write.

Then he did what he did. It was all over very quickly. He had his hand down in the crick of my neck, and then his face was up over mine, a terrible stink of stale fish, and then he had his finger into my mouth, and then his tongue in.

I don't know what I was doing to him. It seemed like a fight for life, more than a fit of horse-play. I could have sworn there was something hard between his legs, too, the same thing I'd been feeling night after night in the heat and privacy of the sleeping-bag.

But there he'd been fast asleep. Now he was wide awake. We were staggering to and fro, slithering over the slime of guts and blood on the snow. One moment we were still upright, and I was sure there was something

235

going to happen that couldn't be put a stop to. Not without blood and death.

Then I heard Fraenkel cry out in pain, and his arms came free, and I saw him tumble onto the ice, doubled up in pain. I stood for a moment breathing hard, wondering what to do. Then I reached down and gave him my hand.

You ought to be more careful, I said. You'll ruin your feet completely if you fool around. We can't afford that.

In the middle distance, I saw Andrée come into sight, poling the boat smoothly towards us around the edge of the floe. Fraenkel followed my eyes. I couldn't tell what he was thinking. Then he shook my hand away, and got slowly to his feet, masking his evident pain with a bout of coughing.

Silly idiot, he said, as if blaming me for his fall. Let's get back to work.

That's all there was, Anna. When Andrée beached the boat, and came over to show us what he'd discovered, we were both hard at work, in silence, cutting meat and pretending that nothing had happened.

I shall have to stop now. There are a couple of ivory gulls circling above the hut, and I think I can get them both with a single shot if I do the alignment right.

Funny how one's mood changes. This is being written a day later, although in the same place, amidst the now rapidly rising walls of my snow-hut. All day I've had the slope of White Island only a short distance away, it seems, to the west. On this side, too, it's rounded like a low loaf, and the shore is no more than the edge of a glacier.

Nevertheless, it's comforting, in a curious sort of way, to have solid land there only a few kilometres away. So near and yet so far, maybe. But there. Something anchored into the bed of the sea, and unmoving. The tip of what would remain as a great mountain if the salt water were drained away.

It reassures me. Sometimes, in the sun, the whole island looks like a solid mass of glass, transparent from above and the side. It shines blue, ice-blue, but with brown strains in it, too, sometimes.

I think of it as like a crystal, a great diamond of many facets, uncut as yet for some ice maiden's wedding ring.

236

You see, I've been growing more poetic in the sun, Anna. A touch of your complaint. A touch of Fraenkel's disease.

But I haven't yet taken to making verses. Not that, thank God. I hope this doesn't sound too jerky. You won't realize, perhaps, that this last page has been written in six or seven pieces.

Every time I get too cold, I have to stop, and do some work on the walls to warm myself up. I estimate that I can rest and write for about three minutes for every fifteen I work moving snow and blocks of ice.

It's getting colder, though. I shall have to make the writing intervals shorter, or give up entirely until tomorrow. I can't face the idea of writing in the tent with the others there.

I'm not sure now exactly what did happen out here amongst the seal-skins yesterday. I was quite clear at the time. I can see that, from what I've written. I want to let it stand.

But tonight I'm not so sure. Perhaps we were both just horsing about. It's easy enough to get into some embarrassing positions when you're fooling around. Wrestling with someone. It happens all the time.

I have to stop and go in. My hands are frozen.

September the 29th. We're in the snow-hut, and I can write in privacy, and with a certain degree of warmth.

It's now just after midnight, and we moved in a few hours ago. The others are already asleep, and I have leisure to say what I want to in peace.

One part of me feels a physical disgust to think what they may be doing to each other there in my little ice bedroom. The other part says, no, wait a minute, Nils. That fiend Fraenkel needs some outlet for what he has inside him. Better he takes his passion out on Andrée, if that's what he has to do.

I have to control what I feel about Fraenkel. Some days I've seen him watching me, Anna, when I bend to lift a block for the hut, and I've seen a funny, soft look run over his face, and I've wanted to take the flensing-knife and slit him in two from the belly to the throat. I know

that Andrée guesses what strains there are. I read the way
he put his fears down in his diary.

'During the last two days the weather has been very
pleasant but on the other hand they have not passed
without signs of differences arising between us. I hope
however that this seed will not grow and develop.'

No, indeed, Salomon August. And so say all of us.

Even as I write, Anna, I see that my knuckles are
whitened through the dirt, and not with cold. With holding the pencil so tight it nearly cracks. Wanting the thin
sliver of wood to be Fraenkel's finger breaking under my
hand.

I don't like being stared at. I don't like to feel that I'm
becoming a piece of meat. Every time I feel his hot eyes go
over me at the table I want to throw boiling fat in them.

I think I'll stop for a moment and patrol outside to see
that all is well.

No sign of any bears. It's a calm, still night, but very
cold. I took a long look over towards White Island, under
the stars. The intervening sea is marked by a range of large
hummocks, and this helps to protect us from ice-
pressings.

But there are dangers. From time to time, the pack-ice
moves under changes of temperature, or slippage in the
water. What happens then is much the same as with a
pack of playing cards built up into a house.

You push, and the cards rise or fall or slide, as individual units, until they form a loose conglomerate mass,
overlapping and jammed together. With ice, though, the
pressure combined with the rigidity is enough to rear
some pieces up into hummocks, into slabs forced onto
their ends.

It makes the landscape we've got to know so well over
the past few weeks. Unfortunately, the process makes our
ice-island, our floe, liable to constant change and cracking.
So far the big hummocks between here and the shore of
White Island are acting as a sort of breaker against the tidal
pressure of the ice-changes. But I don't know how long
that will last.

We're not moving much, but we do move, and the
position of the hummock range will alter. In fact, our floe

does get smaller from time to time. A few nights ago, there was a sharp crack, and we lost a chunk at the edge.

It creaks all the time, of course. Like the metal guttering of your old house in winter. Do you remember how we joked about it, and compared it to an old man groaning? Our ice-floe is much the same, Anna. An old man groaning. Let's hope he doesn't have anything worse to groan about before the winter's over.

Gosh, I'm hungry. I've just finished a caramel I'd saved from dinner, but it hasn't taken the edge off my appetite. It's brought back my memory of our last great banquet, the night of September 18th, when we celebrated the 25th anniversary of King Oscar's accession. Just thinking about it makes my mouth water.

Seal steak and ivory gull fried in butter and seal-blubber. Seal-liver. Brain, and kidneys. Butter and Schumacher bread.

Wine.

Chocolate and Mellin's-food flour with Albert biscuits and butter.

Gateau aux raisins.

Raspberry syrup sauce.

Port-wine 1834 Antonio de Ferrara given by the King.

Toast by Andrée for the King with royal Hurrah.

The national anthem in unison.

Biscuits, butter, cheese.

Wine.

Festive feeling.

Enough of that. I've been writing for hours, and I still haven't done what I promised. I said I'd give you a picture of the hut. So here goes.

From the outside, it's rather low, no more than a metre and a half high, and with rounded sides, like an igloo. There's a low porch at one side, about a metre high, and that leads by a short tunnel to the doorway. This can be blocked by a case of ammunition at night to protect us against bears, and to keep the cold out.

Once you're inside, you stand up in the first of our suite of three rooms. In time, this will be the meat-store, where we hold the stocks of seal and bear meat, and whatever other provisions need to be kept safe, and fairly cold.

239

From this first room, a passage leads through a thick internal wall to the central room, which is where I'm now writing, seated on a box, and using another as a table. I have the lamp lit for illumination, and it throws jagged shadows up and down the ice-walls.

This room will be the main living-room of the hut, and it's a little bigger than the other two. It has all our equipment in, packed up along the walls. The sledges and the boat, of course, are parked outdoors.

Another door leads through a shorter passage to the last of the three rooms, which is mainly taken up by the sleeping-bag. That's where Andrée and Fraenkel are now, only a metre or two away, but further, by miles, it seems, than when we were all together in the single space of the tent.

I can scarcely begin to convey the sense of luxury this three-room bungalow is giving to me, Anna. It makes life cooped up here all winter with the others almost seem like a real possibility. I grow more cheerful every moment I remember that there's a wall of ice between me and them. And another wall of ice between me and the bears. It's a house, Anna. Not much of a house, I dare say, by the standards of Klippan, but to me now, off the coast of White Island, a palace indeed.

I see from my watch that it's after four, and nearly time for Fraenkel to take over. I'd better go in and give him a shake. I feel tired, suddenly. I could do with a rest.

Now that it's happened, I can see that we may be near the beginning of the end.

By a kind of sympathetic magic, Fraenkel's foot seems to have grown unaccountably worse. I can see him through the door as I write, rocking to and fro on the edge of the sleeping-bag.

And Andrée. Andrée's in there beside him, flat on his back on the bag, his hands behind his neck, staring up at the ice-roof. I suppose he's thinking. But he doesn't move. He's just staring at the ice, not seeing anything. It's what Aristotle once called *akrasia*, Anna. Weakness of the will. The lack of the power to *do* anything.

I know how they both feel. I have some sympathy. It

240

was like pushing a huge stone up a hill to take my little book out and begin to write this letter. I'm alive. I'm well-fed. I'm warm, and, for the moment at any rate, I'm safe. But it's hard, almost impossibly hard, to shake off the sense of lassitude. The sense of doom.

The date, you say. What's the date?

The weather first. We had three days of rain, solid, sheeting, and then drizzling rain. An amazing downpour for this time of year. We kept indoors mostly, cooking more than usual, reading and talking, and making improvements to the hut.

It was dull weather, but it bred a kind of contentment. I suppose, more than anything, it was the feeling of cosi-ness from having a roof over our heads.

Anyway, it didn't last. October 1st dawned bright and clear. We ate our breakfast outside again, in the sunshine. Blood-pancakes. They tasted good. I think that blood must contain carbohydrate, because we no longer seem to have such a tremendous craving for bread.

There was a bevy of little guillemots in the water, six or seven, sporting and splashing in the light. I sighted a seal once, in the distance, but it didn't come near enough for a shot. It was like a day in spring, late April or even May, not the brink of winter.

Perhaps that was the trouble. The wrong temperature for the time of year. That, or the tides. The tides, or the will of the gods. At any rate, the trouble came, and it came in the night.

We went to bed a little before twelve. We had all the seal-meat in the food-hall by then. Fortunately, polar bears don't seem to be cannibals, and we thought we could risk leaving the bear-carcases in the open.

You take the middle, I said to Andrée. I'll come soon.

The feeling of pressure from Fraenkel's hot eyes on me had been diminishing for a couple of days, but I didn't want to exacerbate matters by lying down alongside him. I'd had enough of that jumping cock-sparrow of his in the small of my back.

Andrée smiled. He seemed about to say something, and then evidently thought better of it. He reached over and squeezed my shoulder.

241

Goodnight, Strindberg, he said.

It was the one moment of warmth we'd had for weeks. I watched him stoop and go through the door almost with a return of affection.

I thought about this for a moment, looking down at my blackened hands in the flickering light of the oil-lamp. Looking round at the flattened ice-walls that these mis-used hands had built and smoothed. Then I blew the light out, stooped through the door, and slid into the sack alongside Andrée.

I haven't written much about my dreams before. Some nights I haven't had any, some nights they've been very ordinary. Some nights they've been twisted, and gross. This night, though, I had a dream that came with the force of a premonition.

I was paddling across a lead, all alone, with my sledge and all my belongings, not just what I have on the expedi-tion, but all my things, my books from home, my suits of clothes, my ornaments, my family photographs, the Chinese dog my grandfather brought home from Macao, everything I have, everything I hold most sacred and precious, even, in the dream, Anna, a tall gold-framed portrait of you by Edvard Munch, in charcoal on a cream ground, wearing a long red dress, with a string of shark's teeth at your neck, even this.

I knew that I had to get to the other side, that the expedition had failed, except for myself the others had gone I don't know where, not died exactly, but gone home, snatched up to Heaven perhaps in a blaze of fire, or slipped away to Valhalla in a dark mist, I don't know. But they weren't there. At least, not exactly. In a way they *were* there, and watching. But inaccessible.

So I paddled on, negotiating bergs and hummocks of ice, very cold, very tired now, and yet sure I could some-how get across. If only I concentrated. Yes, I could do it. I was sure I could.

And then, in the dream, there was a curious shaking in the timbers of the boat under my feet. A sort of cracking screech of a noise, and then a terrible rumbling. And then I looked up, and a hundred metres away, but coming rapidly closer, there was a great monstrous wave of water, tall as a house, and curling forward like the beak of a sea-eagle to open wide and swallow me up.

Closer and closer it came, sweeping everything aside from its path, bergs and hummocks, even a school of seals, and then a polar bear on a floe. All around it, the sky was thick with the beating wings of gulls, fleeing from the water before it could engulf them.

Overhead they came, flight after flight, the air full of their wild calling, my face tarnished as I looked up by their continuous droppings, bowels opened by the lance of fear as they flew.

And then suddenly, they were gone. And there was only the great wave, now only twenty metres away, gigantic above me, the very tip curling now to plunge down like a dagger and make the first incision for the kill.

Help me, Andrée, I called. Help me.

But there was no one there. No one. Neither Fraenkel nor Andrée, nor you, Anna, nor my mother and father, nor Uncle Johan, nor even God himself. Only the wave and I. And underneath the wave, yes, in the grip of the wave, deep in the guts and maw of the wave, there were Andrée and Fraenkel. Watching. Part of the wave. Helpless in the heart of the wave.

That was why I had called out Andrée's name. He was there. I knew that he was there. But he couldn't do anything to help me. He was powerless. He was doomed.

Then, Anna, the dream became part of my real life, as it must have been when I saw the wave coming, or even before. I was half awake, swimming, it seemed, in the water, with the wave broken to a salt sea around my bones in the very safety of the snow-hut.

Then I was on my elbow, spitting and coughing.

Wake up, Strindberg, Andrée was saying, and I could feel an arm, his arm perhaps, roughly shaking my shoulder.

But that was the least of it. I was in a pool of water, bitter-cold, in the dark. In the sleeping-bag still, I realized. Then I was out and up, blundering for where the door of the bedroom should have been, and smashing my head against the wall, until a sharp pain went through my skull, and the darkness blazed into a firework of dizzying sparks.

243

Jesus Christ, I called out, not just in expletive rage, I think, but in a kind of desperate need.

Then I tried again, and this time, with head down, and my arms up to shield my face, I was through a blank space, and then wading, splashing on, banging my knees against boxes in the middle room, feeling over the ice for the second doorway. And, yes, I had that, too, and then I was through, hearing a splashing in front of me, Andrée maybe, or Fraenkel, I didn't know, didn't care. All that I wanted to do was get out before I drowned.

Help, I remember calling. Help. Help.

Once I went down on my knees, and my head was under water, and I thought I was gone, and that was the end. Then I was up again, and had my shoulders into the final passage to the open air. Andrée, I remember thinking, must have somehow heaved the closing box out of the way. Quite a feat on his own. But panic lends a man strength, for sure.

I shoved and stumbled forward, almost swimming it seemed to me then, water up to my shoulders, as I came through and out into the blissful clear space. I stood erect, gasping for breath, spitting water, soaked through, but alive.

I looked round. The sun was up, and the landscape was bathed in a pure, serene clarity. Visibility was excellent, and the long low bow of White Island shone like a multi-coloured prism of glass where the sun struck the ice.

Andrée was standing a little way away, shaking water out of his clothes. He was shivering, and his teeth were violently chattering. He beat his arms on his sides, and then began to do a rapid dance on the same space to get warm.

Andrée, I said. Thank God you're alive.

There was a convulsive gasp from behind me, and a huge buckled form, shaking water off itself like a dog, came bursting out of the tunnel, and falling onto its knees almost at my feet.

Fraenkel, I said. You, too.

He was rubbing water out of his eyes.

What happened? he asked.

I don't know, I said. I was dreaming. I feel I still am.

244

I had my jacket off, and was peeling my sweater to wring some water out. I put it back on, a little dryer, and bent to unloosen my boots and squeeze the water out of those. Mercifully, the sun was warming the air. It was chill still, but we might be able to dry our things in a moment.

I heard a loud crash, like a clap of thunder, I heard Andrée saying, as he kept his dance up, to keep warm. And then it was like a dam bursting. My God, you both sleep soundly. I had to shake you for hours, it seemed, with the water already over your shoulders. You might have drowned.

I drew my boots on again, watching Fraenkel as he walked a little distance away, and then turned, and lifted his hands in the air.

Kismet, he said, very softly. Kismet. Look at this.

I turned and followed his pointing arm. Then I got to my feet and went over to stand beside him.

Andrée, I called. You'd better come and look.

The worst had happened. The floe had broken on the very edge of the snow-hut. One wall was more or less hanging from the roof over the rim of the sea. The icy waves were lapping under what might have been our windows.

I sank to my knees, put my head in my hands. It must have seemed a theatrical thing to do. But there was no one to care, no audience uninvolved enough to be critical.

Look round, I heard Andrée say. Just look around.

I lifted my head, and turned in all directions. It was worse even than it might have seemed at first. Our huge floe had broken not into two but into several pieces. On one block, already several metres away, there were the carcases of our two bears, enough food to last for nearly three months. On another block, further off, there were our three sledges, our only means of transporting our goods.

The boat, I whispered. Where's the boat?

It was our one piece of luck. The empty hull had caught a jagged hummock and was poised precariously over the edge of our tiny floe, ready at any moment, at the first new shock, to slide off and drift away out of reach in the sea.

I was on my feet, running, calling to Andrée and Fraenkel to help me. I reached the boat in a few strides, hauled the keel back to a safer position, drew it, with Andrée helping, over to the snow-but, and jammed it into the entrance.

We stood, breathless, wondering what to do next. Where to start. Andrée was indecisive.

Right, I said. Let's get the sledges first. Then the two bear-carcases. Fraenkel, you clear the hut, and see what you can start to dry. It will only take two of us to get the sledges.

That was it, Anna. There was no clamour, no dispute. The others had shot their bolt.

So we got the boat into the sea, thank God for the sun, I thought, as we pulled away in a lane of light, and, shivering and half-frozen as we were, we rowed over to the other floe and managed to haul down and load the empty sledges. They were light to move, and they ran well over the clean ice on their iron. We soon had them athwart the seats, and then rowed back and got them, as it were, ashore.

The bear-carcases were more difficult. O, Anna. I feel too tired. You can guess the rest. Labour all day, hauling and dragging. Labour drying and trying to make the primus work. Sleeping another night in the snow-hut, in sheer despair and weariness, unable to contemplate the final effort of raising the tent.

And then today, labour of facing up to what must be seen as our only hope. An attempt to load the boat and transport all our equipment and food across to the shore of White Island. So far as can be seen, it means a single voyage through a jagged, zig-zag lead, and then a landing on the south-east of the island where the ground seems partly clear at the base of the glacier.

I don't like the idea. I loathe it. Perhaps I shall feel better in the morning. It has to be done. I know it has. Goodnight, now.

October 7th. We did land, Anna. Two days ago, in the evening of October 5th, in the last of the fine weather. The following morning the snow started, and we've been in the midst of the blizzard ever since.

246

I'm trying to write this with my hands under the covers to keep warm. I can scarcely hold the pencil, as it is.

God, that wind. It makes the cloth belly in, and it's nearly torn the pole and the weights up more than once. The draught comes in like a long knife slicing along the floor, then it cuts away, and there's a brief intermission. But it's worse that way, in the long run, because we relax and then suffer more painfully from the next slice.

The snow, that's not so bad, indoors. It banks up, and I think the drifts keep heat in. But, alas, whenever I have to go out to meet the needs of nature, the wind catches me, and I find myself lurching up to my knees, even my midriff, in a great freezing bandage. I come in shivering, and it's harder than ever to get warm, or keep my spirits up.

Let me tell you about the landing, Anna. It wasn't hard, that part. We were lucky with the long lead. We got the boat packed on the floe, and all the sledges laid across the thwarts. Then we rowed over, tacking to and fro with the lead, in that marvellous crystalline sun, the very last of the year, I fear.

Strange to have left a floating island and reached an anchored one. At first there seemed little difference. Then it struck me that I could dig, and underneath I'd reach gravel, and not more ice. It was a reassuring moment. I ground my heel down, and there it was, the elemental stone-brash! Not much to crow about, maybe. But not frozen sea. Not salt water turned to ice.

Land. Rock. Earth-stuff. It was the first time we'd set foot on any since July 11th. The first real land since Danes Island. I went down on my knees, Anna, and laid my head on the ground for a moment. I don't know what I expected. To hear a mole digging maybe. To see an ant or a spider. A tiny spore of saxifrage. Anything.

Of course, there wasn't. Just the gravelly, hard earth, and the creamy light along it. We were lucky, as I say, not to need to unpack the boat and trek at all over hummocks. The lead brought us all the way. It was a roundabout route, and it took more than an hour. A long time for such a short journey, no more, I think, than a few hundred metres.

247

But it was well worth the detour to save the labour of all our previous marches over ice. We landed on the south-west shore of White Island, and there was bare soil, we discovered, for about three hundred metres up to the edge of the glacier. The ground was fairly flat, rising by less than a metre until it reached a little range of rocks about two hundred metres from the shore.

Where we came in, there was almost a small bay, a ridge of rock about a metre high, to which we could tether the boat, and then step down and unpack our things in the shallows.

In fact, we contented ourselves with getting the sledges off, and then looking round for a place to pitch the tent. It was late, and we needed to sleep before we made any more plans.

There was a good position in the lee of a group of rocks, facing north-west, and so out of the wind. That's where we now are, cowering from the blast, and hoping the boxes will hold the corners of the tent-cloth firm.

By ten o'clock on the 5th we'd eaten and got the sleeping-bag laid, and Andrée had turned in. I didn't feel in the mood to write then, Anna, and I accepted the situation without argument when Fraenkel chose the middle of the bag, and lay down with his hands under his head. I got in beside him, and closed my eyes.

But I didn't sleep. I soon heard Andrée snuffle and then half snore in that very characteristic way he has when he first nods off. Then I heard Fraenkel grunt, and change his position. I felt myself go all tense, and I lay as close to the edge of the bag as I could.

We shan't survive all this, you know, Strindberg, I heard Fraenkel say.

I said nothing.

Strindberg, I heard him say. You're not asleep, are you? I know you're not asleep.

No, Fraenkel, I said. I'm not. But I'd like to be.

Fraenkel laughed.

What's the point? he said. Of sleeping, I mean. We're all going to die soon.

I thought for a moment.

Andrée, I said, quite loudly. Are you awake?

He's fast asleep, Fraenkel said. You know he is.

I was as far away from him as I could be in the bag. I felt the warmth of his leg touching my calf.

Do you mind moving over a bit, I said, as conversationally as I could. I'm a bit squashed for room.

What does it matter, Fraenkel said. We're going to die soon.

I sat up in the bag.

Fraenkel, I said, steadily. We're not going to die. Our position is better than it's been for weeks. We can build a new hut here on solid ground and last out the winter. In spring we can trek across to Spitzbergen.

Fraenkel laughed again. It was a stagey, theatrical laugh, but it was full of real bitterness.

Why don't you like me, Strindberg? he said.

I suddenly couldn't take any more of this. I got up, and stepped through the flap of the tent into the open air. It was dark now, and much colder, but it was a still, dry night. I groped my way through the rocks, looking for a sheltered spot to ease myself.

I thought that Fraenkel might fall asleep if I stayed outside a few minutes. I shook the drops away, drew my trousers to, and turned to walk along the shore, and check the boat.

Fraenkel was standing in the doorway of the tent. He'd been watching me. I felt a flush of rage mixed with embarrassment.

What are you doing? I asked angrily.

The same as you, he said. I came out for a piss.

But he didn't move to undo his trousers.

You're a bloody liar, I said. You were watching me, you filthy swine.

Something went over Fraenkel's face. I couldn't read his expression in the vague light.

What if I was, he said sadly. Why don't you like me, Strindberg?

I went up to him and took him by the lapels of his jacket.

Because you're degenerate, I said slowly. You and Andrée. That's why.

Then I turned away, and went back to the tent, and got

249

into the sleeping-bag next to Andrée, and turned over onto my face, and, for some reason I don't understand, I was almost instantly asleep. I don't know when Fraenkel came back or if he stayed out all night, and when I woke up in the morning, both he and Andrée were already on their feet, and making breakfast.

Over coffee, we talked about our situation. Andrée began the discussion.

I've climbed the glacier, he said. But from this end of the island it's impossible to make out any sign of the other islands. That may be because they're too far away, or it may simply be that the visibility today is too poor.

The sun was still shining brightly then.

Scarcely that, I said. This is the best weather we're likely to get until the spring.

Andrée shrugged.

So we might wait, he suggested, ignoring my comment. Or we might try an expedition across the glacier to the other end of the island. From there, the main island might just be visible.

Let's do as you say, Andrée, I said, by all means. But I suggest, when we find the right spot, that we dig in. There's no real hope of reaching Spitzbergen before the winter comes. We have to accept the need to winter here, in a snow-hut. The sooner we build something, the better.

It didn't do much good last time, Mr Clever-Dick, now did it? said Fraenkel suddenly. Your precious little snow-hut was pretty soon blown away by the winds, eh?

I looked at him then almost with pity. His shoulders were stooped, his hands trembled, and his bad foot stuck out like a broken branch at a wrong angle. He was a wreck of what he'd been.

Be quiet, Fraenkel, Andrée said. That's a stupid remark, and you know it is.

Now you don't like me either, said Fraenkel. Do you?

Then the big flakes came whirling out of the sky, and there were suddenly huge crystals on our shoulders, and on our cheeks and our eyelashes when we looked up. We'd made no decision, and we had to stop and hole up in the tent again until the storm was over.

I wonder now if it will be, ever. It's been coming down

steadily for eighteen hours, and there's no sign of any change. Perhaps we'll just all three lie here like the babes in the wood until we're covered over with leaves of snow, and we die in our sleep, and they find us one day like frozen statues in the heart of the glacier.

October 9th. I have something very important to say, and I have to say it in the right order. This morning was dry and cold. We all rose at nine o'clock and breakfasted together. By nine-thirty we were finished.

After breakfast, Andrée and I set out to reconnoitre along the glacier. It was a clear enough day, and there still seemed a chance that we might catch a glimpse of Spitzbergen through the binoculars.

It also seemed possible, at least to me, that we might find a better place to make our winter's camp. The tent was very exposed so near to the shore, in the lee of the rocks, and I didn't think the snow-hut we were going to build would be ideally sheltered either.

Fraenkel stayed behind. His foot had become so bad that he could hardly move without wincing. Andrée kept encouraging him to move, to get some exercise, but he lacked much energy to try. He stood in the doorway of the tent as we left, and waved.

There was a watery sun, and no snow for the moment. The remains of the blizzard had blown into long drifts, and much of the ground was clear.

The sea with its leads and floes, its ragged sweep of ice-hummocks, and occasional darker blocks that might be birds, or even a bear or a seal, stretched away on all sides to the misty horizon. Down to our right and left, there was the start of the glacier sheet, and then the tumble of rocks, and the spread of snow-swept gravel and stone-brash to the island's edge.

In the middle distance, the tent stood out as a regular pyramid shape amidst the rock-chaos. Beside it, very still it seemed, there was the tall, stooping figure of Fraenkel. It looked almost as if he hadn't moved since we left ten minutes ago.

He must be frozen, I said to Andrée. Why doesn't he go inside?

Andrée raised his arm, and waved.

Fraenkel, he called. Go inside.

But the figure beside the tent didn't seem to hear. Only the ivory gulls, resting amidst the rocks, rose in a sudden squalling cloud, angry at the noise, and at being disturbed.

The island is a breeding-ground for the gulls, and there are huge colonies everywhere. The ground is a mass of droppings and discarded fish-heads and bones. I lashed out with my boot, kicking some aside as we walked on.

A stench of stale fish rose in the air, a dreadful reek that nearly made me vomit.

After a few more strides, I turned again. I don't know why, something pulled me round. Fraenkel was still there, outside the tent. But this time, he was waving. I waved back. Then he went in.

It was a mixed day. Scatter of snow, then intermittent sun. We did the best we could to examine every possible place to camp. We managed to get down to the shore in two areas, but there were few rocks, and less open space beyond the glacier. Our own spot, it seemed more and more clear, was the only place to build and stay.

After three hours, we gave up. We were both tired, and there was still an hour's trek back. On the way, we passed quite near a young bear, and he paused, snout in air, to stare at us. But it didn't seem worth while to take a shot at him. We'd have had to drag the carcase too far.

At the edge of the glacier, Andrée paused.

You go on, he said, unslinging his shot-gun. I want to take a shot or two at the gulls.

Andrée has become our keenest marksman, over the weeks on the ice. But it seemed a curious moment to choose. I stared at him, wondering if something was wrong.

Go on, he said.

I shrugged, and walked on alone to the tent. It took me a moment to unfasten the flap, which Fraenkel must have tied. Then I stepped through.

He was on top of the sleeping-bag, flat on his back. That was what worried me first. It wasn't like him not to lie prone.

252

Fraenkel, I said.

He didn't speak or move. There was something very odd, very static, as it were, about the way he was lying.

Fraenkel, I repeated, very loudly. We're back.

Then I bent beside him, and shook him roughly by the shoulder. It was like shaking a sack of potatoes. His body felt entirely loose and inert.

I felt a moment of pure panic. I stumbled to the doorway of the tent.

Andrée, I called. Andrée.

He came running, floundering through the snow.

Fraenkel, I said. I think he's dead.

Andrée stooped and lifted the rim of Fraenkel's eye. Then he unbuttoned his jacket, and felt for the heart.

He looked up, his dirty, bearded face very grave.

No sign of a beat, he said. He must have fallen asleep, and died of cold.

I knelt beside him, thinking.

Surely, I said. Nobody dies of cold. Not even Fraenkel.

Something drove me to reach into the pocket of Fraenkel's jacket then, and my hand came out with the bottle of morphine tablets. It was half empty.

Dear God, I said. He must have taken over a dozen.

I stared hard into Andrée's face. He looked back at me, impassively.

You knew, I whispered. You must have known.

I guessed, he said. Long ago.

Then he turned and walked out of the tent. I laid my head on Fraenkel's chest, Anna. There was more than I could take in, at one time. I was too tired for the right feelings to come. I didn't even know what they should be.

Perhaps I closed my eyes. Perhaps I even slept. I don't know. There was grief in me, I know that. And the weariness. And a kind of relief. All that, of course. And horror, too.

That was when the guilt came. The sense of wrong. And I reached up, and laid my bare hand on Fraenkel's brow. And that was when I saw the note-book lying beside him on the sleeping-bag.

I picked it up, and it came open with the pencil he'd been using on the page. The writing was wavering, and he'd obviously formed the words when he was going under. But they were plain enough to read.

'Strindberg doesn't. Why doesn't.'

I tore the page out, and crushed the paper up in my hand. It was quite instinctive. I didn't want Andrée to see what Fraenkel had written.

I got to my feet, swaying slightly. A stab of nausea went through me, and I staggered through the flap into the open air. Andrée was sitting on a rock, staring into space. Overhead a single ivory gull, like a white vulture, was slowly circling. That, more than anything, I think, brought me to my senses.

I went and sat down beside Andrée.

Listen, I said. It's late, and we're both tired, and hungry. The first thing is to make a meal. Then we can deal with Fraenkel. And then we can sleep.

A film seemed to clear over Andrée's eyes.

We have to talk, he said.

I shook my head.

No, I said. We'll talk tomorrow, when we start to build the hut. For the moment, we have to work.

So we got the primus lit, and had fried seal-steaks, and then raspberry syrup, and finally coffee.

We ate, by tacit consent, out on the rocks. It was cold, even huddled very close to the stove, but neither of us could quite stomach the idea of eating our meal beside Fraenkel's body.

Afterwards, we discussed what to do.

We ought to put him underground, I said. It's the right thing.

Andrée looked at me.

Tomorrow, maybe, he said. It would take hours to dig a grave. And I haven't the strength.

I sighed.

No, I agreed. Nor have I. I thought for a moment. Then I looked up the slope of rocks behind us.

There's a fissure there, I said, pointing through the half darkness. We could drag the body there, and cover it over with small stones.

Inside the tent, I lit a candle, and Andrée opened his Bible at the book of Ecclesiastes.

254

'Remember now thy creator in the days of thy youth,' he read out, 'while the evil days come not, nor the years draw nigh, when thou shalt say, I have no pleasure in them.'

I listened while he read through the first seven verses, and the almond tree and the grasshopper took their positions like the stations of the cross in my thoughts. Then Andrée closed the book, and laid it aside, and I blew out the candle.

In the dark we got Fraenkel out of his jacket, and folded it up on the floor. It seemed too valuable a source of warmth to leave to the birds. Then we each took him under one arm, and hauled his great bulk onto the floor.

It wasn't easy work negotiating him through the flap, and up the bank of rocks. But we'd had plenty of practice with dead polar bears, and Fraenkel, heavy as he was, could hardly compete for weight and length with them.

We got him up the slope, and his body fitted easily into the long space. It might not be his last resting-place, but it would do for the moment.

Let's put some stones on top, I suggested, and then get home to bed.

So we each threw handfuls of small rocks onto the corpse, and what had once been Knut Fraenkel, engineer and explorer, a man with a heart that beat and a brain that thought, became only a mass of hardening flesh under a little mound of dust and rubble.

That night, I needed sleep. But there was one thing I felt I had to set right before I lay down.

Andrée, I said, as we made ready for bed. There's something I didn't tell you.

I handed over the crumpled ball of paper that I'd torn out of Fraenkel's note-book.

Andrée read the note, then handed it back to me. His face looked sad and calm in the candlelight.

I guessed what he meant to do, he said. I told you so.

Then why, I began.

Then I stopped.

No, I said. I don't suppose that anyone could have stopped him. He was too far out in his own dream.

Andrée looked at me.

Dream? he asked.

I mean, I said, pausing. I mean, he seems to have had some idea that I didn't like him, and that seems to have mattered to him.

Yes, said Andrée. Well, it *would* matter, wouldn't it? If you were a sensitive chap like Fraenkel, I mean. Writing poetry and so on.

Then he added something.

Did you like him? he asked.

There was a tense silence in the tent.

Andrée, I said, after a while. Did *you* like Fraenkel? How much did you like him? In what way did you like him?

Andrée was getting into the sleeping-bag. He turned on his elbow.

I liked him very much, he said quietly. He was a fine man, in every way.

Then he blew out the candle, and left me to get into bed in the dark.

Hour after hour I dozed or lay awake, thinking about Fraenkel, and, most of all, about what he'd written.

Death is important, but guilt matters even more. So I was happy enough to fall in with Andrée's mood in the morning, and look back at the earlier period of our journey.

You know, said Andrée, I ought to have realized that the calotte would become encrusted with frost. I can see that now.

I rubbed my eyes.

O, you realized, I said. I think we all realized. It was the expedition's Achilles heel. But none of us wanted to give it full value. Because, if we did, it might mean we couldn't go.

Andrée nodded.

Next year, he said, someone else will go. Perhaps with a means of keeping the calotte warm.

I laughed.

Next year you'll come again yourself, I said. But not with a means of keeping the calotte warm. That's impossible, and you know it is.

I put my hand out of the sleeping-bag, and instantly

felt the icy chill on my fingers. The inside roof of the tent was white with rime today.

I brought my freezing hand back into the bag, and thrust it down for warmth between my legs. A black, dirty hand.

Perhaps Jules Verne will write a book about the flight of the *Eagle* I suggested. One with a happy ending. The three faithful comrades planting the Swedish flag at the Pole.

He's too old, said Andrée.

Well, I said. Someone, anyway.

Andrée said nothing. I thought about Fraenkel suddenly, and his pipe. We ought to put his favourite briar in his pocket, the way an Egyptian king would have his sword beside him in the tomb.

Andrée, I said, after a while. Has it ever struck you that there are always three heroes in a Verne novel?

It's a French tradition, Andrée said. The three musketeers. Clawbonny, Altamont, and Hatteras. The intellectual, the man of action, and the dreamer.

I was beginning to feel a need to make water. But it was oddly soothing to lie here and have this absurd literary conversation.

Which one are you, I asked. The intellectual?

Andrée laughed, without humour.

At first, he said, I thought that you were the intellectual, Strindberg, and Fraenkel was the man of action. Now I'm not so sure.

Fraenkel, I said. Fraenkel was always a dreamer. Action was just the sphere for the exercise of his dreams. He dreamed of being a general.

No, said Andrée. I think that he dreamed of being loved. Being a general was just how he thought most people would come to love him.

Later, we rose and there was breakfast, and a nip of brandy to keep our spirits up.

We cleared away the remains of the meal, and it seemed we had to invent jobs for a while to avoid settling down to our main problems. It was a cold day, but without snow, and the visibility was good. We could see the line of rocks over Fraenkel's body quite clearly as we worked.

Overhead the gulls circled, our white vultures. But none

came close, either to the tent or the body. They seemed to be waiting, as if they knew a secret.

Andrée, I said, as we sat warming our hands over the primus. We have to make a plan. Fraenkel dying changes everything. It makes it impossible, in this weather, to move. We couldn't manage the boat and the sledges on our own.

Andrée said nothing. He sat staring down into his gloves. There was frost flecking his beard, as if he was starting to freeze up. I drew my breath in hard, and tried to go on.

Well we could, I said. In the spring, we will. It can't be more than a hundred kilometres to Spitzbergen. Far less than we've travelled so far. But the blizzard will come down really hard soon. We daren't risk being caught on the move. We have to dig in. It's our only chance.

Andrée blew his breath out. He looked up at the sky, an old rock-like man, waiting for the snow to come, that would cover him.

There is no chance, he said, flatly.

I felt the first spurt of anger. I reached over and took him by the chin.

Don't talk like that, I said. I'm as sorry as you are that Fraenkel has gone. But I can't bring him back. He's dead. And the facts of the matter are, that in many ways we're better off without him. It's one mouth less to feed. One third of our winter rations saved at a stroke. Think of that.

One pair of hands less to dig the hut, said Andrée. Think of that.

No, I said, rising, and pacing to and fro. Fraenkel was the hardest worker we had, at first. Of course he was. But he'd gone soft. You know he had. He was good for nothing. Just a drag on our time, and our will. We're better off without him.

Andrée looked up at me. He shook a snow-flake out of his eye. He looked very tired, but not so hopeless, I thought, as he'd done a few minutes ago. I felt energy returning to me.

You're a hard man, Strindberg, said Andrée. Harder than I would ever have known.

I knelt beside him, gripping his gloved hands in mine.

Andrée, I said. We *have* to be hard. There's no other

258

way. Now listen. Only a year ago, and further north than this, Nansen and Johanssen were able to build an earth-hut virtually with their bare hands. And they stayed alive right through the winter, and got home to tell the tale. What they could do, so can we.

It was a whole month earlier, said Andrée. And they had better clothes than we do.

Better clothes, maybe, I said. But no tools. We have a saw and a spade. Listen.

I got up and went into the tent. I scrabbled in my private bag, and there I found the dog-eared green volume, and turned up the passage I wanted. I came out into the cold, leafing over the pages.

Here it is, I said, and I began to read the famous passage. 'We quarried stones up among the debris from the cliff, dragged them together, dug out the site, and built walls as well as we could. We had no tools worth mentioning; those we used most were our two hands.'

I looked up at Andrée, but he hardly seemed to be listening. He was staring up at the circling gulls.

I threw the book down on the rock, and went over to the boat down by the shore. There I unstrapped the rope, and took out the spade and the saw. I tucked them under my arm, and walked back up the beach to the tent.

Here, I said to Andrée, handing him the spade. You start digging just to the west of the tent. That seems as good as anywhere. If we make a trench about a metre deep, I can raise the walls another three with blocks of ice sawn out of the glacier. The eskimos do this every year. It can't be so difficult.

So we tried. It was late in the afternoon then, though, and there's no more than a trench the size of a grave so far. I found it harder than I expected to saw the blocks I needed from the glacier, and Andrée was like a child making sandcastles with the spade. He didn't try.

He's asleep now, sleeping the sleep of the just, or the unjust, I don't know which. It's ludicrous, Anna. We're both so fit. The diarrhoea has gone, and even my foot has healed. We have plenty of food, plenty of matches, plenty of ammunition. The weather is cold, but the wind is low, and there's no snow.

259

It ought to be easy to put our backs into building a hut. After all, on the floe, with my boils and my bad temper, I designed and built the three-roomed ice-hut in no more than ten days. And then I had Fraenkel to contend with, too. Here it's just a matter of hard labour.

Two fit men, and we can hardly make a start. It's as if a kind of rot sets in, or perhaps like that kind of disease that sometimes decimates the chestnut trees. First of all a beetle eats them full of holes, and then a fungus comes and takes root in the space. The beetle of lassitude. That flew to Fraenkel, Anna, and now it's eating away at Andrée. And the fungus of fear. That's cut down one of us already, and it's sending its feelers out through the snow to catch the others.

October 11th. Temperature, minus fourteen degrees. Visibility nil. Wind, gale force. I can hear the whine even here in the sleeping-bag, with my head underneath the reindeer skin. I'm afraid the gusts may tear the tent loose from its moorings.

A few minutes ago there was nothing to see but white flakes. They were being forced into my teeth and eyes the moment I opened the flap and stepped outside. There are still icicles in my hair.

I woke up at ten o'clock. I was freezing cold. There was no one else in the sleeping-bag and I supposed that Andrée must have gone out to prepare breakfast. I lay for a while thinking about Fraenkel, and then I looked at my chronometer again and saw it was after eleven.

I wondered why Andrée was taking so long, and then I grew worried, and then I got up, and drew the tent-flap open. The blizzard had already started, but it was still possible to see a few metres ahead. I didn't need to see any more.

He was lying just outside the tent, face down along the rock. His shot-gun was a few yards away in the snow. I thought at first that he must have tripped while taking a shot at a gull.

I stood up, and felt the force of the gale almost throw me back on the tent-wall. I steadied myself, and leaned forward, shielding my face against the hail of flakes. I turned him over onto his back, and then I knew. He lay like a skin, something stripped off and thrown aside, something no longer needed.

I felt for his heart, under the coat, and there was no heart there. Then I turned his eyes down, and I took the gun out of the snow, and I staggered back inside.

He'll have to be buried later. It's too cold. It's like being out in an ice-box, with a knife shredding frost in the air.

October 12th. Temperature, minus twelve degrees. Visibility ten metres. Wind, near gale force. The blizzard's not so bad, but it's still very extreme. I managed to light the primus yesterday night, and I made enough hot soup to last me, I hope, until it's over. That, and some biscuits, and more of the brandy, should keep me going.

I haven't thought about burying Andrée, or about building the hut.

I've been thinking about how Andrée died. I thought at first that it might be suicide, and I checked the gun to make sure. But neither barrel had been fired.

I think I know what it was, though. He just walked outside into the night, and let the Arctic decide what to do with him.

After all, if Andrée lived, Fraenkel was going to be the hero. The Arctic martyr. Death was at least a way of avoiding second place.

October 13th. Temperature, minus three degrees. Visibility, one hundred metres. Wind, slight. The blizzard is over, at least for the moment. I may have a week or ten days clear, I estimate, to get on with the hut.

A few hours ago, I took out the camera, and examined the mechanism. It's weeks since I bothered to use it. Fortunately, it all seems fine, and I was able to take a reel of pictures.

Rather a morbid set, you may think, when you see them. It isn't often a photographer gets the chance to take pictures of two dead bodies. Particularly when they were his former comrades-in-arms.

I uncovered Fraenkel's body, and laid the stones on one side. It's rather a broad, fine trench he's in, and I think that I may have another use for it.

Fraenkel was just the same as before he died. A sleeping

261

giant, with a long brown beard, and dark skin. The bears have left him alone, so far, and the gulls have been deterred by the stones. I got some good shots of his face, like a death-mask. A kind of macabre calm.

So much for Rossetti, with Elizabeth Siddal in the bath-tub to play the dying Ophelia. These are the real thing. I'm well in the way to meet Max Klinger at his own game.

I feel light-headed, Anna. It must be the morphine. I get bouts of this crazy need to work, and then I fall asleep.

Imagine Uncle Johan's reaction to these photographs! He'll see me as a real rival now, you'll see. A Strindberg to out-Strindberg Strindberg!

October 14th. Temperature, zero. Visibility, several kilometres. Wind, nil. So I can start work. I have an idea, though. It came from removing the stones to take photographs of Fraenkel's body.

The trench he's in is fairly wide, and the rocks at either side form a natural bastion against the wind and snow. If I take the body out, and build round one end with drift-wood and blocks of snow, I can form a small hut far more quickly than down here on the shore. Now that it only needs to shelter one, it can afford to be much smaller.

So with any luck, Anna, your Nils will shortly be laying down his pretty head in poor Fraenkel's grave.

October 16th. Funny, the days are slipping by, and I don't seem to be noticing time any more. It must be the morphine. It makes me feel very good. I've grown full of confidence again. I have plenty of meat, the primus is working well, there are books to read, the sun is shining. What more do I need?

I don't think about Andrée and Fraenkel. Fraenkel and Andrée were degenerates. I feel sure of that now. I examined Andrée's rectum, and there is no doubt in my mind of what I say. I know a rupture of the anus, when I see it. I am very sorry to report this, Anna. But the truth must be known.

He looks very strange without his trousers. I expect those who come later will say that the bears tore them off. I don't know why I did it, really. To pass the time. To know the truth.

I got Fraenkel's body down yesterday, and laid it along the shore, just outside the tent. I mean to begin building the snow-hut tomorrow. It shouldn't take me more than a day or two. Then I can kiss farewell to all my cares and settle in for a long three-month read. It should be pleasant, if a little lonely.

October 9th? I hope that's right. I'm getting a bit confused about time.

I've started to carry driftwood up into the rocks to build my hut. I lay down in the space where Fraenkel was, and it felt very snug. It's a tremendous shelter from the wind.

The gulls bother me a bit. They've started to swoop down when I climb the rocks, and once or twice one has perched on my shoulder, and peered at me.

I saw a bear yesterday night, the first for some days. But I don't need extra meat, and I suppose I ought to conserve ammunition. It came rather close, but I raised the gun to my shoulder, and that made it scamper off.

October 18th. Temperature, thirteen degrees. Visibility, good. Wind, keen. It's several hours since I had any morphine. I need some badly.

I think that I shan't live more than a few days more. I'm not ill. Except for this craving for morphine, I'm not in pain. Even my foot seems to be fine.

But I can't go on, on my own.

I have to stop. I have to have the tablets.

October 19th. Temperature, four hundred and fifteen degrees. Visibility, excellent. Wind, amazing. I feel exhilarated. I've just finished a splendid breakfast of bear's meat broth, Mellin's food pudding, and brandy coffee.

I'm sitting out in the snow − don't worry, it's not very heavy − and playing a game with Andrée and Fraenkel. Dead people are very nice, I've decided, when they don't smell. They do what you want them to. And they don't answer back.

I've been playing a game of forfeits. We ask each other questions, and the one who can't answer correctly has to give up something precious to him. A little book, or a piece of jewellery, or an instrument. Sometimes the forfeit has to be just a kiss or a hug.

I do rather well. I've won lots of nice things. Andrée's

diary, some of his private stock of caramels, and his mother's amulet. I shall give them back, of course. O, yes. It's just a game after all.

I won from Fraenkel too. A book of photographs of nude men in high boots. At least I think they're photographs. I'm not sure. They look very detailed, and realistic.

I don't always win, though. I lost my locket, Anna, with your lock of hair. But don't worry. I shall get it back. I always win in the end. The dead are poor players.

It's getting too cold. I'd better go in and sleep. I have to finish the hut tomorrow.

October 20th? I'm not quite sure whether I've had my tablets yet today or not. I feel very dazed. I know that it's snowing outside, and I think I feel very cold.

I'm going to copy something out to clarify my thoughts. I want to make sure that I can still understand what I'm writing.

It's very cold. I think the balloon must be coming down. I can see snow everywhere. Andrée was very silly not to remember the freezing point of water.

Here it is. We quarried stones. This is Nansen speaking. Among the debris from the cliff. Dragged them together. Dug out the site. And built walls as well as we could. We had no tools worth mentioning. No tools. Those we used most were our two hands. I made a spade out of the shoulder-blade of a walrus tied to a broken piece of a broken snow-shoe staff and a mattock out of a walrus shoe tied to a sledge of a tusk. They were poor things to work with, but I managed managed managed with little by little. With patience, and little by little. Little by little.

Goodbye, Anna.

9
ANNA
1930

I'VE BEEN TRYING HARD to recall the precise feel of that moment when the captain entered my shop. I must have glanced at the ship's clock above the counter, because I know it was just after twenty-five minutes to four. A quiet time.

It was early in October, and we were having a freak spell of fine weather. The sun was dancing in on the tablecloths, and the china looked even more spick and span than usual. I must have heard the latch click when the door opened, but I didn't look round from the till.

When I did look up, my visitor was turning this way and that, in the middle of the room. He looked like a man used to another element, to the rock of the deck and the brush of the wind. As if his gnarled limbs had been chopped or sawn out of the disused timbers of a whaling ship. There was almost an echo – almost a tang – of the salt ocean about his face.

I rose to my feet, feeling dizzy, gripping the edge of the till. Then I mastered the sensation, and went over to his table with the menu. He looked up, uncertain for a moment what to do, twisting his hands together on his legs.

I felt my hands trembling, and I dropped the menu in his lap.

Excuse me, I said, in English.

But he wasn't taken in. He made the same deduction as I had myself.

Miss Charlier, he said in Swedish. Are you Miss Anna Charlier?

267

I touched his arm.

Let me take you home, I said.

Of course I knew why he was there. The first report had
been in the *Scotsman* on the morning of August 23rd. It had
only been a small paragraph, on the Foreign News page,
but I hadn't missed it. BODY OF SWEDISH BALLOONIST
FOUND, the headline had read. I still have the cutting,
dog-eared from rereading, with all the other papers.

'Yesterday afternoon, the skipper of the *Terningen*, a
Norwegian sealing-vessel putting in to Tromsö, declared
that on the morning of the 8th of August he had been hailed
by the captain of the sealer *Bratvaag* off Victoria Island and
told that the ship's crew had discovered the remains of
S.A.Andrée and one of his crew on White Island. They
were returning to Tromsö with the bodies of the two men
and many pieces of equipment from the balloonists' last
camp.'

I'd been reading the paper in the bus, but fortunately I
don't think anyone noticed when I fainted. I came to my
senses two stops beyond the shop, with my head on the
seat in front, and the paper crumpled in my lap. I don't
know how I managed the walk back, or to get the door
open, and drag my way through to the kitchen.

Anna, for the love of God, Jeanette said. You look like
death, woman.

She got me a cup of sweet tea, and sat me down in one of
the bentwood chairs. The heat and the hardness of the
wood revived me, and I managed to put my senses together
again in some sort of normal order.

I've had a nasty shock, Jeanette, I said. Some bad news.

It was true, more true than she'd ever realize. The bodies
of two men, the report had said. Not three men. Just two.
So where was the third?

I drank the last of my tea, and got up to straighten my
dress, and look at myself in the wall mirror. It was an oval,
gilt-framed one, and it showed me, as if in a photograph,
the face of a sharp-lined, once dark-haired woman in her
early fifties, wearing a high-necked black dress, with a
cameo at her throat. She looked old-fashioned, but fit
enough and still handsome.

I looked into the mirror, I say, and I saw the face of my younger self again, ravaged with impossible torment as it had been when I laid the paper aside years earlier in Klippan, and fell back on my mother's shoulder in a paroxysm of weeping.

He's alive, I'd said. Nils is still alive.

I was twenty-one then, in the full bloom of youth, my waist pinched in by a corset that made my bosom float like a swollen fruit.

I remember my mother warming her hands at the tiled stove in the corner, and shaking her head. I knew what she meant. The paper told us only what the aeronauts had written two years before. The buoy they had jettisoned had been washed ashore unbroken at Kollafjord on the north coast of Iceland, on May 14th, 1899. Its message was brief.

'This buoy has been thrown from Andrée's balloon at 10h.55m G.M.T. on the 11th of July 1897 in about 82° latitude and 25° long. E.fr.Gr. We are floating at a height of 600 metres. All well. Andrée. Strindberg. Fraenkel.'

My mother knew very well how little comfort the message could bring. The 11th of July was only the first day of the flight, no more than a few hours after the balloon cast loose from its anchors. It was days, though, before I could digest out the full hopelessness of the message. It was years before that first buoy, and the four others that came later, each one more enigmatic than the last, had lost their power over my imagination, and my heart-strings.

I took the train down to Stockholm, and went to the National Museum of Polar Exploration, and there I stood for an hour on end staring through the glass case at the hand-written message from the fourth buoy, the first they threw over the side onto the ice.

'11 July 10 clock p.m. G.M.T.,' it read. 'Our journey has hitherto gone well. We are sailing onwards at a height of about 250 metres in a direction at first towards N.10 East due course but later towards N.458 East due course. Four carrier pigeons sent off 5h. 40 p.m. Greenw. time. They flew westwards. We are now over the ice which is much divided in all directions. Weather magnificent. Humour excellent. Andrée. Strindberg. Fraenkel. Above the clouds since 7.45 G.M.T.'

That day I was saved by a child. He came over in his sailor suit, with his big serious eyes, and took me by the hand, and led me over to see the model of Nansen's ship the *Fram*, an exact matchstick replica in a special cabinet of its own in the middle of the room. The child's eyes were shining. Nansen was his hero.

It brought tears to my own eyes. That was the second of the buoys to be discovered, and there were two more still to come.

I remember what I felt when I read the news of their finding the so-called Polar Buoy washed up on the east shore of Spitzbergen, in King Charles's Land. I read later all the speculations in Nathorst's book, the arguments about the drift and the currents, the probable time of jettisoning, the reasons for the buoys being found at the times they were. But it made no difference.

I'd seen and touched those buoys before the expedition started. Each one was a tapering, beehive-shaped ball of cork, wound round with a copper net, and containing a closed metal cylinder intended as a letter-box. There were twelve in all. The twelfth, the Polar Buoy, was about five times as large as the others. The idea had always been to throw it down at the northernmost point reached by the expedition. Hence its name.

It came ashore on September 11th, 1899, two years and two months after it had been thrown from the balloon. The copper wire had been torn askew, and some of the layers of cork were injured. But the metal box inside was intact. They broke it open, hoping to find some clue to how far the explorers had gone. But the box was empty. There was no message.

I left home after that, in the spring of 1901, packing my hold-all in the little flowered attic at the top of the house, where the sparrows and martins would come to build their nests. I waited with my father on the wind-swept platform at the end of the town, seeing the smoke from the train approaching in the distance, feeling the rough serge of his official uniform against my wrist.

It was a quick goodbye, waving there at the rolled-down

270

carriage window, and it broke a link. Sweden receded. The voyage from Stockholm to Leith was a secondary parting. I gave up my country when I left the low red roofs of Klippan behind in the mountains. The rest was nothing.

Edwardian Scotland was a rough place for a single girl, and one brought up in rural seclusion, in the heart of her family. I had to fight for life. There were slums and men and raw times and underneath, I could still feel the scrape of those guide-ropes on the pack-ice, and feel the sun steely-white on the ice-pools, and hear Andrée's voice, coarse and domineering, and see Nils as he was in the white flash of his youth, a naked blade in the night air outside my window. But I survived.

Four months of near starvation, and then nine years of slavery in a sordid small hotel. I nearly died, more than once. But at least it dulled the pain, the awful need to lie down and scream for grief. I survived, I say. I even took to eating my food, and walking out, with an occasional sense of enjoyment.

And then there was finding the money, and opening my own shop, and the genial, pleasant bustle again of doing something for myself. It had almost pushed the dream back into the shadows for a while. Until that morning when I opened the *Scotsman* and read the headline in the bus.

The past has a way with it. It never goes. I stared into my drawn face there in that oval, gilt mirror in the kitchen of my shop, and I knew that my own life was bound up now for ever with those three men who cast loose in their balloon from Danes Island on the 11th of July, 1897.

After that first report, the others came thick and fast. The *Bulletin* had a long account, the following day, of what Gustav Jensen claimed he had seen on the decks of the *Bratvaag*. It was all sensational rubbish. That was clear enough from the start.

'The body of Andrée lay there immersed in a block of ice, as perfectly preserved as if he were still alive,' he was alleged to have stated. It was obvious where that fantasy had come from, by one remove or another. Someone had been reading too much Hans Heinz Ewers.

It wasn't until the *Bratvaag* put in at Tromsö, on Septem

271

ber 2nd, that the real story began to come through. From then until all the bones they could find were cremated in Stockholm on October 9th, there was scarcely a day that didn't bring me further news.

After that report in the *Bulletin*, I telephoned to the Swedish Embassy in London, and with their help I arranged to have cuttings from the Swedish press directly sent to me in Moffat. So I was able to follow through each development in full detail.

It was all so dramatic, the way they made it sound. The discovery of the bones and the equipment. The pageantry of the last voyage to Stockholm. The poignancy of the few surviving members of the families greeting the remains of their own.

It made me sick. I could read between the lines, I could guess what so many of the details must have meant. The disposition of the bones, the packing of the sleighs and the boat. It told a story, and one that had to be understood. But the papers weren't interested. All that mattered to them was the glory of Sweden.

I needed to speak to someone who had landed on White Island and seen the camp at first hand. Someone who knew what had happened to the third man, my lost fiancé, Nils Strindberg. Someone who could tell me the truth I had waited thirty-four years to know.

The sloop arrived at White Island, the captain said, as we sat in my darkening parlour, on the morning of the 5th of September, and I went ashore with six of the crew. There were polar bears in the tundra, and we had to shoot three.

I knew already what polar bears had done to the bones in the ice. Thirty-four years of being mauled and thrown about. That was the problem. I felt no sympathy for those great yellow brutes that Stubbendorff and his men had had to shoot.

To the north of us, continued the captain, there rose a little rocky ridge, about five or six metres above the rest of the ground. The crew of the *Bratvaag* had raised a cairn there, to mark the site. It was on the lower ground, between us and the cairn, that the ice was melting. There was a solid frozen stretch and then thaw-patches at the edge, crumbling into old, wet snow. On the stony tundra, and in the rock-pools at the edges of the ice, and visible still within its glaze, we could see a wide range of objects that the *Bratvaag* had evidently missed.

I was lost out there with him on that fine September morning, feeling the hard stone and the slippery ice under my own snow-shoes, ready as he had been, but with how much more passionate reason, to discover whatever was there to be known. I had to shake myself to come out of my trance, and know he had paused.

You see, he was saying, apologetically, the ice was thawing all the time. It had let go its grip on many more things in the few days since the *Bratvaag* was there.

It must have been one of the warmest summers for many years up there, I said. Otherwise, a sealer would have found the camp and the bones before.

I wonder, the captain said.

I watched his face, but the dusk was gathering force, and his features were in shadow. I drew a shawl round my shoulders against the chill. I didn't want to get up to put a light on, or a fire.

It was like a tomb, said the captain. I felt I was rifling a grave, when I touched the first bone, below the cairn. It may be that sailors landed before, and saw the bones through the ice, and heard the gulls maybe, and felt the same weird sense that I did, and then didn't dare to disturb what God had left alone for so many years, and might want left alone for the rest of time.

I heard my clock chime in the hall.

Go on, I said giving him absolution. There was no curse on the bones. You had to do what you could.

I felt something reaching out of the snow to clutch at my heart.

We found many things, the captain said. The bones of one man frozen to the ground. The bones of another scattered. A thigh-bone. A pelvis. A skull.

You found the bones of Fraenkel, I said. His arm was under his head. You had to chip it out with your knife.

Stubbendorff did that, the captain said. It was in a bowl of the rock. We had to work all day, the second day that was, on getting Fraenkel out. The first day we found

273

Andrée's skull, and the sleigh, and some of the books.

I know the details, I had to tell him. I've squeezed the reports like a blood orange, for every drop of juice. I know what the *Bratvaag* found, and I know what the *Isbjörn* found. I know how those two boys came up the shore, after their walruses, and how they rested, and then went to look for drinking water, and found the canvas boat. I can see the ivory gulls, I tell you, pecking at the carcases. I can smell the meat.

I'd spoken fast, in the full heat of impatience. I heard the captain shift his feet. He was feeling awkward, ill at ease.

I'm sorry, captain, I said. I didn't mean to steal your story. You have to understand how much this means to me. I've been through and through the printed words more times than I like to say. You'll forgive an old woman a wee touch of bad temper, I hope.

I reached and poured whisky into the vague shape of his glass on the table. I felt I was giving myself away. I had to go slower. I had to take things more at the captain's pace. I needed to know how far he was someone to trust.

I really am sorry, I repeated. I shouldn't have jumped down your throat like that. I just don't want to waste your time with what I know. Give me the feel of the place, if you can. The look it must have had from the sea.

I heard the captain sucking whisky, in the darkness.

Yes, he said. The feel. It was a dark, strange feel. I've given you that already. There was fog rising and lightning coming by the third day. Rain and snow. We knew we couldn't stay long.

I could hear the slight soughing sound the bottom of the glass made as the captain rubbed it to and fro on the soft leather of the table top.

I wasn't sorry to go, he said, sombrely. Stubbendorff would have stayed another day, I think, and had the ship enclosed in the floes by the north wind for his pains. But I wouldn't let him. The mate gave the storm-signal, and we had to leave. I saw the flare from where I was walking beyond the ridge.

The captain paused.

The look, though, he said, back-tracking. You want the look of the place from the sea.

274

I drank myself, swallowing the hot liquor like a fire, hardly able to restrain my urge to interrupt, to rush him on, past what he knew, past what he had to say, towards what I needed to hear.

Imagine the three sleighs in the foreground, he said slowly. Around them a scatter of bones. Tins. Instruments. The skins of two bears.

Tell me about the bears, I said.

There was something here he could add. I knew there was.

One was an autumn skin, the captain said. The fat had been cut away with a saw. They'd had fresh meat, at the end. In plenty. There were bird-wings, and bone-remains of ivory gulls. And the sawn bones of seals, too.

So it wasn't starvation that killed them, I said.

The captain answered obliquely.

They had plenty of food, is what he said. In the middle ground, he continued, you have to imagine the space the hut was in. Or the tent. There were piles of driftwood at the south and east. A whale-bone in the west. The line of the ridge at the back. In that space were the bones of Andrée and Fraenkel. Or some of them. Andrée against the rock wall. Fraenkel frozen into the ground. The sleeping-bag, frozen and wrinkled, lying between them.

You think they died of cold, I said.

It was more a statement than a question. Everyone thought they'd died of cold.

They had plenty of clothes, the captain said. They weren't warm clothes. But they weren't wearing them all.

So they weren't cold, I said, eager in the darkness.

They were cold, the captain said. But they didn't die of cold. Nobody dies of cold. No Swede, anyway. There has to be something else.

I thought of the Vikings going naked into battle, stripping their breeks off in the face of the enemy. The bare flesh confronting the last extremity.

Aye, I said. There has to be something else.

But the captain was talking on, his broad shoulders only a black square now against the lighter black of the walls.

All round the two sets of bones, he said, there were

things made of metal, and wood, and canvas. Ammunition. Oars. Bits of the boat.

The captain paused again.

Out at sea, he said slowly, duties are what seem to matter most. Duties to the dead, most of all. To those who lie in their graves, at the bottom of the sea, or out on the ice. It's what they want, or what they wanted before they died, that seems to matter, that has to be.

The captain creaked in his chair.

That's why I'm here, he said.

I felt the presence then of something momentous, rising like a great swell from the four corners of the little room in the black dark, something unknown and extraordinary, that would resolve what had to be resolved. I waited for it, knowing the captain was its instrument, and that it would flow from him in its own time.

On the third day, the captain said, I was walking along the ridge, checking the broken ice around a narrow cleft in the rocks. About thirty-five metres from the tent. Under a pile of stones.

I could wait no longer. I leaned forward in the darkness.

What did you find? I heard myself saying. What did you find? Were there more bones? Was there another skull?

I stopped, listening to the sounds of my own breathing, impatient, hopeless.

There were bones everywhere, the captain said. It made no difference. But there were no more skulls. None we could find.

Then the world turned over again, and I let him go on in his own time.

The ice had been thawing more since the previous day, the captain continued. I bent down on my knee, and reached into the cleft, feeling with my hand under the place where the stones had been lying.

I shook the bottle of Scotch in the darkness. It was empty. Later, I thought. I'll get the other one from the cellar. But not now. I mustn't interrupt him.

We'd done the same the day before, the captain said, and we'd found nothing. But today was different. There

276

was something there on the ground, something that didn't feel like a stone. I hoisted it up in my glove, and saw what it was.

I rose to my feet, groped round the table, walked over to the door, and switched on the electric light. As I turned, I saw that the captain was blinking, dazzled for a moment by the sudden blaze.

I took in the whole room. The drab three-piece suite by the fire, too big for the space it had to fill. The table and the cane chair in the alcove. The bulk of the captain, out of place and raw, somehow, in this comfortable domestic landscape. And my own reflection, ragged and threatening, in the central pane of the bay window.

I walked quickly over and drew the curtains, shutting out the cold of the night, hugging my new secret to the warmth of the room. I noticed then that it wasn't warm, not warm at all, and I bent to plug in the electric radiator at the wall. I saw the captain's bag as I did so, awkward and sagging against the leg of his chair.

It was a sort of oilskin parcel, the captain said, slewing round to face me. Very much like the packets of geological specimens that Andrée had bound up with string and stored in the boat. I supposed at first that this was another of those. A particular one that had meant a lot to Strindberg, and been buried with him.

I rose to my feet, then sank into the sofa, turning to face the captain over my shoulder. I knew that the moment had come. I was ready.

Go on, I said.

There was something written on the outside of the parcel, the captain went on. I read it there in the gathering fog, as the storm-flare burst in the sky from the ship, and I saw Stubbendorff signal from the beach for me to come down. I read the words a second time to make sure I'd got them right and I knew then what I had to do. I put the package unopened into the pocket of my fur-coat, and I returned with it, unopened and undeclared, to the *Isbjörn*.

The captain was fumbling with the draw-strings of his kit-bag, reaching in with an awkward, massive hand.

Here it is, he said.

277

I took the package like the holy grail, feeling its weight in my palm, turning it over in the brash electric light to see the words the captain had first read under the dim, foggy blur of the Arctic afternoon.

For the love of God, the message read, and in the hope of salvation, deliver this package unopened to my fiancée, Anna Charlier.

I left the *Isbjörn* at Tromsö, the captain said. It took me some time to find out where you were. I sailed for Leith in the *Haakon*, with a cargo of railway sleepers. I sailed before the mast, for the first time in seven years. To keep faith with the past. To bring you what should be yours.